Panda Books
Mimosa

Zhang Xianliang was born in Nanjing in December 1936. During the political movement of the late 1950s he was labelled a Rightist and detained for over ten years. Following his rehabilitation in 1979, he became an editor of *Shuofang*, a literary magazine published in Ningxia. Later he joined the Chinese Writers' Association and was elected a council member of its Ningxia branch. He is now chairman of the Ningxia Chinese Writers' Association, a vice-chairman of the Ningxia Federation of Literary and Art Circles, and a member of the Chinese People's Political Consultative Conference.

Zhang Xianliang's anthology of short stories *Body and Soul* was published in 1981. The title story won a prize and was subsequently made into a film. Another of his stories, "Bitter Springs" won a national prize in 1983. His novelette *Mimosa* has won wide acclaim since its publication in 1984.

Zhang Xianliang

Mimosa
and Other Stories

Panda Books

Panda Books

First Edition 1985

Copyright 1985 by CHINESE LITERATURE

ISBN 0-8351-1164-4

Published by CHINESE LITERATURE, Beijing (37), China

Distributed by China International Book Trading Corporation
(GUOJI SHUDIAN), P.O. Box 399, Beijing, China

Printed in the People's Republic of China

CONTENTS

Author's Preface

A society and a human being are much the same, in that only after they have matured can they genuinely reflect, can they have the courage to criticize themselves, to honestly and relatively objectively expose the mistakes and the naiveté of their earlier stages of development. In 1958, because we placed too much emphasis on the effect of the subjective will, the movement known as the Great Leap Forward was initiated, and we dreamt of soaring overnight into a "communist paradise". In reality, we had hardly even left the ground, and we paid the penalty exacted by economic laws and ultimately plunged into hell. A dreadful famine spread throughout the country. As *Mimosa* begins, this period of famine is already nearing its end.

I feel sure that readers will be able to understand this book. Although we do have our own special traditions and customs, readers will see that *Mimosa*'s characters have exactly the same needs in life, the same desires and spiritual pursuits as they do themselves.

Mimosa is one part of an autobiographical series of novels and it describes the main character's experiences over a two-month period in 1961 when he is released from a prison camp and sent to a state farm. Zhang is a victim of the 1957 anti-Rightist movement and is persecuted in each of the succeeding political movements. But *Mimosa* does not express any condemnation, nor does it express resentment or indignation. In China, the occurrence of this or that political movement cannot be blamed entirely on any particular person, just as our belief that similar kinds of political movements cannot happen again is not founded upon the verbal assurances of any particular individual. In a country with such a long history, and in such a backward state of economic development, modern political trends may superficially appear to be determined by particular people. In fact, they are governed by a variety of factors answerable to historical categories and not to individual human will. Now the majority of Chinese have emerged from that difficult stage. Consequently we cherish that historical period and must remember what we have learned from it. In *Mimosa* I have tried hard to bring the central character's particular circumstances to life, and in describing a small village in China's northwest, to incorporate a much broader range of social phenomena.

I have always felt that if a character is to be rounded and realistic, the author must not only describe his feelings, his character and his experiences, but also his ideology, his abstract mental processes. The problem lies in effectively integrating this ideology, this reasoning process and character with the contemporary circumstances. It seemed to me that Zhang could only find his lost identity and the meaning of life through the writing of Karl Marx. Some people have expressed doubts about this and have asked whether or not somebody who has been declared an enemy of the people and who hasn't got enough to eat can genuinely think of reading Marx, indeed can genuinely accept Marxism. They have asked whether or not this was done just to make sure the book got published, whether it was the same old stuff. I think that one ought not to underestimate the readers' powers of imagination. In foreign countries, there is, apart from judges and lawyers, a group of people who assiduously study the law, i.e. the criminals who run the risk of being punished by it. In each of China's past political movements, intellectuals have always been first in the line of fire, and many of those who were declared "bourgeois Rightists", "anti-Marxist" or "reactionary academic authorities" were labelled as belonging to Marxist categories and punished. Whether in order to try and get out of the way to defend themselves or to come to some kind of individual understanding, these intellectuals all tried to determine in their own minds the true nature of Marxism. They did this with a thoroughness that would exceed that of any defence lawyer, because during that period almost nobody would come to the defence of besieged intellectuals. As a consequence, they incorporated both the status of criminal and lawyer in one, possessed twice the degree of enthusiasm. Marxism, however, is not a series of legal statutes, it is a philosophy of social struggle, a philosophy of the oppressed, and its powerful revolutionary enthusiasm proved to have an irresistible appeal and inspiration for intellectuals. Frequent political movements produced the dramatic effect of a Shakespearean comedy: the prosecuted became the prosecutor, the prosecutor the prosecuted, and intellectuals who had always been "enemies of Marxism" became genuine Marxists.

It should be explained that Zhang has only just begun to become familiar with Marxism. There is a point at which he thinks he genuinely is a "bourgeois Rightist" and the book describes his inner confusion over the "theory of descent" popular at the time. This is a genuine psychological process. Political movements, in the guise of mass movements, used seemingly orthodox Marxist idioms to lend themselves validity, and the victim frequently had to sincerely believe that he had committed an "ideological crime" and repent. In order to eliminate this ideological pressure, it was necessary to show him the concern and attention of ordinary workers, who were honest and rational and who had great empirical experience in differentiating what was right from what was wrong. He was also required to understand Marxism in the way that a lawyer understands the law. Once he gained this understanding he would have a positive and critical world view and methodology; his consciousness could be raised from that of a criminal up on to a whole new plane.

Some readers may not understand the ending of *Mimosa*. This is because I want each part of this series to be able to stand on its own. Chinese readers like their stories to have a discernible beginning and end, and I must accommodate their tastes. All in all, the series will be divided into nine parts, and once it is completed, then the principal character's experience will be set out in chronological order. I plan to write one book every two years and estimate that I have a couple of decades of creative energy ahead of me. When the last part is completed, I will be able to use Marx's final line in his *Critique of the Gotha Programme* as a conclusion:

"Dixi et salvavi animam meam."*

---

* I have spoken and saved my soul.

I hope that some of the people I met during my trip to Europe will read this translation. Through its imagery, the book can perhaps underscore some of my answers to the questions that were put to me about why Chinese intellectuals, who have suffered so much, are so unswerving in their loyalty to their country, and about the degree of liberalization in Chinese cultural life today. Now Chinese writers seek only authenticity, and whatever realities particular social phenomena may reveal, that is what they will write about.

Mimosa

"THRICE wrung out in water, thrice bathed in blood, thrice boiled in caustic." This is Alexei Tolstoy's description in Vol. II (1918) in his *Ordeal* of how hard it is for an intellectual to remould his thinking. Of course he had in mind bourgeois intellectuals brought up in tsarist Russia.

However, this description also applies to those of my generation who, like myself, indiscriminately absorbed feudal and bourgeois culture. So it occurred to me to write about a young Chinese from a bourgeois family, brought up on hazy notions of humanism and democracy, who after a long "ordeal" finally becomes a Marxist.

This book, entitled *The Making of a Materialist*, will consist of a series of nine novelettes. One of these, *Mimosa* is what I am now presenting to my readers.

I

The cart, after lumbering over a creaking hump-backed wooden bridge, reached the farm where we were to work.

Beneath the bridge the river-bed had dried up for the winter. The withered, frozen grass on either side was motionless. The soil scattered over the rickety bridge had been ground up by cart-wheels. The rushes spread beneath were of different lengths, some of them jutting out to make the bridge seem wider than it really was. But the carter did not dismount, though his three panting horses floundered left and right, their eyes rolling, steam spurting from their nostrils. He remained seated upright on the shaft, gripping it between his knees as he drove steadily, expertly forward.

The horses were in no better shape than I was. One metre seventy centimetres in height, I weighed only 44 kilos, little more than skin and bones. When he weighed me, the doctor in our labour camp had congratulated me, "Not bad! You've survived." It seemed to him such a miracle that he felt entitled to share in my pride. But no one showed any concern for these three horses with their bony heads, scraggy necks and sunken eyes. As they strained forward, their gaping jaws showed gaps between their discoloured teeth. The mouth of one roan had been gashed, and the red blood trickling from it stood out sharply against the brown soil.

Still the carter sat on the shaft, staring grimly into the distance. The horses twitched their ears in desperation as he mechanically cracked his whip. The roan with the bleeding mouth looked particularly frightened, though the carter had no intention of lashing it.

I could understand the carter's callousness. Hungry? So what? While there's life in you, keep going. Hunger, far more terrifying than his whip, had long since driven all compassion from our minds.

Still, the sight of the emaciated creature made me ask:

"Master Hai, is it much farther to the farm headquarters?"

He completely ignored me, didn't even look contemp-

tuous — the greatest sign of contempt. His black padded
jacket with its dozen or so buttons down the front
reminded me of the coat of an eighteenth-century
European noble. And he carried himself with dignity
even though he only drove three scrawny horses.

I was so used to contempt, it couldn't dampen my
spirits. Today I had left the labour camp to embark
on a new life. As our political instructor said, I would
now be supporting myself by my own labour. Nothing
could depress me.

In fact we had only just reached the boundary of the
farm where we were to work, and were still a long way
from any settlement. There wasn't a building in sight.
The boundary between this farm and our camp was a
stream, yet setting off at nine we hadn't reached it till
afternoon, judging from the sun's position. The soil on
both sides of the stream was the same, but on this side
was freedom.

The road was flanked by paddy fields. The tall
stalks standing there had ragged tops, obviously reaped
with blunt sickles. Were the farm-hands here the same
as we had been, too lazy to whet their sickles? I didn't
mind this, but was sorry that these weren't fields of
maize. Then we might have scavenged a few kernels.
Too bad! No maize fields around here.

The sun was warm. Mist rising from the foot of the
western hills was painting the rolling mountain ranges
a soft milky white. The cloudless blue sky stretched as
far as the eye could see, its colour gradually fading to
a pale vaporous blue at the horizon. The bare fields
were strikingly brown. I began to itch. Now that it
was warming up, the lice were coming out from the

seams of my clothes. When lice don't bite they can be quite lovable, they used to make me feel less lonely and destitute. I had my little dependants too!

At a crossroad the cart turned off down a rutted dirt track. I discovered that my companions were no longer trudging along beside me. They had ducked off behind the paddy field and were searching for something. Hell! My short-sightedness always made me too slow off the mark. They must have found something to eat.

I parted some withered reeds, crossed a ditch, and hurried to catch up with them. The Boss, holding a carrot, was scraping off the mud on it with his pocket knife. He glanced at me and chortled:

"My luck's in."

"My luck's in" was what you said in the camp if you got an extra large barnyard-millet bun, were assigned a light job where you might get some pickings, or got given sick leave. . . .

I looked: a good-sized carrot! He was always a lucky devil! The Boss was a "Rightist" too, but from what he'd told us I thought he had been wrongly labelled and should have been called a "degenerate". He felt he'd been unjustly treated. Said that the department store where he worked had made him a "Rightist" to fulfil its quota. In one of our come-clean meetings he learned that my great-grandfathers and grandfathers had all been officials or minor celebrities, while my father had been a capitalist running a factory. After the meeting he'd confided in me, rather enviously:

"You're a real 'bourgeois Rightist'. You've been around, lived on the fat of the land! Me, I started life as a beggar, then joined the army. How the hell can I be called a 'bourgeois Rightist'? If I'd enjoyed just one day of bourgeois life, I wouldn't complain. . . ."

That didn't make him treat me any better. Quite the opposite, he lost no opportunity of jeering at me to show his own superiority. A lot older than me, he was a lot weaker too. He had a sparse, dirty beard and snotty nose. Not daring to fight, he tried to make my mouth water by flaunting his outside aid and his good luck. I couldn't steer clear of him because since both of us were "Rightists", we were always in the same group. Now that we had been released, we had both been sent to work on the same farm since he'd lost his job in town.

A field of carrots is different from a field of turnips. Carrots aren't grown in plots separated by ridges but sown all over the field. If they're sown too densely they get thin and small, so that some of them are easily missed by harvesters. But since this field had been ransacked many times, and the ground was frozen hard, I squatted down and scrabbled about without finding a single carrot.

When our Boss had scraped off the mud, he stood near me crunching his carrot as if it were crystal sugar, munching loudly to show how crisp, juicy and sweet it was.

"Tastes great," he gloated.

That kind of carrot can only be found in a crack made by the frost. Knowing this I searched different cracks carefully, but in vain. Very few would have been left. You needed the Boss's luck to find one.

Still, today I wasn't put out about it. Standing up, I forced a smile as I passed him and took a short cut to catch up with the cart.

2

Yes, I was in good spirits today. That morning, at our last camp breakfast, I joined a friend I had made in hospital in front of the kitchen window since those of us who'd been discharged no longer had to eat with our team — he was a lecturer in philosophy from a well-known university in the northwest.

"You leaving, Zhang Yonglin?"

Even though he had on a camp uniform with soup stains all down the front, he congratulated me and shook hands like a gentleman. For me such politeness belonged to a different world. Yet this common courtesy immediately carried me back to that world once so familiar. So I did my best, in the din outside the kitchen, to talk to him like a scholar.

"What about your book?" I asked. "How can I get it back to you? Shall I post it?"

"No need!" A bowl of soup in one hand, he brushed this proposal aside with the other. "It's a present. Maybe...." He looked round in a detached way. "Maybe you can find out from it why we're where we are today."

"We? You mean us? Or...." I too looked round at the men queueing up for food. One was complaining that the cook's ladle had been tilted, hysterically demanding his full share. "Our — country?"

"Remember," he pointed at my chest, also covered in soup stains, and went on in a professorial manner, "our fates are closely bound up with that of our country."

This pronouncement and his attitude impressed me. Here, where men had no freedom of action, their thoughts were free to take flight. To prolong this intellectual pleasure, though I also kept glancing at the hatch (if you left it too late the cooks wouldn't serve you, or would punish you by giving you short rations), I answered equally seriously:

"But the first chapter's very hard to understand. Marx's dialectics ... the use of abstract theories to describe the formation of specific values. . . ."

"Read Hegel," he advised me, looking surprised, as if I had a library and could read anything I wanted. Then he frowned. "You must read Hegel. Marxism is an advance on Hegel's theories. Once you've read Hegel you'll find that first Chapter 'Commodities' easy to understand. You'll have no difficulty either with Chapters 2 and 3 and Part II 'The Transformation of Money and Capital'."

"Very well." I nodded politely, as if in college. "I find just the author's preface fascinating. It's a shame I only studied literature. . . ."

We concluded this cultured discussion at exactly the right time. After he had said goodbye and carefully carried off his bowl of gruel, I rushed to the hatch and thrust in my can just as a cook was about to close it.

"Where the hell have you been?"

"I've been helping load our baggage." I put on a submissive, ingratiating smile. "This is my last meal here."

"Oh." With a glance at me, the cook took my can and after serving my ration added nearly another ladleful.

"Thank you! Thank you!" I hastily nodded.

"Wait a second." An older cook wiped his wet hands and came to the hatch to have a look at me. "Are you that son of a bitch who crawled out of a pile of corpses?"

"That's right." His friendly tone surprised me, raised my hopes.

"Dammit, that took some doing!" Sure enough, from the steamer by the hatch he took two barnyard-millet buns left over from the day before and slapped them down on my skinny palms. "Take these!"

Before I could thank them again they slammed the hatch shut. They didn't care much for thanks, were sick of them.

This was a real stroke of luck! In my can I had nearly two ladlesful of gruel with vegetable leaves in it, in my hand two buns. Two! Not just one! Two buns were a day's ration: one in the morning, one in the evening. And the gruel was thick, almost as thick as paste. Sometimes the cooks stirred the gruel before serving it, bringing the thicker part to the top, so that the first-comers were in luck. If they ladled it out slowly, the thicker gruel sank to the bottom and the last in the queue had all the luck. This usually happened when the cooks had been too busy to eat before serving us, and wanted to leave the thick at the bottom for themselves. They liked us to race to the hatch, so that they could serve us quickly and knock off. But you could never be sure. Besides, as there were swarms of us and a dozen big wooden barrels in the kitchen, there was no knowing in which they would keep the best for themselves. . . . So getting thick gruel was more difficult than predicting changes in the world economy — it was a matter of luck.

Today my luck had been fine.

Just on the day I was starting a new life.

A good omen.

Hence my high spirits.

3

Actually I usually had more to eat than most of the other convicts. If we were served gruel, not buns, I generally got about 100 cc more. The secret was my can.

After the labour camp kitchen stopped serving rice in the spring of '59 and gave us gruel instead, we started using basins to fetch it rather than bowls. The cooks slopped it out so fast that if you used a container with a small mouth the gruel at the bottom of the ladle would drip back into the barrel, whereas if you used a basin you'd get your full serving. It had to be smaller than a wash-basin but bigger than a bowl — a child's wash-basin. In the hard years such basins were hard to buy. But our Boss had a way. I suspected that he'd smuggled out all the children's things from his department store, and that he had accomplices still at large. In any event he got his wife, who paid him monthly visits and was equally obnoxious, to offer to sell one to everyone in our group. Of course he expected something in return. He used to boast that although he was shut up here he could still pull strings outside. He spun this web to catch flies and wanted to catch me too so he could jeer at me. But I didn't rise to the bait. I hadn't a penny, and didn't get any food from outside which I could give this broker. My mother in Beijing was living with a friend, weaving plastic string bags for the neighbourhood committee. Since she only made a dozen yuan a month, I couldn't ask her for help. But I had my own way out. I had brought with me a five-pound milk-powder tin, my sole legacy from my bourgeois family. I tied a wire tightly round the top to make a handle, and this can was much bigger than most enamel mugs. Though its mouth was the size of a bowl, and the gruel outside the ladle was lost, because of its depth it contained more than a mug. The cooks, deceived into thinking that they had given me less than other people, always added a little more. And this "little" was a lot more than what spattered outside.

Each time we went back to our quarters from the kitchen, the Boss used to swagger up to me holding his new child's wash-basin which had a design of a kitten washing its face on it. It was easy for me to see that his gruel came up to the kitten's middle. Once when all the others had gone off to work, and I was alone on sick leave, I put in my can as much water as my usual helping of gruel, then poured it into his basin. The experiment proved that I got 100 cc more. The water was up over the towel in the kitten's paw.

I got that 100 cc by taking advantage of an optical illusion.

That was where my education came in handy.

However, a basin had its advantages too — it could be licked clean. The Boss's way of doing this was unique. Instead of lowering his face to the basin, he held it above him, stuck out his tongue and deftly turned it round with both hands. Before long other members of the group began to do the same.

I couldn't lick my can, that was a real shame! After finishing off the gruel I washed the can with water, then drank the water. A tin can, unlike an enamel basin, will rust unless wiped dry. So after each meal I dried mine scrupulously with a towel and put it on the dry, airy window-sill. Of course that annoyed the Boss. At our weekly meetings to criticize each other's conduct, he condemned me for not reforming my "bad bourgeois habits, so thoroughly different from the life-style of the labouring people".

Although secretly ashamed, because there was some truth in this criticism, the thought of that 100 cc comforted me.

Our relationship continued like this: he felt superior to me both morally and materially, while I felt much the same about him.

Now I'd got the better of him again. For breakfast I'd had nearly a whole ladleful of extra gruel, thick gruel, which was still not fully digested in my stomach, was still supplying me with calories. All he'd got was thin gruel. Although he was smacking his lips over a carrot, did he have buns in his pocket? No. Certainly not. I had two substantial millet buns. Could eat them whenever I wanted. But I didn't choose to just yet. If you over-indulge yourself, your good luck's bound to turn bad. Four years in the labour camp had taught me that.

"Get moving! The cart's way ahead!" I shouted over my shoulder to the others, who were still looking for carrots.

I felt superior for another reason too. I realized that *today* I could leave the highway and cross the ditch to scour a field for carrots (irrespective of whether I found any or not). *Today* I could catch up with the cart whenever I pleased, *could do whatever I pleased*, instead of being at the beck and call of the team leader.

Although the Boss was doing the same and had even got one up on me, he wasn't conscious of having acquired this freedom and that set me intellectually above him.

Although I had found no carrots I still felt content thinking of my superior status. I hurried after the cart, proud to have won a moral victory.

"Come on! The young master's orders!" I heard the Boss yelling behind me.

They soon caught up with me.

4

The cart jolted steadily forward. The roan's mouth had stopped bleeding, the black blood on the gash had clotted. Every wound can heal. Tomorrow it would be back in harness again.

It would go on drawing the cart, bleeding, drawing the cart, bleeding ... till its dying day.

The carter was still sitting brooding on the shaft. He paid no attention to us, as if we didn't exist. His silence worried me. The farm had sent him to the camp to fetch us, but we didn't know whether he was a cadre or a farm-hand. He was good at harnessing and driving the cart and fastening on the baggage. Had a Hezhou accent but seldom spoke, and then only very tersely, as if there was something weighing on his mind. He neither ordered us about nor showed us any sign of goodwill. Cold and harsh, he ground his teeth grimly whenever he cracked his whip. He looked forty or thereabouts but might have been younger, as northwesterners have weather-beaten faces. Big and burly, his eyes, nose and mouth seemed etched on his bronzed, handsome face, which hadn't a trace of softness about it.

As I sized him up I analysed the reason for my uneasiness. I decided that I was used to being supervis-

ed and ordered around. Though today I'd got my
freedom, it would still take some getting used to. I still
needed someone to boss me about.

Mortified by this discovery, I defiantly moved off to
walk by the roadside.

The horses staggered along, jolting the cart, their
hooves and the wheels leaving tracks on the lonely road.
The rest of us followed in silence. A breeze sprang up.
At the foot of the hills a whirlwind swirled yellow dust
like a jade column high up into the air. After a bit
two eagles flew over to soar above us.

As if in response to the cries of the famished eagles,
the carter, motionless as a stone statue, suddenly burst
into song:

Ah!

His voice was laden with grief.

The carter has snapped his whip,
The horses are out of step.
Three days Brother has been away,
Farther from home each day.

His rich voice was constrained, as if it was forced
out of him; and the last word in each line slid down the
scale like a groan, to drift across the boundless fields.
The changing tempo was so charged with vitality that
even when the last note had died away I felt as though
the beautiful melody was still floating in the air. I have
heard recordings of many famous singers, but none of
them had moved me as much as this song of his. Not
simply because it smacked of Central Asian and old
Oriental music, but because of its passion, its simplicity

and desolation, which seemed one with the vast gloomy plain, seemed one with this loess plateau.

He went on:

> Ah!
> The moth has burned itself in the lamp,
> The frog has hidden itself in the camp;
> I stayed awake thinking of you all night,
> Thinking of you until the day was light.

The melody, rhythm and his local accent all carried the flavour of the steppe. Just as Neapolitan folk songs conjure up the blue Mediterranean, and Hawaiian songs palms waving in the breeze, so this song brought to life these fields, the clouds scudding before the wind, the sky and the eagles soaring overhead, with their compelling vitality. I was suddenly captivated by the magnificent landscape.

His singing had awakened the poetry which had lain dormant so long in my heart.

Ah, today I was a free man. With my chapped bloodless lips I wanted to kiss this soil!

I listened in absolute silence as he went on:

> Ah!
> The horse has galloped far away,
> The foal behind must stay.
> I've left the housework all undone,
> Thinking of you and you alone.

Grief is the soul of song. I was thoroughly riveted by the poignancy of his singing. Not so much by the words as by the tune and rhythm. His longing for someone, perhaps some imaginary figure, aroused in me too a yearning which the pangs of hunger had driven from my mind. I felt wretched, but this time it was a human wretchedness, not the wretchedness of a famished animal.... The tireless eagles followed us as the wintry sun sloped westward.

He broke into a livelier song, though it too was tinged with sadness.

> Ah!
> The black cat curls up on the stove,
> Round a bowl its tail it twines.
> Sister is lying in Brother's arms —
> Press your sweet lips to mine!

When I realized that this was a love song, my imagination, long as inactive as a wounded bird on a withered bough, was startled into life to spread its wings and fly far, far away. Looking back I saw green grass sprouting under a tree which had been blasted by lightning. The song, with its expression of undisguised sexual desire, swept my heart clean of the filth of the camp which had been choking it. It seemed to me so bold and unabashed that by comparison *O Sole Mio* was insipid and colourless. Though I was twenty-five, my blood was very thin from malnutrition, yet it now coursed more swiftly through my veins, mounting to my head to conjure up formless fancies, until I felt I was on fire. . . . I discovered that tears had welled up in my eyes.

This was my first day of freedom.

5

But this day, so important to me, so memorable — December 1, 1961 — was to others no different from any ordinary day.

That rather disappointed me.

When finally at sunset we reached a village — where someone hailed the carter as Xixi — there was no one to welcome us. We didn't even see a dog or a hen, just a few old men in ragged clothes lazily sitting on a concrete bridge basking in the evening sunshine. They didn't so much as glance in our direction.

This village was laid out just like the labour camp, with barrack-like rows of adobe cottages. They were in an even worse state than those in the camp, with some of the walls crumbling away. In the camp there had been a labour force available to do repairs. Here, however, they did have a couple of stacks of firewood, sodden by rain or snow, outside each small wooden door as well as clothes-lines which made the place seem a little more homely.

The cart passed a row of cottages in front of which were nothing but stacks of firewood. There wasn't a soul in sight. We seemed to have come to a deserted village.

"Dammit! Is everyone dead! Where are they to be quartered?"

Hai Xixi the singer had switched back to being a carter, who now growled out unprintable obscenities. He was obviously furious at having had to fetch us. He jumped down from the shaft, tugged the horses forward and looked right and left. From the way the old men on the bridge had addressed him we knew he was not a cadre, and that diminished our respect for him. We ignored him. He could take us wherever he pleased.

When we reached the last row of buildings he halted in front of what looked like a storehouse, then quickly unhitched the horses and led them off, leaving us without a word.

We felt a bit let down by this casual treatment, and by this time were famished. I thought of eating my buns, but resisted the temptation. Eating, the greatest enjoyment, should be in a quiet place free from interruption, to savour the full flavour of the food. Since we hadn't yet settled down and could be moved on any moment, to eat now would be a great waste.

"Hey, mates. This is probably the place." The Boss had poked his head through a broken window. Because he never admitted that he was a "Rightist", he kept taking small liberties. While the rest of us stood there helplessly he had been scouting around.

"This isn't the farm headquarters," he said. "Just one brigade. Look! This must be our dorm. Hell, it's worse than the labour camp! There at least we had a heated *kang*."

We peered through the paneless window. On the earthen floor was a row of fresh straw pallets. No furniture of any kind. The brown adobe walls were peeling, straws sticking out. What a dump.

"This is obviously a poor place," said the newspaper editor from Lanzhou. "Just like the village I was in before."

"Would they send us anywhere good?" swore the Lieutenant, a Korean War hero. Despite three years of labour reform, he still expected preferential treatment. "Blast it, we've simply moved from the eighteenth stratum of Hell to the seventeenth."

"Well, it's no use grumbling." The Shanghai bank accountant adopted a fatalistic attitude. "Let's make the best of it. Since we won't be here long we can put up with it."

The others cheered up a little, describing the strings their families were pulling for them. Yes, they wouldn't be here long. They had homes in cities like Shanghai, Xi'an and Lanzhou, where their wives were arranging for them to be transferred to farms in the suburbs. The Boss would soon be able to go back to the suburbs of the provincial capital. They all wanted to rejoin their wives and children, and this was in line with the state policy. So they were just here in transit from Inferno to Paradise. I was the only one who would have to stay on here, maybe till I died of old age. My mother in Beijing had no way of getting me transferred back; my bureaucrat-capitalist home had been destroyed by Japanese gunfire, all its members scattered. Just as it says in *A Dream of Red Mansions*:

> When the food is gone the birds return to the wood;
> All that's left is emptiness and a great void.

Unable to join in their talk about bright futures. I squatted down to one side thinking. This, my first day of freedom, had been marked by various good omens (apart from my failure to find a carrot), and this encouraged me. Since I had crawled out from a heap of corpses, I could surely live on. Might even live another sixty years. I was still active, could see the sun, hear songs. I was lucky, had got off lightly, so hardships and poverty should not make me despair. True, my home had turned into "emptiness and a great void", leaving me to go "naked without impediment". So, although disappointed, I was not particularly discontented. I had learned to be patient and stoical.

After about half an hour, we saw people with shovels coming back from the fields and voices sounded in the next row of housing. Work was over for the day. A middle-aged cripple limped towards us.

"So you're here." Without looking at us, he selected a key from the bunch in his hands and opened the door, then turned to leave.

"Hey, where's the team leader!" the Lieutenant called after him. "Don't we have to check in?" As soon as he'd left the labour camp he had reverted to his army ways.

"The team leader will come over when he's rested," the Cripple answered without looking round.

There was nothing to wait for. Since I was meant to live on I had to be resourceful. I was the first to get up on the cart to take down my tattered quilt — all the property I had. Clutching it under one arm I dashed inside and kicked one pile of straw as close as I could to the wall to make a thick pallet, making sure that the pile next to mine was equally thick. Honour among thieves. Live and let live.

Then I put my quilt at the foot of the wall. I had staked out my claim.

"Hey, what are you up to? The team leader hasn't told us our places yet." The Boss was annoyed that he hadn't grabbed a place by the wall himself. Though he was always trying to take small advantages, if somebody else did so he would report them. This morning he'd put his things in the bottom of the cart to make sure they wouldn't be shaken off. So now, by the time he brought in his bedding, the floor space by three walls had been occupied. Too bad, you'll have to sleep in a draught by the door. Never mind. Live and let live. He had a quilt and mattress as well as a sheepskin jacket; it was only fair for him to sleep by the door. I unrolled my tattered quilt and stuffed Volume I of *Capital* under one end as a pillow, then stretched out on my "bed", ignoring everyone else.

The foot of a wall is the best place to sleep in a dormitory, because on one side there is no one to disturb you. If you have a sewing-kit, shoes and socks or — by some stroke of luck — some food, you can stow it under the straw by the wall. If you have other possessions, you can hang them on the wall. If you want to read or write a letter home, you can turn your back on the world to concentrate. After four years in the camp I understood why monks face the wall to meditate.

6

We'd just spread out our bedding, and dust from the straw still hung in the air, when the Cripple came back to announce that the team leader wanted him to take us to get our food.

Food! Great!

The village had come to life. The golden rays of the wintry evening sun were gilding the brown adobe walls and the ramshackle window-panes. Smoke rising from the small chimneys of each cottage filled the air with the scent of mugwort and artemisia. This rural scene, so different from the camp, elated me. What did poverty and hardship matter now that I was back in a normal environment.

The kitchen was small, which rather worried me. The fewer the people eating there, the more the cooks would squeeze from each of them. Still, now that we were workers we could go into it. While the Cripple — I'd heard that he was storekeeper — was telling the cooks how much grain we were to have, I peered short-sightedly around the kitchen. The cloth from the steamer thrown on the chopping-board had morsels of steamed buns sticking to it. In fact men like the Boss were stupid. They wrote so many complaining letters home that their families tightened their belts to help them out. Instead of troubling my mother I used my wits to scrounge at least as much extra food as they received from outside.

Our ration was four ounces: a millet bun and a bowl of cold soup made with salted vegetables. Standing last in the line, I asked the cook with a smile, "Can I scrape that cloth from the steamer instead of taking a bun?"

"Sure." Raising his eyebrows he handed me a scoop. "Go ahead."

I carefully scraped the cloth clean, filling my can to the top with bun scraps. I got at least a pound.

That was a stroke of luck!

Though they smelt of water from the steamer, they tasted good.

Only free men could go into the kitchen. How good it was to be free.

After supper the team leader brought us a lantern. "So you're here, good. . . ."

He produced a box of matches. At once I went over to hold the lantern while he lit it, then hung it on a hook above my pallet — it would be half mine. Life in the camp without any help from outside had sharpened my wits. The Boss and the others could only rely on support from their families.

"Are we to sleep any old way like this, team leader?" asked the Boss.

"Just sleep wherever you want, it doesn't matter." The team leader sat cross-legged on his pallet, not grasping what he meant.

"Isn't there a better room than this, team leader?" asked the Lieutenant grumpily. "There isn't even a *kang* here."

"Just make the best of it. It's up to you to fix it up." The team leader sounded annoyed. A thin middle-aged man, he told us his name was Xie. By the dim light of the lantern I saw that he was bearded, looked exhausted, and was wearing a patched padded cadre suit. He said, "You can't build a solid *kang* in winter. It'll have to wait till spring."

But by spring we wouldn't need one.

Some men asked him the postal address of the place. Where was the farm headquarters? To whom should they apply to transfer their residence registration? Team Leader Xie realized that they didn't intend staying long. He looked at me, sitting in the shadows. Narrowing his eyes he asked:

"Hey, you, what's your name?"

"Zhang Yonglin." I leaned forward, rustling my pallet.

He held a paper up to the light and strained his eyes to read it.

"You're from Beijing? Just twenty-five?"

"That's right."

"You're the youngest of the lot. Well, do you want to leave too?"

"No, I don't."

"Good. Then mind you do a good job here." He sounded pleased, and added amicably, "This isn't such a bad place, better than where you come from. You'll get 25 catties of grain a month and two packets of cigarettes. The pay is 18 yuan for the first grade, 21 for the second. You'll start off with 18. After half a year we'll see how you're shaping. . . ."

"Yes." I nodded to express complete satisfaction. The others were leaning back against their quilts listening glumly. In the dim light their faces looked like masks.

In fact there was nothing to be pleased about. Except the pay, which we didn't get in the camp. And in those hard times 18 yuan wouldn't buy ten catties of carrots. Besides, you didn't get your clothing issued here. The grain ration was the same as in the camp, and what with various deductions the most we'd actually get was 20 catties. (25 catties a month would be enough normally, but we had no other foodstuffs, no oil or vegetables, and were doing manual labour. On top of which we'd been undernourished for years. The ration in 1960 had been only 15 catties.) What pleased me most was the way the team leader had avoided referring to the camp.

From his pockets Xie now produced some cigarettes, and gave each of us two packets, for which he charged 16 cents. Eight cents a packet. Splendid! It was real tobacco, not the leaves of sunflowers, cabbage or eggplant. . . . To me cigarettes meant almost as much as grain. But I couldn't help feeling jealous when I saw that the Boss, a non-smoker, was given his share. When you were desperate for a smoke, he would sell you one cigarette for 20 cents. Share and share alike also had its drawbacks.

"Breakfast's at nine, off to work at ten. We knock off at four. There's not much to do in winter. You'll start work tomorrow and keep at it till your day off." The team leader stood up and brushed off the seat of his pants. He had said "day off" not Sunday. Which was the day off?

"Team leader, since there's no *kang* can't we have a stove? This room must be freezing at night." The Lieutenant, his quilt around him, made another special request. A collective needs someone like this.

"Yes, you must build a stove. There are adobe bricks around. But we only have coal, no charcoal." Xie tucked his hands in his sleeves as if he felt cold. "And you must paper the windows. Go to the office tomorrow to fetch some old newspapers, then get some paste from the kitchen."

"I know how to build a stove," I volunteered. With two buns in reserve I didn't mind doing the job.

"You do? It's not the same as a brazier." Xie eyed me in surprise. "All right, tomorrow you stay at home and see to the stove and windows. Oh, another thing, you'll need a group leader. Zhang Yonglin can take that on."

Fine! My first day of freedom and I was a group leader!

7

That evening I burrowed cautiously into my quilt. Mustn't stick my toes through the holes or I'd make them bigger; and I must keep the quilt well tucked in or the straw would prick my back. Last of all I took from my padded jacket, spread over the quilt, the two buns I'd got that morning. I sniffed them appreciatively under the quilt, then wrapped them up in my towel and hid them in my pallet.

The night was utterly silent. Unlike the camp where at midnight you heard the steps of the patrol.

Then I began thinking. My mind, splintered by the pain of an incomprehensible reality, started tormenting me like spikes of glass. Night was the time when I felt most wide awake.

In the daytime my instinct of self-preservation drove me to ingratiate myself and resort to all kinds of tricks. At night I was horrified by my contemptible behaviour, revolted by my conduct during the day. I shuddered and cursed myself.

I was fully aware of just how low I'd sunk.

I don't believe that decadence is entirely due to objective circumstances. If that were the case and will-power counted for nothing, then men would sink to the level of beasts. True religious believers can lay down their lives for God. Materialist poets take high ideals as their god. Since I was not dead, what was I living for? Just for the sake of living? If so, how utterly futile.

But right now I was living for the sake of living.

What new ideals should I have, what new aim in life?

I had been told that the aim in life of someone from my sort of background should be to remould himself. Today I had gained my freedom. If I had been punished for my crimes, by now surely I had atoned for being a "Rightist". If my release signified the end of one stage in my remoulding, how should I live from now on? I had to think this over. But on this farm I didn't know how to test the extent to which I had been remoulded.

Although free I didn't feel that I had my feet on the ground, more that I was floating in the air. . . .

I turned my face to the wall. It smelt mouldy, smelt of rat droppings and also, faintly, of straw. Next to me the old Accountant was grinding his teeth, as if over our wretched future. My quilt felt icy, I was numb with cold. How could I have landed myself in this predicament? It was a mystery to me. Sometimes my life before the camp seemed like a dream; sometimes the present seemed a nightmare from which I would wake to find myself back in the classroom teaching Tang and Song poetry, or sitting at my desk reading my beloved Shakespeare. However, my belly gave me the most practical advice: Face up to reality or you'll go hungry.

That was the truth of the matter.

Was this fate? But hunger was a fate shared by millions. As the philosophy lecturer had said, "Each individual's fate is bound up with that of the country."

I felt for *Capital* under my head. "Perhaps you can find out from this why we're where we are today." This book was now my sole link with the rational world of the intellect, the only way I could rise above buns, carrots and gruel, could become different from a starving beast. . . .

Gradually my quilt warmed up. I felt cosy and relaxed, aware of my own existence. What is existence? Descartes said: I think, therefore I am. How good to be alive, to be able to think! I didn't want to sleep, but I dozed off anyway.

8

First thing the next morning I received a staggering blow — my two buns had been eaten by rats!

Eaten by rats, not stolen, because my towel had been gnawed into shreds as well. I rolled it up and stuffed it into my pocket. I couldn't let the Boss know, or he would have gloated over my misfortune.

Breakfast wasn't till nine. I leaned against my folded quilt feeling faint. If I hadn't lost those two buns I would have felt all right, even if I hadn't eaten them. But this disaster made me ravenous. Hunger can become a palpable weight pounding against your stomach. Can scream to each nerve in your body: I want food! Too limp to move, I decided to make up the loss.

Once again survival became my sole aim in life.

When we had fetched our food back from the kitchen, we sat on our pallets to devour it in silence. My can had failed me. The cook here seemed to have no optical illusions. He trusted his ladle, gave me no extra helping. Never mind, I had thought of a way out.

After breakfast Team Leader Xie sent a grim-looking farm-hand to take the rest off to work. The crippled storekeeper arrived with a bundle of old newspapers under his arm. Having put this down he told me where to find bricks and a barrow, then took me to his store-room to fetch a shovel, a small bucket, a mason's trowel and some iron bars to make a grating. He told me to go to the kitchen for paste — he had notified the cook. If I needed anything else, I could find him in the office.

Building a stove is a job for two, but I preferred to do it single-handed. The adobe bricks were just outside our quarters. Earth I could easily dig up in the yard. The soil here, being alkaline, hadn't frozen. The less water I used the better, or it would take hours for the stove to dry. As soon as the Cripple left, I went off with a newspaper to the kitchen.

"I've come for paste, master," I told the cook with a smile, as if I weren't ravenous.

"Help yourself." He was sitting with a full stomach sunning himself on the doorstep. "Just don't take too much."

"Look." I held out the newspaper. "I'll wrap it in this."

On the chopping-board was a wash-basin half full of grey barnyard-millet flour which he had apparently put out for me. I unfolded my paper and poured it all out, then bundled it up and carried it off.

It wouldn't occur to someone with a full stomach that barnyard-millet isn't cohesive enough to make paste. It would flake off as soon as it dried. My first concern anyway was the stove. In the camp I had spent a month building stoves for the cadres there with an engineer who specialized in heating systems. He was a "Rightist" too. As his assistant I learned the simplest way to make stoves, which he was able to do with only a shovel. His stoves burnt well and economized on fuel. It was all a question of the depth of the flue. After less than two hours' hard work, by which time I was sweating profusely, I had made a simple yet scientific stove.

Without stopping to rest I pushed the barrow to the kitchen to half fill it with coal — I couldn't have pushed a whole load. On the way back I pinched some kindling from someone's woodstack.

With trembling fingers I struck a match and lit the

kindling in the stove. Flames and smoke belched out. After a while the smoke disappeared and the wood crackled merrily. As soon as there was a good blaze I shovelled in some coal and, as if by magic, out billowed black smoke which was promptly sucked into the flue. Flames were still coming out from cracks in the stove. In less than five minutes the fire had turned scarlet.

My next concern was to ensure that nobody could see what I was up to. I went to the office, where the Cripple was sitting idle, and asked him for some small nails, some old cardboard and a pair of scissors. Since I hadn't tried to scrounge anything to eat, he readily handed these over, and back I rushed. I cut the cardboard into narrow strips to hold the newspapers in place, and nailed them firmly on the window-frames.

Now the place looked like a dormitory. Or as Team Leader Xie had said, a "home".

I had the whole operation down to an art. By now the stove was bright red, smokeless and very hot. After washing the shovel clean, I propped it against the mouth of the stove, poured some millet flour into my can and stirred in enough water to make a paste, then sloshed this on the hot shovel. The shovels they use on the steppes are flat, like the bottom of a frying-pan. My dough spread out evenly, the bubbles at its edge quickly subsiding, so that in less than a minute I had a pancake.

This was the treat for which I had worked so hard.

I ate the pancake, cooked another and ate it. . . . Each one tasted better than the last. While the pancakes were cooking I blocked up the rat-holes by my pallet. Finding rats here was a surprise. There had been none in the camp — they had nothing to eat there and were in danger of being eaten themselves.

The adobe cottage warmed up. So did my stomach. I sat down by the stove feeling drowsy. But this was no time for sleep. I took a pack of cigarettes from my quilt and lit one from a cinder which had fallen out through the grating. I didn't exhale a single wisp of smoke. I swallowed it all. At once I felt pleasantly intoxicated.

Then, for some reason, my heart began to ache.

Stop brooding! I should have known that as soon as my belly was bloated my heart would ache with a pain worse than hunger. Hunger was easier to take. I carefully stubbed out my cigarette and put the butt back in the packet. I must find something to do. After putting away my tools, I wrapped up what was left of the millet and hung it on the wall. I stoked the stove, picked up my patched mittens, brushed the dust off my clothes and left "home".

9

The weather was exceptionally fine. The loess on the steppe was all tinged a lemon colour. The only trees round the village were a few leafless white poplars thrusting proudly like silver shafts towards the warm sky, casting elongated shadows. The sun was to the west. Yesterday at this time Hai Xixi the carter had burst into song. Now, full, I thought of some verses by Pablo Neruda.

Often on a full stomach I have strange mental associations. And Hai Xixi's song reminded me of the fearlessness of the American pioneers. The song, the eagles, the far-stretching landscape with its rolling mountains . . . filled me with exhilaration.

I walked cheerfully towards the stable, wanting to see the horses. I love horses. They always make me think of the heroism involved in opening up borderlands.

However, in front of the stable some farm-hands were forking manure. Among them were the Boss, Lieutenant, Accountant and Editor. It was too late for me to beat a retreat.

"Fixed up your home?" Team Leader Xie was standing on a dunghill with a shovel.

"Yes."

"What have you come for?"

"I. . . ." I could hardly say I'd come to look at the horses. "I've come to do some work."

"Fine." His bearded mouth split open in a grin. "You can shovel down dung for them."

I looked in the direction he was pointing and discovered that there were women here too.

I had never worked with women. Had seen very few during my four years in camp. Head lowered, I shuffled over.

"Fetch a shovel, and we'll sieve what you shovel down," one of the women said. "Don't wear yourself out.   You're as skinny as a monkey, so take it easy."

Her voice was soft; I was touched by her concern. It was so long since anyone had spoken like that to me. I was more used to hearing, "Get a move on!" I blushed, not daring to look at her, determined to do my best.

I asked the team leader where I could find a shovel.

"Why the hell didn't you bring one?" he bellowed. "Can't eat without chopsticks can you?"

The women beside me giggled. I flushed and inwardly cursed the team leader for his sudden changes of mood.

I was wondering what to do when the woman who had first spoken gave me a key. "Here, fetch a pickaxe from my place. Behind the door. It's handy."

I sheepishly took the key.

"The first door in the front row of cottages to the west. You can't miss it. Just turn the corner and it's the first door."

"It's marked 'American Hotel'," another woman tittered.

"You bitch, giving it a name like that!"

I left while they laughed and traded abuse.

The copper key, home-made, was bright with use and still warm from her pocket.

I turned it over to examine it, and stroked it gratefully as if it were her hand.

There was no "American Hotel" sign on the door which, like all the rest, had a black stack of firewood and a clothes-line outside it. Going in, I found the place smaller than ours, half taken up by a *kang*. The mud floor had been swept very clean and was as flat as a cement one. There was no wooden furniture. Table and stools were all made of clay. A sort of kitchen cupboard had been built by the *kang*, its top shelf covered by an old floral curtain. All these furnishings were immaculate. The table glittered with empty wine bottles and tins. On the *kang* was spread a shabby rug, which had a neat pile of patched quilts and clothes on it, among them a child's. The *kang* had a gay curtain, and over it were pasted colourful photographs.

On the stove by the *kang* stood a pan with a wooden lid.

This was the first time I had set foot alone in a stranger's home. Her trust in me warmed my heart.

I raised the lid of the pan and lifted the curtain, unable to resist seeing what there was to eat.

How shameful!

Quickly taking the pickaxe from behind the door I headed back to the stable.

"Did you lock up?" she asked as, head lowered, I handed her the key.

"Yes."

I started swinging the pickaxe. A woman near by warbled:

> Three times I loitered by Sister's gate,
> But caught no glimpse of her lovely face!

"Just you wait, you. . . ." The other woman called her such a dirty but colourful name that all the rest burst out laughing.

I shot her a glance, not knowing why she was so angry. As she had her back to me, all I saw was two black plaits and a flowered padded jacket, patched with a darker material.

Horse-dung mixed with soil was used here as fertilizer. We had to hack down and break up frozen chunks of it, then cart them to the fields and cover them with earth, to be scattered in spring. After eating all those pancakes I worked all out and in no time had supplied them with a big pile.

"Slow down, you id-i-ot!"

She dragged out the word "idiot" so touchingly that I had to smile. I glanced at her again. Her head was bent over her work though, and she didn't see me.

"First steep the millet, then simmer a thick gruel. . . ."

"Best to top it off with shredded carrot."

"Diced carrot looks better."

"Carrots aren't as tasty as beets."

After their slanging match the women by the dunghill had started discussing cooking. She turned to them and cried:

"Hell! I'd rather eat one bite of a peach than half a crate of rotten pears. I'd choose cooked rice every time!"

"Ha, who can match you, with your 'American Hotel'. . . ."

"Don't give me that nonsense." She straightened up. "I know how to make millet taste like rice."

"Make some for us to taste then."

"To taste? Suppose you lost your way and ended up on someone else's *kang*?" Her laughter rang out again.

This was followed by another exchange of good-natured abuse.

Just then Hai Xixi came back with his cart, cracking his whip at his scrawny team as he sat bolt upright on the shaft.

"Are you knocking off already, you bastard?" demanded Team Leader Xie, his shovel still for a second. I'd noticed that he got through more work than the farm-hands.

Hai Xixi, taken by surprise, quickly jumped down and pulled up his cart.

"The horses are tired, team leader."

"Are the horses tired or are you slacking, you swine? Eh?" Xie narrowed his eyes. At once he grew in stature in my eyes, while hefty Hai seemed to shrivel. I was sorry for the carter: He looked so taken aback.

"Want me to settle scores with you, you bastard?" Hai looked even more at a loss than I had when I'd suddenly found the team leader there.

Xie bellowed, "Unhitch your team and fetch a
pickaxe. You're to hack me down two cubic metres of
dung before you knock off, you son of a bitch."

The team leader's invective made everyone laugh.
Even Hai Xixi had a hint of a smile. That cheered me
up a bit. Xie's abuse of me had been mild by comparison.

Hai Xixi drove his cart into the stable, coming out
again with a pickaxe.

"Where shall I start, team leader?" He looked ready
for anything.

"Here." Xie pointed in front of himself. He sounded
tired. "There's a whacking big block here I haven't been
able to bite off."

Hai Xixi spat on his hands. "Leave it to me." He
went straight into action.

Soon they were working together in perfect harmony,
shovel and pickaxe co-ordinating smoothly.

"Trashy good-for-nothing!" the woman next to me
swore. I'd no idea who she was cursing.

I concentrated on hacking down frozen dung. When
she couldn't keep up I helped her break up the hunks
and she shovelled them aside.

Then she leaned on her shovel and sang softly:

> Don't laugh if I sing,
> Singing to drive care away;
> It's care that makes me sing,
> Don't think I'm singing for joy.

Like Hai Xixi the day before, she was singing a
popular folk song, but it was one I'd never heard before.
Though her voice was completely untrained and we
were surrounded by dunghills, I felt transported to

mountains beneath a blue sky, felt my horizon expanding. There was something saddening too about the casual way she sang, because while giving me such pleasure she herself had no idea what a lovely song she was singing. Just like Hai yesterday, she took no pride in her singing.

That afternoon we forked a whole pile of dung. When Xie made a tour of inspection he was especially pleased by what we had done and shouted:

"Knock off!"

Everyone scattered to their homes. Out of politeness I said to her, "Thanks.   Let me carry this pickaxe back for you."

She turned from wiping her shovel to eye me in surprise, as if unaccustomed to such courtesy.   Then she grabbed the pickaxe from me and answered rudely:

"*You* carry it! Look at you, you skinny monkey, gray in the face."

10

Back in our quarters I found the rest of my group delighted with our "home". The Boss took his wash-basin over to the stove, saying it was now warm enough to have a bath.

At supper time we all gathered round the stove.   Its warmth knit us closer together, made us more talkative. The Editor, true to his profession, had collected a good deal of information. According to him this was a very large farm with over a dozen teams scattered beside the mountains from north to south. They were at least ten *li* apart, and it was twenty *li* to the farm headquarters. The most remote team, at the foot of the mountains, was a day's journey away. Headquarters had a shop, but as at present it only stocked salt the farm-hands called it the Salt Store. To buy anything you had to go over thirty *li* to South Fort. You could take a train east for thirty *li*, to a place where there was a one-minute halt. A freight train passed there at four a.m. every day. Our team had no Party secretary and the deputy team leader was bedridden with dropsy, so Team Leader Xie was in charge of political work and production. The farm-hands said, "If you don't get on his bad side, Xie's a good sort." The team at the foot of the mountains was the worst. So strictly run that you had no freedom of movement. The farm-hands called it the Gate to Hell. All the trouble-makers got sent there.

The Editor also told us that most of the farm-hands here were local people or came from Gansu and Shaan-xi. Xie had been the Party secretary of one brigade in a former commune here. Other new teams were very mixed: young people from Zhejiang, demobilized soldiers, men who had served their time in labour camps, and redundant factory workers.

"Well!" exclaimed the old Accountant. "It's more of a melting pot than the camp."

"Better hurry up and leave this hole," grumbled the Boss, washing his feet. "You could leave the camp after serving your term; you may be stuck here for life."

I felt too limp to listen to their chat. Exhausted. But I couldn't sleep. Sometimes for an extra bite to eat you have to expend more calories than the food supplies. It really wasn't worth it, since you grew weaker and weaker. Today, as that woman said, I had worked myself "gray in the face".

The fearful thing about debility is your full awareness of each minor symptom. It isn't painful, doesn't make you faint, but saps all your strength. I'd rather faint. It appalled me to find myself so weak at only twenty-five, with no organic diseases. . . . Death holds no terror at such a time. What I dreaded was the awareness that each step I took was taking me nearer my grave, that my life was being reeled off like raw silk from a cocoon.

Ah, Lazarus! Lazarus!*

II

I woke the next morning ravenous, aching all over. That was proof that there was life in me still.

I must at all costs find some pretext to stay at "home".

After breakfast I told my group that the stove had cracked in some places. Unless filled up these cracks might let out carbon monoxide. "And that would be no joke, going back to Hell straight after leaving the camp." I asked them to tell Team Leader Xie I was staying in to fix it.

Because I was "group leader" and, even more, because all of them prized this stove, the Lieutenant said, "OK. I'll tell him."

I guessed that Xie wouldn't just take their word for it. I slowly fetched water and dug up some earth. I

---

* The Bible says that Jesus raised Lazarus from the dead, and so he became the patron saint of invalids.

was mixing mud when, sure enough, Xie came along with his shovel.

"Well I'll be damned!" He examined the stove with an expert eye and squatted down to warm his hands by it. "So you can make a simple stove that saves fuel and burns well."

"It's not hard once you get the hang of it." I explained with a smile who had taught me.

"Well I'm blowed! You 'Rightists' are all so smart. Our local people have built stoves for eight generations, but all in the same old way. Wasting mud and bricks. Solid as a city wall, giving off precious little heat."

Now that Xie was warm his eyes began to water. He wiped them with his sleeve. His rough hands were badly chapped. Years of outdoor work had ravaged his hands and face. He suddenly struck me as not a bad old geezer with his kind, wrinkled face.

"If your stove doesn't burn well, Team Leader Xie, I can come and fix it for you," I volunteered.

"No need," he said quietly. "We burn wood, can't afford coal. As bachelors you're entitled to a coal stove. Not the others. Haven't you seen those stacks of firewood outside their doors? They use it to cook, to heat the *kang*, so that they sleep snug at night. Xixi built my stove for me. He's a clever devil."

"Isn't Hai Xixi a cadre?" I asked plastering over the cracks, "We all thought he was when he fetched us yesterday."

"A cadre? Hell no!" Xie laughed. "He arrived this spring from Gansu. Studied in a mosque as a boy, but didn't get anywhere so he started roaming the country. He's a good worker, strong. He'll go out on long trips and not mind going hungry."

He laughed, I couldn't imagine why. After a bit, he continued:

"You'll get your pay this evening, tomorrow you have a day off. You can go wherever you want."

"To South Fort?"

"Sure, anywhere you like."

I suspected that he said this to let me know my changed status. Yet I found it hard to believe that someone who looked so uncouth could be so considerate. I glanced at him. His expression hadn't altered. Still, I felt grateful.

Having asked about my former job and my family, he went off with a parting shot:

"Don't make this place too hot, watch out for fumes. Better make a hole in the paper on your windows."

He didn't tell me to go to work after finishing the job.

I filled up the cracks in no time. Washed the shovel and propped it on the stove, took down my package from the wall, poured some millet into my can and made myself some more pancakes. . . .

When the millet was finished, I shook the paper and nailed it to the wall beside my pallet. That gave me a clean patch of wall. Afraid to go out again to see the horses, I lit the cigarette stub left from yesterday and stretched out comfortably.

By my head Castro was calling for world revolution; Kennedy was expounding his New Frontier policy; western countries were talking about a "welfare state". All this seemed extremely remote. So what about my life in these new surroundings? Though so poor, crude and backward, as if forgotten by the world, abandoned by civilization, I found a novelty and warmth about them. When as a child I had run off to play in the servants' quarters, the heads of the family had scolded me, "Why keep such low company!" The intellectuals I later came in touch with visualized working people as wearing white shirts, blue overalls and cloth caps, striding proudly with plump ruddy cheeks along a broad sunlit highway. We were called upon to learn from the "labouring people", but I had no clear idea of what they were actually like. In the camp there had been only intellectuals and hooligans. Here I was among working people. I found them uninhibited, optimistic, quite different from the camp inmates. That was fine. Quite unexpected. So no matter how poor and backward these villagers were or how crude their behaviour, they were rough diamonds. Remembering what I'd seen and heard at work the previous day, I smiled.

12

South Fort fell so far short of my expectations, I was sorry I'd walked the thirty *li* there and got blisters on my feet.

This so-called market-town, a stockaded village built by some cattle owner in the old days, stood on stony, sandy ground at the foot of the mountain, surrounded by weeds. Its earthen wall enclosed about a dozen cottages, fewer even than in our village. The gate in the wall had been removed, so that the entrance looked like a gaping jaw. Still there was a small post office, a credit co-op, a shop and a police station, making it a political and economic centre. Since today was market-day it was swarming with people and reminded me of a small Arabian bazaar in a Hollywood film.

I went first to post a letter to my mother, telling her that I had left the camp and was now a *bona fide* worker; that I was eating well, had put on weight and become tanned.

I had no money to send her, only good news.

My group, including the Boss, had asked me to post their bulky letters for them, letters filled no doubt with complaints and requests to speed up their transfer.

By the post-office door was pasted the provincial newspaper of the previous week advertising the Soviet film *Red Sail*.

It took less than ten minutes to stroll down the street and back. The shop had only a few dusty bolts of cloth, a few blankets and, of course, salt. On the smoke-blackened wall was the notice: Good news: Iraqi dates, one yuan a catty. The red paper had faded. An old man by the stove told me that this announcement was six months old.

Twenty or thirty old peasants had stalls in the market, mostly selling wizened carrots or potatoes. One had brought a lean old sheep, which was snapped up for 150 yuan by some quarry workers. I reckoned that at the most it would provide a dozen catties of mutton. I watched the workers carry it off — they wouldn't even let it walk by itself, and my mouth watered. I didn't dare price any meat.

My objective was carrots. Potatoes were too high-class. I went up to a stall of fairly fresh carrots.

"How much a catty, grandpa?"

"One sixty."

Not surprised, I pointed to the potatoes next to them.

"Potatoes?"

"Two yuan."

"That's far too much!"

"Too much? If you had to grub about in the fields you'd charge even more."

"Come on, don't give me that, I've been through tougher times than you. Don't you believe me?" I glared at him.

He snorted sceptically. I gave an ugly laugh.

"I'd have you know I've just come out of a labour camp."

"Oh, then. . . ." The old man looked afraid.

"What about dropping the potatoes' price a bit." I deliberately threw him off balance with this switch. "Other people trade three catties of potatoes for five of carrots."

"Nothing doing." He wasn't afraid enough to bring the price down. Still he fell into my trap. "Bring me three catties of potatoes and I'll let you have five of carrots."

"You mean that?"

"Sure!" he said irately.

"All right." I put down my crate. "Weigh me three catties of potatoes."

I paid him from the eighteen yuan I'd got the previous day — a month's pay for one day's work, that wasn't bad! After we had haggled over the weight and he'd emptied the potatoes into my crate, I said:

"Here you are, now give me five catties of carrots."

The old man did so without any hesitation. I emptied the potatoes back in his basket and made off with the carrots.

I was gloating over the success of my trick.

I'd had a lot of dealings with local pedlars in the camp. I knew how their minds worked. They could be mulish, insisting on one point regardless of everything else. This made them stick up stubbornly for their interests but also made them easy to fool. So I often outwitted them.

What sort of man was I really?

13

The sun was warm. I crunched across the pebbles and sand. There was no-one in sight for a dozen *li* around. I was free, all on my own! After four years of sleeping in a concentration camp, lining up to go to work, back to our quarters or to fetch food, what bliss it was to be striding all alone through these big open spaces.

Brooks rushing down the hills had scored them with what seemed like stony paths. Stones and pebbles glinted in the sunlight. The barren slopes below had a grim look. The only moving creature was a brown lizard which flicked its tail at my approach and then darted off in fright. At this time of year there were no wild shallots or other edible plants I could pick to munch on. Wasn't I free, on my own? Even the air was mine! But only weeds and wild dates grew here, and the dates were covered in thorns. I hitched my crate higher up my back and strode on, thinking of my five catties of carrots.

In front stretched a ditch two metres wide. When I crossed it that morning it had been frozen solid, but now bubbles had appeared in the ice, which seemed to be thawing.

Since there was no bridge across, I found a place where it was slightly narrower and threw a clod of earth on to the ice. The clod broke up without cracking the ice. I decided to risk crossing.

If I had been as fit as I'd boasted to my mother, I could have jumped across. Or if I hadn't had that crate on my back. As it was, I landed 30 centimetres short of the other side. The ice cracked! I fell over backwards, crate and all, making a big hole in the ice.

I stood up in the icy water, which was up to my knees, and saw there were only a few carrots left in my crate.

Since my jacket was soaked, I didn't roll up my sleeves but groped desperately in the ditch. By the time I had salvaged half I was numb with cold and my legs were seized with cramp. I had to reluctantly clamber out, putting my remaining carrots in the crate.

On the bank I shivered like a drowned rat. I went on, looking back from time to time, as if the carrots in the ditch might hop ashore like frogs.

14

That night after my soaking I ran a fever and woke up parched. A northwest wind howling outside flapped the newspaper nailed to our windows. I had spells of dizziness. Now that I was so run down, I'd discovered the falsity of novelists' descriptions of dizziness: crashing on to the floor or collapsing on to a sofa were simply putting on an act. I felt dizzy just lying in bed, and instead of making me lose consciousness vertigo woke me up. My head was swollen, the blood in my brain too little and too thin, like a trickle of water swirling in a big vat.

Of course there was nobody to give me any water. I just had to put up with my thirst. I was used to that. Sometimes I was touched by my own fortitude. That was the case now. Stamina can't be measured like strength; it's partly a matter of will-power. Some men can bear mental pain but not material deprivation; some, vice versa. I was fairly good at both, with only death itself setting a limit to my endurance.

Had I been born with such stamina so that I could just drag on ignominiously? Couldn't I do something useful for mankind?

My conscience began to prick me. The loss of those carrots struck me as retribution. The peasants had a hard life. One yuan sixty cents was not too much for a catty of carrots. The peasants near the camp had asked up to two yuan. I'd exchanged my good watch for thirty catties of carrots and a bowl of mouldy sorghum. But I'd fooled that honest old man with the wrinkled face, and prided myself on it. . . .

The blood kept swirling in my brain, bringing another memory to mind. In a spacious room with sky-blue wallpaper and elegant furnishings, one of my uncles had sat on a dark brown leather armchair while I sat on a hassock on the carpet. Twiddling a cocktail glass with ice in it, he had told me how the Morgans had made their fortune. According to him the old man arrived in the States from Europe without a cent, and with only one pair of trousers. Later he and his wife had started a little grocery. When he sold eggs he never touched them himself but made his wife show them to the customers. Because her little hands made the eggs seem bigger. It was this shrewdness of his that had enabled his son to build up their financial empire.

"That's the spirit a businessman needs!" this manager of a stock exchange advised me. "To make a killing you must bankrupt your rivals."

. . . As this memory receded I suspected that my scheming was linked with my bourgeois family background. Both Morgan and I had made use of optical illusions as well as our native shrewdness. I'd substituted nails for barnyard-millet, and swopped three catties of potatoes for five of carrots, making two yuan on the deal. . . . The struggle for survival takes different forms depending on your training. Though I had no capital I had picked up bourgeois ways. I had not believed the charges brought against me in 1957, though I did finally accept them completely, as well as the Boss's malicious carping. Someone brought up as a beggar instinctively hates someone brought up as a young gentleman. I was not conscious of being a "bourgeois Rightist" because this was congenital. I was so parched that my mouth felt as if it was on fire but I put up with it, thinking it just retribution. It reminded me of Dante's *Divine Comedy*.

My class was doomed. My place was in the Inferno.

15

The next morning snow fell from the slaty sky. Nature hadn't forgotten this poor, backward village but impartially covered it with pure white snow. Wisps of smoke from small cottage chimneys made it seem like a scene in a fairy-tale.

My cold had cured itself. In my experience, if you coddle an illness it will grow even worse. If you ignore it, or can do nothing about it, it will clear out.

The Cripple was limping about blowing his whistle to announce that we had the day off. That was good news.

I had dried my padded clothes on the stove. The Boss complained that I was stinking the place out. I ignored him. If he fell into the water he had another pair of padded trousers as well as a sheepskin jacket. In my eyes he was a bourgeois — our class relations had been turned upside down. The trouble was that my padded clothes, when dried, were as hard as a suit of armour. They didn't keep me warm, and because I had no underclothes they chafed my skin. After breakfast I stripped and wrapped myself in my quilt, with only my hands sticking out to hold a book, my back against the peeling adobe wall.

I solemnly set about reading *Capital*.

I read it avidly all morning. First the different prefaces. Their arguments confirmed my conclusion of the previous night: the class to which I belonged was doomed. I was simply the last of the species. It comforted me to regard myself as a lamb being sacrificed to the new age. Through no fault of my own, I was atoning for the crimes of my forbears, like the son of alcoholics or syphilitics. There was no escaping from my wretched fate.

By noon, though, I couldn't go on. The worst thing about a day off was having nothing to eat. At work hunger was not so unbearable. When you were idle you felt ravenous. I could really believe Chaplin's portrayal of that famished prospector on a snowy mountain who mistook a man for a turkey. That wasn't a stroke of imaginative genius, Chaplin must have heard about it from somebody who'd known what it was to starve.

When I read, "Commodities come into the world in the shape of use values, articles, or goods, such as iron, linen, corn, etc.", I savoured the word "corn" instead of concentrating on the meaning. I had a mental picture of bread, steamed buns, flapjacks, even cream cakes which made my mouth water. Then came the equation:

$$\left.\begin{array}{r} 1 \text{ coat} = \\ 10 \text{ lbs tea} = \\ 40 \text{ lbs coffee} = \\ 1 \text{ quarter corn} = \end{array}\right\} 20 \text{ yards of linen}$$

A "coat", "tea", "coffee", "corn", what a feast! Imagine wearing a spotless white coat (instead of huddling in a quilt), with some Keemun tea or Brazilian coffee in front of you (instead of an empty tin), cutting up a cream cake (not a carrot) — that would be a feast fit for the gods! My imagination enabled me to amalgamate all the banquets I'd ever attended, seen or heard about. But all of those delicacies distracted me from "The Fetishism of Commodities and the Secret Thereof". And on that cold silent winter day there wafted over the appetizing smell of the food I'd been imagining. I started to have stomach spasms.

The Boss got up to his tricks again. He rummaged in his little box and produced a brown pancake. This he offered not to the Lieutenant, Editor or the rest of us, only to the old Accountant who slept beside me. He knew the Accountant's rule, "Don't touch anything of mine, and I'll touch nothing of yours." The old fellow carried this to ludicrous extremes. For instance, the demarcation line between his pallet and mine was like the border between two hostile countries, although in fact we got on well together. If a corner of his quilt happened to touch my pallet, he snatched it back as if it had caught fire. If some cotton from my ragged quilt stuck to his mattress, he solemnly returned it to me like a lost wallet. I couldn't understand how somebody so timid had become a "Rightist".

"Go on, eat it, never mind." The Boss carefully broke the pancake into two and tossed one half on to his pallet.

"Oh no, no. . . ." The Accountant frantically tossed it back, as if it were a ball of fire.

"Go on, what's stopping you?" The Boss tossed it over again. It was so hard and dry that no crumbs dropped off.

"No, really, eat it yourself." The Accountant uneasily threw it back.

"Eat it, I'm telling you. Who isn't hungry?" The Boss hurled the pancake back.

This time, though, it fell on my pallet just by my feet.

The Accountant eyed it apprehensively, twitching. Should he pick it up? It had fallen on my pallet. Maybe he was sorry for me, wanted me to have it. But it had been meant for him. He didn't want to be indebted to the Boss.

The atmosphere was tense. Although the others ostensibly went on with what they were doing, mending socks, writing letters home, thinking about things, they all kept an eye on the pancake. The Editor and Lieutenant paused in their chess game on a home-made board. Everyone was waiting to see what would happen.

The pancake must have weighed about an ounce. It had been kept so long that it had the dull sheen of a slab of chocolate. It was perched there on my pallet, putting me in a difficult position. I'd boiled and eaten my remaining carrots the previous evening, and had nothing to stop my mouth from watering desperately. Tears of resentment, self-pity and shame started to my eyes.

The room was deadly quiet.

Light reflected by the snow filtered through the papered windows, making all our faces deathly white. Finally the Accountant decided that this wasn't in his territory and had nothing to do with him. He closed his eyes and tucked his hands inside his sleeves, like a monk practising yoga. The Boss looked as calm as he had before throwing the pancake, sitting cross-legged on his pallet; but he kept his eyes fixed on his bait to see what prey he could catch.

Just then we heard footsteps approaching through the snow and light-hearted, unrestrained singing.

I recognized the voice of the woman who had given me her key two days earlier.

Her footsteps came straight to our door, to everyone's surprise. All eyes turned in that direction. Even the Boss relaxed and pricked up his ears.

Next we heard a crash and the door was flung open; but no one came in.

For a few seconds we stared foolishly at the doorway, as if waiting for some miracle to happen. Then, as if overcoming her hesitation, the woman strode on to the threshold, her hands on the frame, and looked around the room.

"Which of you is the 'Rightist' singer? I've got a job for him."

It was her!

And she must be looking for me.

"There." The Boss pointed me out and chortled, "You're wanted for a job, Zhang Yonglin."

But from her tone, expression and laugh, I sensed that she didn't want me for any job. I was overjoyed that she had come to my rescue.

"Is it me you want?" I couldn't be sure, because she had said "singer" not "poet". "What for?"

She chuckled, swaying forward and back still holding the door frame. "I guessed it was you. They say you build good stoves. I want you to build me one."

How had she guessed it was me? Since she had shown concern for me I was eager to work with her. Even working on an empty stomach was better than doing nothing. I said, "You go first. I'll come as soon as I'm dressed."

She chuckled again, probably thinking I cut a funny-looking figure.

"Hurry up then. I'll be waiting for you. You know the way."

She went out and closed the door. As I scrambled into my padded clothes, I kicked the pancake into the space between my pallet and the Lieutenant's as if by accident.

16

Outside everything was white. This first snowfall had levelled the vast plain, camouflaging gardens and villages alike. The lovely, dazzling scene made it hard to believe in the farce which had just been enacted.

Her footprints on the white snow gave me a feeling

of buoyancy and warmth. Even and regular as a string of pearls, they gracefully rounded each corner. I carefully traced her steps, as if to pick up each pearl and store it away.

I knocked on her door. Instead of "Come in" she shouted from inside, "The door's open, just give it a shove."

She was seated sideways on the *kang* playing with a little girl of about two. The child's tiny padded jacket was of the same material as hers; but her hair was cropped like a boy's, her thick eyebrows were boyish. At the sight of me both of them laughed; but when I smiled the child clung to her mother in fright. It dismayed me to think that even when I smiled I was such a fearful sight.

"Where do you want your stove?" I asked. "Have you got a trowel? And I'll need some bricks."

"What's the hurry." Stroking the child with her long slender hands she beamed at me. "For a bag of skin and bones you're a glutton for work! Sit down first."

The "bag of skin and bones" sat on the one clay stool. The room, with no stove in it, was as warm as our "home". A pervasive warmth, not like the heat of a stove which bakes you on one side only. That was thanks to the *kang*. That poor neat *kang* suddenly made me feel homesick. Four years in a labour camp where I'd nearly died of hunger had driven all impractical ambitions and romantic dreams from my mind. Now all I dreamed of was "A wife and a big beef and cabbage stew".

She paid no attention to me and fondled the child. I sat there glumly hanging my head. The indescribable warmth of this shabby cottage drove my own wretchedness home to me.

Whether she sensed this or not, after comforting the child she laid her down and jumped lightly off the *kang* to raise the lid of the pan on the stove. She took out a white bun and offered it to me.

"There!"

Stunned, I looked fearfully from it to her as she stood there calmly, unable to hide the warmth and pity in her eyes, yet with no trace of contempt.

I dared not accept the bun. In those days it was something too precious, something priceless. My head whirled with misgivings and undreamed of joy.

"Mama," called the little girl, and started crawling towards the edge of the *kang*. Her mother stuffed the bun into my pocket, then turned to pick up the child, butting her with her head as she rocked her to and fro.

> Let's grind some flour for supper,
> Uncle's coming to our place;
> If we give him chaff to eat
> We shall lose face!
> Let's boil a pan of noodles
> And kill a rooster too;
> A bowl of noodles for Uncle,
> And a big bowl for you!

Instead of reciting this like a nursery rhyme, she sang it to a lilting tune, the child in her arms as she seesawed to and fro. Their innocent laughter floated through the cottage. Only someone still a child at heart could have played like this. She obviously had had no ulterior motive, but had given me that precious gift simply out of kindness.

Still I hesitated:

"I'm not hungry, let the child have it." I offered the bun to the little girl.

"She's just had one. Go on, eat it."

But the child reached out crying, "Me eat!"

"Now Ershe, be good!" She lifted her back out of reach of the bun, then opened the steamer again and took out a potato.

"Look, Ershe, what's this? It's for you."

With a smile the little girl took the potato and awkwardly peeled it with her chubby fingers.

That made me still more unwilling to take advantage of such generosity. The value I set on that bun held my hunger in check. I mustn't waste it. Could fill up on something less costly. I longed to exchange it for two of the potatoes — short-sightedness hadn't stopped me from spotting them. But I didn't want to suggest this.

Seeing me holding the bun, she pointed at me and said to the little girl:

"Say, 'Uncle, eat it!' Go on!"

The little girl pointed one sticky finger at me.

"Eat, you eat!"

"I don't want it," I told her. "I'll leave it for your dad, how about that?"

Her mother laughed. "Her dad? He's in Java! Go ahead and eat. Why are you scholars always so formal?"

I could only guess at what she meant by "in Java". In the classics "Java" is always used to mean somewhere remote or non-existent, and the colloquialisms of the peasants here still retained many phrases from classical Chinese. Did she mean that her husband was far away? Or that her child had no father?

"Well then . . . keep it for yourself." I looked at the

pan, meaning to put the bun back. If she insisted, I'd ask for two potatoes.

"You wretch!" She flared up. "You're hopeless! All right, then put it back and clear off!" She turned to hug her child, not looking at me.

I held the bun awkwardly in both hands, as if it were a brimming bowl of hot soup and I didn't know where to put it.

"Didn't you want me to build you a stove?"

"Of course not!" She burst out laughing again. "Xixi built my stove, it burns fine. Here's what happened. On our day off yesterday I ground some wheat he'd given me into white flour and steamed five buns. One for Xixi, one for me and two for baby. The last one I decided to give to you. But I couldn't find you. . . . I didn't have any yeast, so it's unleavened. Just make the best of it. I've still got some flour left and I'm fermenting yeast now for another batch."

Another batch! I didn't like to ask what had made her think of me. It must have been pity. The Boss, Lieutenant and Accountant as soon as they left camp had changed into cadre suits sent them from home. I was still wearing my camp clothes, with a collarless jacket as conspicuous as the brands they used to burn on the faces of criminals. The shoddy material, not much stronger than surgical gauze, was in holes after just a few days. And now it was hard as armour. Hunched in this padded suit, I was like a larva frozen in its cocoon.

When she saw that I seemed ready to eat the bun, she drew back the curtain over the stove to get out a dish of salted carrots and a pair of chopsticks. Having wiped these she put them next to me.

"From now on come here when you're hungry. That

day I first saw you you looked just like a ghost." She burst out laughing again, but broke off quickly, pursing her lips to sit on the *kang* watching me.

Now of course I had to eat. But I felt embarrassed — ashamed to let her see how I wolfed down my food.

She didn't realize this, didn't know that it was rude to watch a guest eat. "What are you waiting for?" she asked in surprise. "Hurry up, someone may be coming."

Yes, I was afraid of that. What would people think if they found me eating there? I couldn't take this precious bun home either, where I was watched by so many pairs of eyes.

I slowly tasted it.

It was hard but snowy white. She must have sieved the flour twice. Being unleavened it was very solid, half a catty or more in weight, the consistency of a softball. I nibbled at it and chewed, nibbled and chewed, trying my best to eat in a civilized manner. For four whole years I'd not eaten any white flour, and it melted like snowflakes in my mouth. It was redolent of wheat, of summer sunshine, of the loess of the steppe, the sweat of the reapers, the pristine fragrance of food. . . .

All of a sudden I noticed a distinct fingerprint on the bun, the small whorls in the middle fanning out like the ripples fish make in a pond.

A tear fell on to the bun.

She probably saw it. Not smiling or watching me, she stretched out on the *kang* holding the child and sighed:

"Ah — what a life!"

Her sigh, expressing sympathy rather than pity, somehow opened the flood-gates of my tears. I had never wept when goaded by the Boss. Now my tears poured out in silence. I was too choked to even finish off the bun.

The cottage was strangely still. Outside snowflakes occasionally fluttered against the window. On the *kang* the child was quietly smacking her lips. Inwardly I heard the strains of Verdi's *Requiem*:

Ah, save me! Save me! . . .

Presently she said softly to the little girl:

"Ershe, tell Uncle: Don't worry. So long as I have food there'll be some for you. Go on, say: Uncle, don't worry. So long as I have food there'll be some for you."

I heard the child turn towards me.

"Uncle, don't worry. Don't worry. . . ."

She seemed to find it amusing to repeat words which she didn't understand. Standing up and stepping to the edge of the *kang*, she pointed a small finger at me.

"Uncle, don't worry. Don't worry. . . ."

"There's more," her mother reminded her. "So long as I have food there'll be some for you."

The little girl stammered, "You have food, some for me."

Her mother hugged her, laughing, and started tickling her.

"Little wretch! You got it the wrong way round!"

The two of them rolled over and over laughing. Their gaiety comforted me. I quickly finished the bun and the salted carrots.

"There are potatoes too." She sat up brushing back her hair and smoothing her jacket, then pointed at the stove. "Just help yourself."

It was only then that I took a good look at her.

To my surprise her features seemed rather southern:

clear, sparkling eyes; long eyelashes; a straight, finely chiselled nose; a full, expressive mouth. Many novelists concentrate on women's eyes, but I discovered from her that the mouth can be just as expressive. A whole gamut of emotions flickered across her finely curved lips. She had a ruddy complexion, slightly freckled. The faint shadows under her eyes were a foil to her brilliant black pupils. The harmony of her features was very pleasing. From the little she had said to me, and what I had seen of her, she struck me as a strong character, forceful, frank and lively. This was borne out by her appearance. Later I learned that these features which had struck me as southern had come originally from Central Asia.

I put her age at between twenty and twenty-five.

Her name was Ma Yinghua — Mimosa.

17

After eating her bun and potatoes I didn't like to go back to her cottage, though she had invited me repeatedly.

After breakfast the next day I lay on my pallet reading the Chinese translation of *Capital*. But this time I kept my clothes on.

I didn't like to go, yet I longed to go.

The snow had stopped and lay a foot deep on the ground. On the paths between buildings the dirt and snow had been trampled solid. Dark clouds still hung in the ashen sky, as if it might snow again at any moment. After breakfast Team Leader Xie had looked in to tell us that we had the day off. He commented that this was a timely snowfall. This year no one had the energy to work hard and there had been a drought; but this snow should make up for it and we could expect a good harvest. The surly Lieutenant retorted, "So what? However good the harvest, we'll still have the same piddling ration of grain." At that Xie went off in a huff, though I'd seen that he'd meant to stay a while to ask what I was reading.

The Lieutenant, after his demobilization, had been a section chief in some government office. Now that he'd left the camp and had his "Rightist" label removed, his old comrades-in-arms were manoeuvring to get him a job in the suburbs of Beijing. Since he wouldn't be here long he didn't mind saying the most outrageous things.

Still I was surprised. Surprised that the team leader, though furious, hadn't told us to hold a meeting to criticize the Lieutenant. In the camp he'd have had a beating.

That brought home to me my new freedom. By now I was reading the footnote:

> Savages and half-civilized races use the tongue differently. Captain Parry says of the inhabitants on the west coast of Boffin's Bay: "In this case (he refers to barter) they licked it (the thing represented to them) twice to their tongues, after which they seemed to consider the bargain satisfactorily concluded." In the same way, the Eastern Esquimaux licked the articles they received in exchange.

I thought: No doubt free men also use their tongues differently from those in confinement. That's nothing to be afraid of.

At noon, the same time as yesterday, she came back.

I recognized her step. As the drifted snow lay deeper, the sound was crisper but her step was still light.

She flung open the door and called to me:

"Hey, what's the idea? You can't leave the job half done."

The Boss sniggered. I would have to work while they rested — fine!

I put down my book with a show of reluctance and slowly rose to my feet, then followed her out.

Once round the corner she started to laugh and nudged me playfully. That reminded me of how my girl cousin and I had played truant as children, running off to a secret hideout in the garden as if by tacit agreement. I laughed too.

But today she really had dismantled the *kang*.

Hai Xixi was squatting in the doorway. Arms folded, thin lips pursed, he was glowering. Some mud had been mixed outside. The whole top of the *kang* had been removed. Bricks had been set out too — all ready for me to start.

"You tell Xixi what to do," she said. "He's as strong as an ox. Have some potatoes first, both of you, to warm up. When you're through I'll steam some buns."

"Him — tell *me* what to do!" Without so much as looking at me, Hai Xixi spat on the ground. He didn't take the potato she offered him.

"Since everything's ready, let's start," I proposed. "When it's done we'll have to light a fire to dry it."

He squatted there without moving. His laziness and contempt for me spurred me on. I stepped inside the framework of the *kang*.

"I can handle a little job like this by myself," I announced confidently.

"Aren't you going to lift a finger?" She glared at Hai.

He leapt up like a dog that's been kicked and rolled up his sleeves. "Hell! I'll do it on my own."

"You're a blockhead, he's got brains." She thrust a potato into my hand as she teased him. "Today you can be his assistant."

When I was eating potatoes here the day before, I'd told her that her stove wasn't scientifically built. The villagers made the chimney directly opposite the stove door, so that most of the hot air escaped through it and only the front part of the *kang* was heated. A flue that ran round the whole would be more scientific, more economical. I sketched a diagram on the floor to show her. "This way you can heat the whole *kang*," I explained. "I can easily alter it for you." She had taken me at my word.

I ate the potato while working. As a boy I'd enjoyed watching film stars work while eating, or sailors chewing bread as they rushed up from the hold to swarm up the mast. To me this suggested virility, drive, professionalism and disregard for one's own comfort. But in those days I hadn't worked. Later, doing manual labour, I'd nothing to eat. Today I worked with a will. By the time the job was done my stomach was full.

Hai ate nothing, either considering it beneath him or because he wasn't hungry. Glowering, he kept me supplied with mud and bricks, muttering that if this bricked-up *kang* burned well he'd jump into the river. I turned a deaf ear. When the top of the *kang* was finished, I jumped down and told him:

"All right, plaster it."

He squatted down squinting this way and that to find fault. By now she had put the buns on to steam. She scolded:

"What are you squinting at? Can't you do a mason's job? Start plastering from the stove here. I want to light the fire."

She fetched some bundles of kindling with which she deftly lit the stove. To start with smoke puffed out of the cracks in the surface of the *kang*, but as Hai plastered these over it disappeared. When he leapt down, the blazing fire inside was roaring through the flue and the *kang* was steaming, the brown mud slowly turning white as it dried.

"Go and jump into the river!" she mocked him. The fire lit up her expressive face. It was a long time since I'd seen such a beautiful, radiant colour.

I sat on the clay stool smoking and taking it easy. This was the first time my work had won me respect. This made up to some extent for the shame I'd felt at accepting her charity the previous day. I thought: I'm supporting myself now as a farm-hand. I must try to become a good worker and settle down to farming. What I learned from that engineer changed my status vis-à-vis Hai Xixi today. A couple of days ago I looked up to him, but today he's served as my assistant. That shows that here, in this poor village at the back of beyond where I may spend all my life, it's manual labour that a man is judged by. And so long as I get enough to eat I should grow as strong as Hai, able to tackle any job I'm given.

She had steamed two tiers of buns and stewed some

cabbage and potatoes. When she'd fetched Ershe back from the neighbours we started our meal,

And what a meal it was! I hadn't eaten so well in years.

"Here, start with this." She gave me a big bowl of stew as well as a large white bun. "First eat two buns, I'm keeping more for you. I'll heat them up when you come."

Hai squatted grimly by the stove, not hiding his jealousy as he watched her serve me.

I paid no attention to him. I'd earned this meal. Villagers always feed a man who helps them build a *kang* or house. So I had an easy conscience.

After the meal I went "home" and ate another barn-yard-millet bun from the kitchen. I knew the difference now between being "full" and being "bloated".

I lay down on my pallet under the lantern and curled up to sleep, feeling blissfully well-fed, drowsily trying to work out how much I'd eaten. Being well-fed I could think of other things apart from food. I thought of her and Hai Xixi. They obviously weren't married but on close terms. I knew instinctively that she wasn't his woman. If she were, he wouldn't obey her like a dog or put up with her taunts. They both intrigued me, Mimosa especially, so kind yet so caustic. . . .

As for Hai Xixi, in some ways I envied him. He was such a skilled workman. He had plastered the top of the *kang* so rapidly, without a single wasted movement. And had dirtied neither his clothes nor his hands in the process. The villagers set great store by this. Some women kneading a catty of dough finish up with two ounces on their hands, in the basin or on the rolling-board. But good housewives end up with clean hands, a clean basin and a clean board. It's the same with other manual work. Neatness, efficiency and speed are the criteria, just as succinctness is most prized in writing. And this doesn't come solely from experience. People who haven't worked on the land think that if you have the physical strength then practice will make perfect. Not so. I've seen old peasants whose work is still sloppy, just as some professional writers remain long-winded.

Simple manual labour reveals a man's intelligence and character.

I drifted into sleep, and dreamed that I was a skilled worker. But, strange to say, my face was the face of Hai Xixi.

18

We went back to work before the snow had melted.

I love snow. My first sight of it was in Chongqing. One morning when my nurse had dressed me and I got out of bed to pull back the curtain, my eyes were dazzled by a silver light. The wretched hovels and sparse clumps of bamboo at the foot of the hill were as lovely as a dream. The whole spotless world around me filled me with awe and the longing to become one with Nature, so that tears welled up in my eyes. I could say that it was snow that made me precocious, made me later become a poet. . . .

The snow on the loess plateau is superb. More magnificent than the snow in the south. Snow in the south tells you that winter is here at last, whereas in the north it turns your thoughts to spring. Snow on the loess plateau heralds spring.

Today I was going to help cart the manure we had earlier broken up. The snow had apparently swept away everything superfluous from the far-stretching fields. The angles of hills, ridges, gullies and gnarled branches had become strangely lustrous and rounded, as if covered by fluffy down. The snow seemed warm rather than cold, making me want to press my cheek against it.

I was accompanying a cart driven by a man in his fifties. This old fellow, incredibly taciturn and slow, made only two trips for five of Hai Xixi's, though his horses were in better shape.

"Silly fool! Lashing his team! We'll take our time." He scowled at Hai who had passed us, and nursed his freezing red nose in one hand. That was all he had said today. To him, going all out on a job put other people's backs up and was simply asking for trouble. That was his philosophy.

Well, by going at this snail's pace he gave me time to day-dream as I sat on his jolting cart. Snow reminded me of Hans Anderson, Pushkin, Lermontov. . . .

> Ah, you created Pushkin!
> You drift down
> Surely not from those slaty clouds
> But plucked by jade-like fingers
> From some orchard of pear-blossom.
> Give me a snowflake, one
> To moisten my heart.
> It was you who saved Zhang Yonglin!
> When you stretched out your hand
> I could not believe you had grown up in the wilds,

Your bewitching eyes so radiant,
In your heart the riot of colours of the South.
I shall always remember
Your gem-like fingerprint.

The cartwheels came up against a ridge. The carter
decided to stop there. He remained hunched up on the
shaft nursing his nose. In the camp we'd called slackers
like him "dead dogs". No amount of threats or persua-
sion could make them move any faster.

I left him alone. I was wondering: Why call her eyes
"bewitching"? "Compassionate" would have been more
appropriate. Now that I was well-fed, something long
submerged was tugging at my heartstrings. My heart
was like a spider's web, sparkling with raindrops, swaying gently under the eaves.

For no reason at all I blushed.

She and the other women were turning over compost
by the stable. The compost stained the white snow in
an ugly way, but made it easy for Team Leader Xie to
see how much work they'd done. That afternoon when
our cart creaked back he called cheerfully, "Knock
off!"

The farmhands scattered as usual to their homes. She
waited for me with her shovel by the dunghill.

"When you've rested come to my place."

"What? Got a job for me?" I asked sheepishly as
I jumped down from the cart.

"What?" she mimicked laughingly. "The fire in
the *kang* doesn't draw well."

After supper I went to her cottage, my departure unnoticed by the rest, all busy with their own affairs.

Her window, like those of the other cottages, was fitted with broken panes of glass. Probably bought at a discount by the farm. She was sitting on the *kang* mending Ershe's clothes under a paraffin lamp made out of a medicine bottle hung on the wall. The child was sleeping under a small faded quilt.

"What's wrong with your *kang*?" I asked as I stepped in, pretty sure that the flue was drawing perfectly.

"What?" she mimicked me again. "Why are you so late?" The light lit up her small teeth as she laughed. One lower tooth protruded a little. But this in no way detracted from her good looks, in fact it only served to set them off. Her laughter woke Ershe. She jumped up then to fetch me a bowl of cabbage and potatoes, as well as two white buns which she had steamed.

I smiled, scratching the back of my head, and softly protested, "With grain in such short supply, how can I keep eating yours? Keep that for Ershe."

"Wha-at!" She spluttered with laughter again, I couldn't think why.

"Don't talk such nonsense," she scolded. "You don't have to worry. Don't they call this the 'American Hotel'?"

She behaved so naturally that I didn't feel embarrassed by her pity, compounded as it was with childlike mischief and womanly wilfulness. Nor could I ask her where she got her grain. That was understood. All families had ways to get extra food, but not we bachelors eating in the canteen. We had no vegetables to eke things out . . . and we watched each other like lynxes.

We chatted as I ate. She told me she came from Qinghai, had only an elder brother, a factory worker in the county town who had married a local girl. Because she didn't get on with her sister-in-law she had come here a few years ago to work on the land. Not wanting to talk about this, she launched into reminiscences of her childhood. Said all the girls in her old home could embroider, embroidering even the soles of their socks. Next time we were paid she'd buy me a pair and embroider them for me. I said there was no need, who could see the embroidery on the sole? She looked at me searchingly without a word, wondering, probably, what I needed most. Next she spoke of her mother, well-known for her singing when young and "prettier than a peony". She then began to sing:

> Green scallion grows in the yard;
> Don't cut it, let it grow here.
> He's a ditch, she's a brook;
> Don't dam the ditch but let the brook flow clear.

"Like it?" she asked, her eyes shining.

I had finished eating and was listening quietly. Her lilting song, the snug peaceful room, Ershe's soft breathing, the mellow golden lamplight, and the good meal I had eaten all made me feel as if this were a dream, or as if I were drunk. The real world had blurred, had taken on all the colours of the rainbow. My heart seemed like a sponge soaking up fresh morning dew. The tune she had sung, running up and down the scale, expressed her people's frank, fearless character, their passionate search for love. I had never before been so carried away by a song, not even by a symphony. I felt as though I had been given a shot in the arm.

"Aren't you a singer? Sing something," she begged with a smile. Like a child saying, "Now it's *your* turn."

I told her I wasn't a singer but a poet. But I found it hard to explain "poetry" to her. The poetry taught in college loses its purity and simplicity. I began to understand why it is not enough for poets to mingle with the working people: they must share their destiny, enter into their feelings. So in the end I said lamely that poems were like songs. She could sing what I had written, but I could only recite it. "Well then, recite me one," she said, and settled down to listen attentively.

I cleared my throat. What could I recite? I realized I had published nothing but doggerel. It couldn't be spoken with genuine feeling. If I recited my verses she would be puzzled. And I was no good at reciting, which meant I was no real poet. My lack of depth put me to shame. Finally I chose one of Li Bai's most popular poems:

> Before the bed bright moonlight
> Like frost on the ground.
> Head raised, I look at the bright moon,
> Head lowered, think of home.

She seemed to be moved by it. But she started chuckling, then bent over double to laugh, falling on the *kang*.

"Oh my! What a joke! . . . What 'frost on the ground'. 'Frost'." She sat up again and opened her mouth wide to imitate my pronunciation of "frost".

"That one's no good," she said. "Recite another."

Li Bai's poem had saddened me, making my voice mournful. He could "think of home" but I was homeless. The native place listed in my file was our ancestral home — I had never been there. And my mother was living with strangers in Beijing. What was wretched wasn't "thinking of home" but having no home to think of. I had no roots. But her laughing face cheered me up, as she meant it to. I was very touched by her kindness and had to check the urge to pour out my gratitude.

Since it was a snowy night, I remembered a poem by Lu Lun:

Moon obscured, wild geese fly high
As the Hunnish chief flees by night.
We give chase with light cavalry,
Snow shrouding our bows and swords.

I was explaining this to her when the door was thrown open and Hai Xixi came in. By the flickering lamplight I saw him dump a bulging sack behind the door. Because he was so hostile to me I ignored him. She didn't seem to have noticed him come in, didn't even greet him. He squatted down as usual with folded arms, then viciously spat on the floor.

"Hell! Give chase with light cavalry! You couldn't catch him, not even with a plane!"

"What do *you* know?" She glared at Hai. "Filling your belly is all you understand."

"Filling your belly." It had taken me twenty-five years to learn the importance of that. I had found this truth more difficult to grasp than Aristotle's *Poetics* — it had nearly cost me my life.

Hai glared back, baring his wolfish teeth. "Takes some doing, filling your belly. Some people don't even know that."

I glanced at him in surprise. What was he insinuating? I felt we had something in common. But he had annoyed her again. She turned away to grab a brush and furiously swept the *kang*.

"Clear out, both of you! I want to sleep."

19

She told me to go to her place every day after work. If I didn't, she'd come to fetch me. Not wanting her to do that and arouse the suspicion of the Boss I took to going regularly each evening. There, feeling abashed, I first tucked in to a meal, a good square meal. She had a store of flour, rice, glutinous millet, maize, sorghum, soybeans, peas ... whatever grew on the steppe. And she often cooked a mixture of rice, glutinous millet and soybeans which was more appetizing than just rice. In those days the mass media called on everyone to make the most of coarse food grains. A cook in our camp was sent to a conference of model workers because he had managed, with only one catty of rice, to boil up seven catties of mush. But she cooked real solid rice, each grain plump and glistening, instead of a "supersaturated solution". Of course I also ate her barnyard-millet "rice", which she cooked more skilfully than that camp cook.

Barnyard millet had never ranked as one of the Five Cereals until the Big Leap of 1958. During the nation-wide movement that year to smelt steel, all the peasants and farm-hands started mining coal and building furnaces. As the furnaces in the hills blazed, the paddy in the fields burned up as well for lack of water. Not a grain was harvested. But the barnyard millet had grown extra large ears and stood like a forest, too dense even for locusts to fly into. That gave the local authorities a brilliant idea: eat barnyard millet! It could be delivered too as grain for the state. This was an emergency measure. So barnyard millet joined the honoured ranks of commodity grain, soon taking pride of place there. It was usually milled husks and all — this was the flour we ate every day. Since it lacked cohesiveness, only gravity held the steamed buns together. If you were more fastidious and milled it like rice, then, as the women turning compost had said, all you could make was gruel. Yet Mimosa steamed "rice" out of this despised grain — surely a record achievement!

My bashfulness was not put on, I was really ashamed of taking advantage of her. Yet her home drew me like a magnet with its dream-like happiness, its comfort and freedom. Several times I urged her not to give me grain, just cabbage and potatoes. She would reply:

"The idea! You need feeding up. If I didn't have grain why would they call my place the 'American Hotel'? Can't you see how sturdy little Ershe is?"

Yes, sweet little Ershe was sturdy, a ball of energy. Not an undernourished child watching greedily when other people ate. If she was awake while I ate there, she played happily by herself on the *kang* with the little clay stove and pots Hai Xixi had made for her. A two-year-old doesn't pretend and isn't polite. She didn't care what other people ate — a sure sign that she was well-fed.

So I concentrated on building myself up.

As time went by I learned what the other farm-hands meant by "American Hotel". It was just a figure of speech based on their understanding of the world. It wasn't a hotel in the usual sense, but anyone could drop in for a chat; so it was more like a teahouse. And the men who frequented it showed their appreciation by keeping her supplied with extra grain. The intriguing thing was the use of the adjective "American". To the farm-hands America was an outlandish, promiscuous, immoral country, but so rich that no one worried about food and clothing. They weren't insulting Mimosa, just poking fun at her.

Team Leader Xie's attitude to her was typical. Once when our cart returned to the stable for more compost, the two of them were having a slanging match.

"You say I run an 'American Hotel', well, why don't you try it!" Standing on the dunghill she giggled.

"Hell!" Xie went on forking compost. "I'm just not interested."

"Oh you!" She wagged a finger at him. "You'd be drooling, wetting your beard!"

While swearing Xie had sprayed spittle in all directions, so that his beard was wet. The farm-hands standing round all roared with laughter.

Mimosa had got the better of him. But I knew that Xie had never been to her cottage. And if she and the women were working on a job, he always sent able-bodied men to help them. He never even gave her a serious telling-off let alone taking "reprisals".

If a village woman with no husband brings up a fatherless child on her own and has many male visitors, there is pretty sure to be gossip. But the farm-hands made allowances for Mimosa. I realized that her popularity did not depend on her attractiveness or any special inducements. It was her friendliness and sympathy that made everybody well-disposed to her.

Sincerity and goodness can lend charm to unconventional behaviour.

I had gathered from the farm-hands that recently Hai Xixi had virtually "monopolized" Mimosa, who had few other visitors. So the name "American Hotel" belonged to history now, like Babylon. But I knew that Hai had not monopolized her. He had a rival in the crippled storekeeper. One day when I went there the cripple was sitting on my usual stool while, with her back to him, she rolled out dough. On my arrival he left in a huff, first picking up an empty sack and stuffing it in his pocket — he had evidently taken her something. Another time, when we were chatting after my meal, we heard limping footsteps outside, and she at once jumped off the *kang* to bolt the door. When he called out she answered, "I'm already in bed!" I held my breath, my heart pounding. When the Cripple hobbled away, she smiled mischievously and told me to finish my story, saying nothing about his visit.

The more I saw of her, the more convinced I was that she was not a loose woman. She was innocent, straightforward, mischievous, gay. . . . Still, there were sides to her that I didn't know.

20

She never shut Hai Xixi out. He would swagger in as if he owned the place. When he found me sitting on the only stool he would squat on the floor, a grim look on his face.

We met there nearly every day, although he came much later as he had to feed and water his horses or repair the harness. By the time he arrived I had eaten. Yet he always made me feel like a thief caught red-handed. So each time he came in I flushed and lost interest in what I'd been saying. The bowl and chopsticks not yet cleared away seemed evidence of my crime.

Mimosa wasn't a gossip like some women. She liked to hear fairy tales or fantastic stories. These unusual tastes of hers made her seem a different person from when she was laughing and scrapping with her friends. She pestered me for stories, and by telling them I repaid her in a way for her hospitality. My stories would set her fancy wandering. Of course everyone has dreams. But it's rare to be able to accept and understand the dreams of other people. Mimosa listened raptly to *The Ugly Duckling, Cinderella, The Mermaid* and Pu Songling's *Strange Tales*. She was barely able to read yet could respond to stories from other lands or ancient times. I am not a good story-teller, I often leave out incidents, and just give the gist of the plot. But Mimosa had enough imagination to fill in the gaps. She asked me pertinent questions and told me her reactions, which often coincided with the originals. She had never seen the sea yet was able to imagine its changing colours, the roar of its billows, and how sailors were bewitched by the songs of sirens; could imagine mice being transformed into horses. . . . This never ceased to amaze me.

Hai Xixi was just the opposite. He kept contradicting me or picking fault with my stories. Squatting on the floor like a wolf, his ears pricked up like a fox, if I faltered, put off by his presence, he would lick his lips as if he heard some small creature stirring in the undergrowth, and when I had finished he would pulverize my story like an elephant running amok in Versailles.

"Hell! A wild duck hatching out a swan's egg!" he sneered. He never looked at me, only at Mimosa, as if I weren't there. "Some duck that! A swan's egg is much bigger than a duck's. If there were a swan's egg in its nest, the duck would fly off bloody fast!"

"Shit! A carriage made of gold!" he scoffed after hearing *Cinderella*. "What idiot would bankrupt his family by making a carriage of gold? You can't fool me. No team of horses could pull a golden carriage. Why, a gold ingot this size" — he held up two fingers — "weighs over a hundred catties."

His comment on *The Mermaid* was even more scathing. "A girl with a tail like a fish! Where would it grow from? How could you tell a merman from a mermaid? How could she have babies? Bloody nonsense!"

I put up with his abuse and didn't talk back. He was nearly twice my weight. Mimosa was usually lost in thought by then, as though smacking her lips over the taste of an olive. She paid no attention to him. But now that I was slowly regaining my strength, his rudeness, jealousy and contempt set my blood racing. I would turn scarlet, tears of rage starting to my eyes. I had lost what little respect and liking I had once had for him. But although he provoked me, certain qualities of his attracted me too. His crudity and fearlessness fitted in so well with our surroundings, making life more colourful. To him I was a weakling, a coward, like a shrivelled bedbug. So my tears of rage were also tears of self-pity and resentment. I measured my wrist between my thumb and forefinger, determined to take him on!

Anyone living for any length of time in a village is

bound to be influenced by country ways, and I was deliberately trying to pick them up. To fit in here, I thought, you had to be tough, proud, fearless and ready to tackle any work. Had to be like Hai Xixi. To hell with culture! There are no mediocre jobs, only mediocre people. If that carter with whom I'd teamed up were better educated and became a writer, I couldn't see him writing anything original — he'd be a "dead dog" writer. But Hai Xixi, if he wrote, could astound the world of letters.

I secretly considered Hai my rival.

By now I had grown much stronger.

Mimosa said, "Grain, that's what you must eat. Vegetables can't take its place. Spuds and cabbage may fill you up but don't build you up. The more you stuff yourself with them, the flabbier you get...."

There was truth in that. Each time I stoked up with real grain there, I felt myself growing stronger. It wasn't just my imagination either. Though we had no mirror at "home" and I didn't like to use hers, I could feel my cheeks filling out, feel my good muscle tone. For the first time in my life I was full of energy. This pleased me more than had I been transported into a garden full of rare flowers, because this change had taken place inside of me. Many novels describe the sound of plants growing at night or shoots breaking through the soil; but I had the unique experience, as I lay in my ragged quilt at night, of hearing my own cells divide. Modern medical researchers are looking for ways to make people fit, but unfortunately for them they haven't discovered my experience: first starve a man for three years, then feed him up. Then, without any medicine or tonic, in a flash he will be transformed like Monkey King into a giant. Because his voracious digestion will instantly convert all that he eats into cells. To exaggerate a little, each catty of grain I ate could become a catty of flesh. My stomach no longer discriminated — all food was grist to my mill.

21

The loess steppe is very arid. After a couple of weeks most of the snow on the fields had evaporated. Evaporated, not melted. There was only a sprinkling left in damp ditches out of the sun, while the dirt roads were dusty again. And once again whirlwinds raised columns of dust at the foot of the hills. The boundless plain to the east, gleaming like gold, held an intimation of spring. When a wind swept across it, mist swirled like stampeding horses.

Hai Xixi was driving his creaking cart faster than ever. His lean horses looked more jaded every day, but he made them keep to the pace. Unless one dropped dead he would never let them slow down.

Each carter has his own way of driving.

No one could keep up with Hai for more than two days. "He drives like hell, knocking us out!" swore the men teamed up with him. While carting manure his team mate was changed at least ten times. When it came to our group's turn, the Lieutenant was sent out with Hai for one day. He came back cursing, "The bastard! Is this a time to try to show off? Dammit if he doesn't make five trips to other carters' two. He nearly killed me. Someone else can go tomorrow. I'm off to South Fort."

The next day I volunteered to accompany Hai.

The stable was in a big square yard. The carts were lined up by one wall. On the other three sides stood three rickety old sheds. I went there with some other farm-hands in tattered padded jackets, and squatted down in the morning sun waiting for the teams to be harnessed. The carters, yelling orders, led their horses out one by one. Some carters still looked half asleep; the faces of most were glum. The horses too looked reluctant to set off and stood as if rooted to the ground. The carters had to lash and swear at them to get them between the shafts.

Only Hai Xixi, chest thrown out, ignoring everyone else, used the tip of his whip like a circus master to marshal his well-trained team. Without a single crack of the whip, he harnessed them to the cart. This done, he vaulted on the mud wall and squatted there looking arrogantly down, a posture with which I was all too familiar.

One by one the carts were driven out, a farm-hand sitting on each. Soon Hai and I were the only men left in the yard.

He stood up then on the wall, shading his eyes to look round. Outside the stable women were forking compost. Their bickering and laughter sounded like the cheeping of sparrows. He jumped lightly down and strode towards a haystack.

He emerged from behind it with a sack which looked as if it weighed at least forty catties. This he stowed away in the rack below the cart. Then, having brushed some straw from his sleeve, he flourished his whip. "Giddap!" The cart rolled through the gate.

He didn't greet me as he passed me. And I leapt

on to the back of the cart without catching hold of the rail, to show him that I wasn't a lame duck.

I knew that sack must hold fodder: soybeans, peas, sorghum or the like. Well, I wouldn't give him away. I'd seen plenty of pilfering like this in the camp. It was a carter with whom I'd traded my watch, who had produced carrots from a sack in the rack below his cart. We had no scales but haggled over the weight. And where had those carrots come from? Obviously from the field where he had just been. In this way he had acquired my good Swiss watch for next to nothing. But you couldn't report him, that would be against our tacit agreement on barter, and you would go hungry!

The weather today was fine. By ten all the frost had melted, leaving straw and wooden rails moist and brown. The sky was a translucent blue, the road dry and hard. The spongy piles of compost were steaming. I was in high spirits and felt a secret excitement, a sense of anticipation. . . .

As a rule carters load their own carts, their team mates simply helping out. If the two of them hit it off well, it doesn't matter if one works harder than the other, so long as they get the job done. No one is born a good carter, it comes from practice. If you're handy and quick-witted and help to harness and unload the cart, taking over the driving sometimes on the road, you gradually get the hang of it. No driving licence is needed, nor do you have to pass any test. Your team leader can see when you're proficient. It's much easier than learning to drive a car. Where skill comes in is in training your team — this is much more difficult than handling machines — and in coping with breakdowns or dangers. At such times clear-headedness and quick reactions count for more than experience. So a carter's status will remain high until we have mechanized farming.

Hai Xixi as a skilled carter ranked very high in this farm.

... Having driven the cart to a compost heap surrounded by a fence, he jumped down and squatted at the foot of the fence making a show of mending his whip. He intended me to load the cart by myself.

I took a pitchfork and spat on my palms, the way he did, then set to work with a will. When the cart was loaded I stuck the fork into the compost and jumped up to sit on the shaft, swinging my legs as I smoked one of my precious cigarettes.

"Sit at the back!" he growled, flicking his whip as he came alongside. "You're making the front too heavy."

I knew this wasn't the case. He just wanted to drive me to the back. On a cart, the front is like a "soft seat" carriage in a train. Sitting behind, when the cart jolts, is worse than "travelling hard". But loading the cart had given me confidence. Sweating a little from every pore, I felt that I still had great reserves of strength. It was a discovery that pleased me enormously.

With a tolerant, contemptuous smile, I jumped off the shaft to seat myself on the tail-board.

> Ah, I must remember
> Your gem-like fingerprint.

In the fields he didn't help unload the compost, just fiddled with his whip. Each time I'd unloaded one cartload he pressed on quickly. Each load of compost was dumped in four heaps. He was faster than anyone

else.   Returning from our first trip, we left the other
carts far behind.

Now we were the only cart loading up by the dunghill.   By our third trip all the farm-hands there forking
compost, among them Team Leader Xie, could see that
something was up.   Hai parked the cart then brashly
walked off to squat down at one side, making no at-
tempt to hide his hostility toward me. He didn't smoke,
just gripped his whip as if prepared to thrash me if I
slacked. The farm-hands chuckled, exchanging whispered
comments.   And I played up, going all out, not just to
take up his challenge but because I was brimming with
energy.   I had unbuttoned my jacket, baring my chest
to the warm winter sun.

Horse compost, being mostly straw, isn't heavy.   I
forked up great hunks of it, a hundred or so of which
filled the cart.   Work seems heavy only when you are
half-starved.   I could take this job in my stride, having
figured out the most effective, effortless way to co-
ordinate my movements.

After our fourth trip I knew that I had triumphed!
I still felt practically as energetic as during our second
trip.   Some of the women watching laughed at Hai,
calling him unprintable names.   Team Leader Xie kept
swearing, "Hell!"   But which of us he was cursing I
couldn't tell.   Unwilling to go on squatting by the cart,
Hai wandered off.   And now that I'd passed the goal
I'd set myself, I wanted to do more.   To challenge him.
To turn the tables on him.

On our return from our fifth trip, other carts had
mostly made three, the Dead Dog only two.   Team
Leader Xie looked at the sun and yelled, "Knock off!"
But I yelled back:

"No! I haven't had enough; let's make another trip!"

When we came back from our sixth trip, the wintry sun was setting behind the hills. Their bare peaks, free from clouds and mist, were black. Crows and sparrows, unable to find any grain in the stable, flew past the dirt track through the fields and alighted, cawing and twittering, on some bare trees. The clammy air made the dust thrown up by the cartwheels settle quickly and was chill on our cheeks. I pulled my tattered jacket tightly round me as I sat on the cart rail. Before me was Hai's hunched back. It made him look dispirited, disgruntled. For some reason I felt that way too. Felt down in the dumps.... My sense of triumph had vanished, as if I had fallen into an icy well.

In the deserted fields we were engulfed by a violet evening mist. Just the two of us on that desolate dirt track.

22

After we had eaten our barnyard-millet buns from the kitchen, the Editor gave me half his wash-basin of water. I took off my jacket by the red-hot stove and had a good rub-down. Under my once flaccid skin I could now feel muscles. This meant that I had the strength to make my way in the world. The discovery spurred me on.

The past was over, done with. I must bid farewell to the Muse of Poetry. Here there was no need for culture. Knowledge couldn't benefit me, could only upset me. Torn between grief as if leaving my nearest and dearest, and joy as if going to see the one I loved most, I went to call on Mimosa.

I couldn't define my feelings. I seemed to be plodding along in a most fantastic yet thoroughly rational dream.

Today while I was washing at "home", Hai Xixi turned up. Strange to say, instead of sitting on the only stool he squatted in his usual place, holding Ershe and absent-mindedly playing with her.

The lamp hanging on the wall flickered. The room was filled with steam and the smoke of firewood. Mimosa, half hidden in the steam and smoke, made it seem even more like a dream. The frenzied rhythm of life reminded me of a song sung by Louis Armstrong. Only a few weeks ago I had come here a timid, uninvited guest, eager to raise the lid of the pan and draw back the curtain on the sly; but now I sat myself down without any hesitation as if I owned the place. That stool which seemed to have been left for me suddenly changed my attitude to Hai, making me respect him and sympathize with him.

Mimosa quickly brought me a steaming bowl of rice, glutinous rice and soybean, as well as a dish of pickles. This was my favourite meal. As usual she wiped the chopsticks with one hand. I was afraid to look at her, Hai or Ershe. I had thought that, after my triumph, I'd be able to put on a bold front, but I felt more inexplicably bashful than ever.

I pecked at my food. Although hungry, I couldn't eat. I was thinking that no work of literature can fully reflect the drama of real life and a man's complex changes of mood. The elusive quality of life, invisible and intangible, is hard to put into words, to draw or to enact on the stage. For instance, as Hai behind me softly teased Ershe there was something forced and distressing about his laughter, as if he were under pressure. And there was something disturbing about the chink of the bowls Mimosa was washing. Presently, prompted by Ershe, Hai started singing rather listlessly:

A scarf floats on the water,
I sing to ease my heart.
One straw won't make a gate,
The two of us must part.
Sweet pears, red apples too,
But nothing pleases you.

By the last line his voice had grown youthful and strong. Ershe clapped her little hands. "Go on! Go on!" I felt a pang of jealousy. Not just because he had such a ready imagination, such skill in conveying his feeling; but because Ershe had never shown herself so fond of me. When I told stories she fell asleep in the middle. Had I lost the ability to communicate with children?

Then I heard Hai whisper to her. She piped up: "Mum, sing to us. . . ."

I didn't look round. Mimosa had probably finished washing up and was sitting on the *kang*. I heard her laugh — it exasperated me that whatever happened she could always laugh. She said readily, "All right, I'll sing."

Her voice was gay, soft but untrained.

A scarf floats on the water,
I'll sing a song for you.
Thirty-three grains of buckwheat,
She may be sweet but she's not yours to woo.
Sesame yields fine oil.
If I can't find a husband, a friend will do.

Their singing conjured up for me a picture of two eagles soaring one above the other in the clouds. It struck me how well matched they were! In the flickering lamplight and smoke of this rustic cottage, I was completely superfluous. A fly that had blundered in to eat then fly off again. I had no place of my own and didn't belong anywhere. Wherever I went I would be superfluous. Doomed to be a Wandering Jew, an outcast all my life. . . . Now they had fitted me in so that I thought I had found my niche; but in fact I was disrupting and spoiling their lives.

A good meal should make one comfortable and cheerful. Instead I felt more depressed. I decided that it was better for me to go hungry. Otherwise I would only make trouble for other people.

After eating I pushed away my bowl, not looking at them, and started out, saying my group was waiting to consult me. Outside, the cold crescent moon was half hidden by clouds as ragged as my padded jacket. The ranges of hills on both sides were a forbidding black, like judges in black robes. There wasn't a breath of wind. The air was bitterly cold and dry. Though dim lights still showed in some cottages, the village was silent except for my shuffling footsteps. I felt wretched but not resigned. Just then Hai came out of her cottage. He cleared his throat, then hurried off quietly to the pitch-black stable.

I felt resigned then, but more wretched than ever.

23

The next day, sitting on Hai's cart I felt rather guilty. But I realized to my shame that this compunction wasn't genuine.   I could no longer claim to have drifted into an ambivalent relationship. I was deliberately setting myself up as his rival.

But Hai's attitude to me had worsened. His feelings were less complex than mine. It was as if he were the sky high above us, in which any wisp of cloud could cast a shadow. And his face today was stormy.

After loading up for the first time — naturally all the loading was done by me — I sat on the tail-board as I had the previous day. The cart jolted out of the village on to the dirt track.

Crack!

His whip lashed my face! I clapped one hand to my burning cheek and looked at Hai. His back to me, sitting on the shaft and driving just as usual, he seemed quite unaware that he had lashed me. Such accidents do happen. The thongs of whips in the northwest are three times the length of the crop, so that a careless carter may hit someone sitting behind. A carter in the labour camp had had his sentence extended for a year because by mistake he struck a cadre to whom he was giving a lift. He explained to us tearfully that it was an accident. His wife and new-born son were waiting for him to go home for the Spring Festival. . . .

Never mind whether it was an accident or not, I picked up the pitchfork stuck into the compost and held it in front of me as a shield.

Hai knew how to handle a whip, how to hit a target behind. Presently he lashed out again. The pitchfork twanged as I deflected the blow. He had struck harder this time, aiming for my face.

He did this again and again, but each time I parried the blow. This farce infuriated me. His hunched back no longer struck me as disgruntled, but as vicious, murderous! I hadn't done anything wrong. Had nothing to be ashamed of, especially vis-à-vis Hai. Since fate had thrown us together, why should I feel guilty?

As I loaded our cart for the third time, the others were returning from their first trip. They gathered — all but the Dead Dog's cart — by the dunghill near the stable. Men shouted, whips cracked, hooves clattered, the women forking the compost kept up their banter ... it was a bustling scene. At this point Hai Xixi, his face black, got up from where he'd been squatting by the wall and bore down on me menacingly.

"Get a move on, damn you!" He flourished his whip, his coarse hair bristling, the veins on his temples standing out. "Quit slacking and get moving!"

At once silence fell, as if a stone had been thrown into a pond of croaking frogs. All eyes fastened on the two of us. I panicked for a moment. Suppose he beat me up. . . . But I knew that Mimosa must be watching too, and self-respect got the better of my panic. I threw my pitchfork down in front of him, and stepped away as if to take a rest, actually to get out of his reach.

"Too slow for you?" I fumed. "Why the hell don't you lend a hand then? You can load it."

"Don't give me that bullshit! . . ." He strode up to me. "This is your job, you *ka-fei-le!*"*

The farmhands roared with laughter. I had no idea what *ka-fei-le* meant, and assumed it to be some kind of obscenity. At the same time his threatening attitude alarmed me, and I wanted to find a way of shutting him up. So I ignored the obvious and shouted:

---

* *Ka-fei-le* is the Arabic for "infidel".

"I know why you're foaming at the mouth like a mad dog. Because yesterday I caught you stealing!"

To my surprise, instead of silencing him, this made him shake with fury. He pointed at me, his lips quivering as if chanting. Then he roared:

"*Ka-fei-le, du-si-man*!* You've gorged yourself long enough! Today I'll bleed you!"

His voice had risen to a screech. He dropped his whip and charged me. Catching hold of my jacket he swung me into the air and whirled me round and round, then dumped me like a dead hen on the dunghill.

This caught me by surprise. I'd expected a whipping. Or somebody in the crowd, Team Leader Xie at least, to intervene. Then I could have exposed Hai's behaviour on the road. Now I was a sorry sight, covered with mud and horse-dung, like a donkey that's rolled in the dirt. For a few seconds I lay there catching my breath, too dizzy to think clearly. I saw the baleful gleam in Hai's eyes, heard the laughter of the onlookers. But fury filled me with a strange excitement, the sort a man may feel when he first sees the ocean he has long dreamed of and, throwing wide his arms, leaps in to swim. "Come on!" I told myself. "Come on!"

I rolled over to where my pitchfork lay, picked it up and sprang to my feet. Leap into the ocean! As I sprang up I let fly the pitchfork. It whizzed straight at him.

The farm-hands cried out in surprise and admiration. Hai ducked. The pitchfork made four white dents on the mud wall before clattering to the ground.

---

* *Du-si-man* is the Persian for "enemy". Both *ka-fei-le* and *du-si-man* are still used as terms of abuse in Ningxia.

I had heard approval in the farm-hands' voices, had seen alarm in Hai's eyes. That bolstered my courage. Leap into the ocean! I bounded to the wall and retrieved my pitchfork to attack him again.

Hai hadn't imagined I would fight back so fiercely. He stood gaping by the wall, as if waiting for me to strike him. I thrust out at his thigh. He grabbed the pitchfork, then hesitated, not knowing what to do. With my left foot I kicked him in the groin.

He groaned, bending double, head lowered as if to see where I had kicked him. Then he looked up, his eyes glittering savagely, his face contorted. My pitchfork in one hand, he held out the other like an eagle's talon. He was such a hulking great fellow, it was my turn to panic. I froze.

By now, however, the farm-hands had gathered round.

"That's enough, Xixi! You swung him round and he kicked you, so you're quits."

"Dammit! He's a scholar, knows more characters than you'd ever learn in eight lives. Why pick on him?"

"Why the devil couldn't you help load the cart? Why make him mad?"

"Enough's enough. How much energy do you both have to work off?"

". . . . ."

Team Leader Xie was the one with authority. One hand behind his back as if holding some powerful weapon, he pointed at Hai with the other and said as if scolding a child:

"Don't you dare make any more trouble, you rascal!"

Hai glared at him furiously, then stared at me with blazing eyes. He tugged hard on the pitchfork handle. I let go of it before he could pull me over. Then, grinding his teeth, he hurled it high into the air. It whirled round and round before falling into a ditch some distance away.

Everybody relaxed. Someone picked up my padded cap. With its torn ear-flaps it looked like a half-dead crow. One youngster laughingly crowned me with this dead crow and gave me an encouraging pat on the head. I took a look round. I wondered what Mimosa had thought of all this. She'd turned her back to the rest and was walking towards the ditch. My group, adopting a neutral attitude, were standing by the dunghill watching with interest.

Of course, after that I couldn't go out with Hai. Team Leader Xie assigned the Boss in my place, and told me to go back to the Dead Dog. When the Boss refused this assignment, Hai spat on his palms and picked up his own pitchfork:

"Hell! I don't need anyone. I'll do it alone!"

Working like a maniac he loaded the cart in no time, then cracked his whip and drove off.

Mimosa brought over my pitchfork and handed it to me like a banner brought back in triumph.

"Here you are!" she said softly. "Look, all your buttons are missing. I'll sew them on for you in a bit."

I looked down and saw that my chest was bare. Hai had ripped off all my buttons.

24

That evening I called on Mimosa as usual. I had fallen into this habit, and people are creatures of habit. Besides, I went not only to eat but to satisfy the longing in my heart. Being with her, even if Hai came between us — actually I came between the two of them, but I no longer thought that — I could find what my heart craved. A little warmth, pity, sympathy and respect, a little . . . undefined love.

When I was a boy my family lived near a temple. Halfway up a hill, its red walls were hidden in a bamboo grove. At dawn each day we heard the deep, long-drawn-out toll of its bell, and in fancy I followed the sound till it was lost in the misty Jialing River. . . . The next toll of the bell would carry me right out of this mundane world to an imaginary unpeopled realm. Somehow Mimosa's cottage reminded me of that bell. Perhaps because when I was so wretched, so downtrodden, she had rescued me from our crude bachelors' quarters and taken me to her cozy home. Besides, she was a lovely, lovable woman. So leaving my mundane world of straw pallets for her room with its flickering lamplight, I felt a strange content, and the whole world assumed a fresh significance for me.

I alone was able to grasp the significance of returning to normality: not leaving the world but coming back once more to the world of men. My recollections of the past had been swallowed up in darkness, like the moon obscured by galloping black clouds. But in Mimosa's place there was always something, sometimes her childlike yet fertile imagination, to link together fragmented memories and make me realize that I was a normal man. Even my fight with Hai today, I thought, was normal behaviour for someone in my situation, an important indication indeed that I was back to normal. The farm-hands' approving laughter and Team Leader Xie's initial non-intervention but final blast at Hai were evidence that they all believed that this was the right outcome. I had passed the test set me by my surroundings. And they, normal people who had grown up in these surroundings, had accepted me as one of them.

Mimosa was putting Ershe to sleep. Village children always sleep early. As soon as I went in she jumped off the *kang*. First she bolted the door, then turned, wiping her hands on her jacket.

"Here, let me see how badly that swine beat you up."

Only then did I realize that my face was smarting painfully. Our fight had made me forget the weal on my cheek.

She turned my face towards the lamplight, and studied it carefully with her lovely flashing eyes, giving little exclamations of dismay. Head lowered, I let her stroke my cheek. When her fingers caressed my weal like a gentle breeze, I felt the world could hold no greater consolation, and could hear strains of Brahms' famous *Lullaby*.

Fate had been kind to me.

Her actions and expression revealed a deeper feeling for me than pity. Being loved, I could sit down without any scruples on the stool and wait for her to serve me.

Today she looked even more radiant than usual. Her lingering glance was more ardent. Her long eyelashes fluttered bewitchingly. Even when silent her finely curved lips remained slightly parted as if in anticipation.

While I was eating I told her about the day's events. I knew she had bolted the door, the first time in more than three weeks that she had shut Hai Xixi out. Still I kept a wary eye on it But he didn't come near all the time I was there.

Paying no attention to anything outside she commented on what had happened, expressing great maternal concern and roundly cursing Hai. Actually that upset me, since I thought it was unfair.

"Weren't you on really good terms with one another?" I asked. "I thought you were close friends."

"Friends!" she fumed, flushing crimson. "That good-for-nothing! . . ."

She broke off abruptly like a car suddenly braking. Then she sat down on the *kang*, picked up her mending, and went on with it in silence.

I realized my gaffe. I had used "friends" in the ordinary sense, but to her it meant something completely different — lovers.

This confirmed my intuition.

People make a strange distinction between love and paintings. The more seals there are on a scroll, the greater its value; but love has to be virgin. Whereas in fact mature love is the best.

Mimosa's love was mature.

After a silence she raised her head. No longer blushing but with flashing eyes. She laughed sweetly and blurted out:

"You, you're just like one of us!"

I smiled as I caught her meaning. "Like one of us." That meant so much. It included all working people, manual labourers, farm-hands, even the descendants of settlers from Samarkand in Central Asia. It enabled me to understand why only today had she expressed her feelings so explicitly. To her, a "scholar" who could only tell stories would at most arouse her pity; but to win her love a man must be able to work, to fight back if attacked and use force to safeguard his manhood. That was the way of descendants of Samarkand!

She told me she hadn't found enough black buttons yet for my jacket — in those days even buttons were in short supply. She'd find some more tomorrow and sew them on for me. From under her pillow she took a girdle plaited out of remnants of cloth, and told me to wear it for the time being.

"You," she chuckled, "I know you haven't even got a piece of string."

True, I hadn't even a piece of string.

"You know a lot about me." Since I knew she loved me, I didn't have to be ashamed of my poverty. I went on, speaking casually, "But there's a lot I don't know about you. Tell me, who is Ershe's father?"

She hung her head, smiling in silence. Then started laughing softly again.

"I can't have anything to do with men. If I do it's bound to go wrong."

This staggered me. She hadn't answered my question. I had hoped she would tell me her story, a sad one or a tragic one maybe; but instead she had glossed over it, as if cheerfully consigning all her memories of that period to oblivion. Judging by her tone, she didn't think she had hurt anyone, not even herself. . . .

Damn it! Though she had brought me back to normality, brought together my memories of the past and my present experiences. her behaviour took me aback. There was so much about her I didn't understand, that was at variance with my old moral standards. Yet in her it seemed so good and beautiful that I always felt she was right, above reproach.

She and Hai Xixi had unconsciously infused me with

the spontaneity of the people of the steppe. And this just at the time when I had become a normal person again, which made it doubly potent.

25

For the first time I was aware of the joy that good health brings. I felt I had inexhaustible strength. As Walt Whitman wrote:

> O the joy of the strong-brawn'd fighter, towering in the arena in perfect condition, conscious of power, thirsting to meet his opponent.

In my arena I had evened the score with one of the farm's best workers, a giant feared by all! Brimming with energy, I could almost hear the virility surge in my blood.

The next day Hai drove and loaded his cart by himself again. And once again I accompanied the Dead Dog. When our carts passed, Hai didn't look at me, but he couldn't hide his dejection. He had got over his hatred and was simply sunk in gloom. This Herculean giant had turned overnight into a reed blighted by frost. Not because I had kicked him, but because of the bigger blow to his pride.

Ever since childhood I've been sensitive to the sufferings of others. This isn't pure sympathy. Sympathy leads to action, sensitivity to fear. If I read about a paralytic, I feel half paralysed myself for some days; if I read about a blind man I dread turning blind myself. And my fear for myself surpasses my pity for others. This strengthens my instinct for self-preservation and my unwillingness to make sacrifices. So I no longer felt sorry for Hai but was afraid I too might be unlucky in love.

This vicious streak in me, combined with my distorted view of "manual labourers", was making me sink very low.

When our shift ended I jumped off the Dead Dog's cart. She was standing in front of the stable with something in her hand — I guessed it was buttons — which she held up to show me. After supper I went to her place.

By now about half of our group of eight had stopped working. . . . They kept going to the farm headquarters or to South Fort to look for registered letters. The trip to both was sixty *li* there and back. Our team was a cultural desert. Since coming here we hadn't read an up-to-date newspaper, hadn't heard a single radio broadcast. As the Boss said, this place wasn't up to the camp. They were busy trying to get their residence permits transferred so that they could leave as soon as possible. So they paid no attention when I went out each evening. For them our "home" with its straw pallets was simply a temporary lodging-house, and they didn't care what other transients were up to.

Today I was in high spirits, in a sort of a spin, but certain that this would be an important evening. I was drunk with sweet and disturbing fantasies which floated over the plain like the evening mist.

I went into her cottage. My face must have been shining, my eyes unnaturally bright, because her eyes flashed strangely as she regarded me closely. Her long eyelashes and the dark circles under her eyes made them seem very deep-set with pupils brilliant as stars. She was lying on the *kang* putting Ershe to sleep, as she had been yesterday. With an enigmatic smile she pointed towards the stove. Then, still mechanically patting Ershe, she sat there staring at me woodenly, as if she had something on her mind.

On the stove was a mixture of maize flour and soybean flour. I helped myself to a bowl. As I ate this slowly I tried to suppress my feelings and cool down. Patting Ershe, she sang softly:

> Gold hills, silver hills,
> Treasures in each.
> Others pair off, I'm all alone,
> Poor brother, she's out of reach.
> On White Cliff a dove nests,
> A cock-dove or a hen-dove?
> Last night I counted the stars in the sky
> And couldn't sleep for thinking of my love.

All the ideas about love which I'd been taught were completely different from the love in which I was now immersed. My concept of love had been an enduring close affection, charming yet tinged with heartache and melancholy like a fragile, dewy carnation. But the love expressed in her song was frank, open, crude, filled with inexhaustible passion. As hard to withstand as the wind in the wilderness.

Ershe fell asleep while she was singing. Then Mimosa quietly got off the *kang*, straightened her jacket and smoothed her hair with a captivating smile. For the first time she looked bashful, flushing crimson, her blush deepened by her dark complexion. She arched backwards, raising both hands behind her head, her whole attitude, it seemed to me, that of someone worn out by love.

"Well?" she asked with a smile. "Take it off, or how can I sew on the buttons?"

A threaded needle in her hand, she came up to me. The high colour in her lovely face flustered me. I stammered, "I ... I'll keep it on. I've nothing underneath. ..."

"You!" she giggled, pulling me off the stool. "You wretch. I shall have to make you a vest.... Well then, undo that girdle, go on."

She ordered me about with wifely concern. So as if it were the most natural thing in the world, I took off the girdle and stood facing her without any embarrassment. I was glad to be able to put myself in her hands, I had such trust in her, such fondness for her.

Not needing to stoop, she sewed on the top button. Her hair was very thick and curled naturally. It had a faint bluish sheen in the yellow lamplight. Her dainty ears were very well-proportioned, as if carved. I looked from her slightly prominent forehead to her eyebrows, so even and bewitchingly arched. Her jacket, unbuttoned at the top, showed the hollow of her throat. Her long, rounded neck, as smooth and white as marble, reminded me of a swan.... Irresistible excitement made me lose my reason just as I had when Hai whirled me in the air. I threw my arms around her.

She gave a soft cry, looking up in bewilderment. But I dared not meet her eyes. I hung my head, burying my face in the hollow of her throat. She didn't struggle but nestled up to me, gasping. In less than a minute, though, she broke loose, brushing her jacket as if to brush off dust. Blushing, she glanced at me sideways with fearful, misty eyes. She stammered:

"All right, don't do that. . . . Don't get hurt. Better stick to your books!"

26

Ah!

I staggered "home", my head reeling. Groped my way to the wall and flopped down fully dressed, pulling my tattered quilt over my head without caring whether or not I ripped it.

Soon all the others turned in too. Having put out the light over my head, the old Accountant burrowed into his quilt. Silence reigned. I felt I was already dead!

I really was tempted to die. How easy it would be to step across the border-line between life and death. To end everything, the shame, the remorse, the suffering.

I'd thought she might refuse me, might slap my face, but had never dreamed she would say something to put out the fire in my blood.

"Better stick to your books!" That was more staggering than a slap on the face. I trembled.

Die and be done with it!

I really felt dead. That passionate embrace seemed to have sapped all my energy. My mind was thrashing about between my temples as if trying desperately to split my skull open. I didn't dare look back on my behaviour here; but, inevitably, shameful scenes kept coming back to me. The more tightly I closed my eyes the clearer they were. Hai Xixi shaking his fist. "You've gorged yourself long enough!" I'd trembled as if at the thunder that comes before lightning. Whose loving-kindness had restored my health? To cadge food from her like a beggar, I had offered to rebuild her *kang*, had gone to tell her stories. . . . Outwardly I had played the part of a mendicant monk, while at heart I was still a profligate parasite. Goethe once called "ingratitude" a virtue. Said the unwillingness to express gratitude was confined to the poorest of the poor who were forced to accept favours, favours poisoned by the contempt of their benefactors. But I was the reverse: my contempt had poisoned my benefactors. As I regained my strength a demon had leapt out of me like that genie from the bottle on the beach who threatened to kill his deliverer. Why? Because I hadn't started life as the poorest of the poor. The son of rich parents, when he falls on hard times and is rescued by a poor woman, will immediately repay her by trying to lay her — isn't this an old, old story?

By now all of my longings of the night before had turned into a Buddhist monster, a man with the head of a beast, and Mimosa was struggling in the clutches of this vicious, hideous monster.

Yet her final advice to me had shown her kind-heartedness and moral strength. This made me even more ashamed of myself.

I wanted to repent, to pray, but as a materialist, an atheist, there was no one to whom I could confess or pray. I had no belief in spirits. After my first "death" I had lost all respect for religion. So to whom could I pray? To the people? They had cast me out. "Serves you right! Your present behaviour proves we were justified. It wasn't the decision of any one leader but of the whole people. You've been crucified for good!"

I heard a sinister hissing from the corner, seeming to emanate from a world of utter darkness. It was neither God nor the Devil, I knew, it was Death calling me. Death had long had a strange appeal for me: I loved it as dearly as life. Because it is something that none of us can ever grasp in our lifetimes. This eternal riddle exerts an eternal attraction. Most people overlook the fact that death is an important component of life: those who love life most are least afraid of death. To an atheist like myself, especially, death is the easiest way out. Everything ends when your heart ceases to beat. Well then, let me present the world with an eternal mystery. Tomorrow morning when the sun rose, the wind blew the clouds away and the farm-hands went to the fields — all as usual — I would have become a lifeless heap of flesh and bones like a dead sheep, a dead dog. Not a trace would remain of my remorse and shame, my self-reproach. My secret would go with me to the grave, an eternal mystery.

When half-starved I had wanted desperately to live, but now that I was well-fed I wanted to die. In previous spells of frustration, poison, ropes and knives had held a powerful attraction for me. Now, in the dark, I fingered the girdle she had given me. It was soft and elastic. Its length, width and tensile strength would make hanging comfortable. How strange and unpredictable life is! I had a picture of the previous evening when she gave me the girdle to help keep me warm. Now I meant to use it to end my wretched life. She said I hadn't so much as a piece of string, and had taken pity on me, yet had given me the wherewithal to commit suicide. Holding her in my arms had been bliss, but it had led to remorse, the longing to die. . . . My fate was extraordinary. The last of my family, born into a moribund class, I could never enjoy happiness because anything good that happened to me turned out badly. . . . The only final release for me was death.

So, I died!

All that was left of me, my head, was drifting through a black, forbidding forest. Disembodied, it could only skim through the air. I floated on, flew on. . . . I was hemmed in by dense trees. Their towering crests shut out the sun, but no leaves or branches brushed against my cheeks. They parted like water weeds at my approach. I had no goal, knew only that some force was buffetting me forward, drawing me this way and that. . . . The translucent darkness shone with a spectral blue light. The huge trees were not three-dimensional but as flat as backcloths on a stage. This forest had no end. All the vegetation in it was motionless, moving aside only when my head approached, then closing in again. . . . There was nothing specially sinister about it. What was sinister was the ghostly blue miasma which spurted out of my head to fill the spaces between the trees. There was no sound, but my head had ears. And now a roar like thunder made itself heard:

"Why must you die — die — die —"

"Die — die —" The tinny sound drifted through the trees.

I laughed sardonically. What was there to be afraid of? I feared no one, not even death.

"That's what I want to ask *you*!" my head called

back, rolling its eyes to track down the sound. But it was echoing everywhere. I yelled:

"Why must I live — live — live —"

"Live — live —" My cry, too, echoed through the forest.

Silence! Silence fell. I laughed. So you have no answer, eh?

I went on careering through the forest. Enjoying death.

But the huge dark trees grew denser. Above and below me their boughs formed an impenetrable net. As they closed in, there was less and less room for my head. Finally I was forced to hang motionless in the air, my two eyes rolling wildly, my mouth wide open, panting. I had no arms with which to resist, no legs with which to kick out. I waited: what devilish tricks could be played on a dead man?

The sound started up again like an echo in the hills, a spectral, muffled voice:

"Go to heaven! Go on — go on. . . ."

"Heaven?" My head had broken out in a cold sweat, but I wasn't afraid. "Where is heaven?" I shouted indignantly. "There's no such place. I don't believe in any damn god!" Why try to fool a dead man?

"Transcend self — transcend self — transcend self — for you that is your heaven. . . . Transcend self."

The phrase made me suddenly burst into tears. My tears plopped down into the miasma. "Transcend self!" This hadn't been the spectral voice, it sounded more like the dear one I had lost.

"Transcend self, that is heaven."

"How can I?" I sobbed despairingly. "This poor dump

at the back of beyond is like me, cast out by the world. How can I transcend self here?"

"Integrate yourself with the wisdom of mankind. What did she tell you? Remember what she said!"

The voice sounded faint and far-off, then died away completely. My head, streaming with sweat, thumped down now like overripe fruit, as if it had been that voice which had kept it afloat.

I seemed to have landed on a soft patch of damp soil. I felt moss against my cheeks, and dew dripping down my face like tears. The cold moist air brought me peace of mind.

Peace returned to the vast forest. The thick mist lifted, a ray of sunshine filtered through the treetops like a flashing golden sword. The soft notes of a piano could be heard. Fate knocking at the gate! It sounded uneasy yet strangely resolute. Presently a French horn trumpeted a charge. Powerful, stirring music engulfed me like the waves of a sunlit sea. It seemed to be expressing Beethoven's determination to grapple with fate and not let it subdue him. . . .

By now I was wide awake. My face was covered with tears, and tears had soaked the bedding under my head. I felt for the thick hardback copy of *Capital*.

27

The next day the sun rose as usual and wind blew the clouds away. Golden sunlight penetrated the old newspapers on our window, dappling the walls and straw. For a while the memory of the folly I'd contemplated the night before depressed me. But I quickly realized that if my room-mates got up to find me dead, apart from a spell of flustered surprise it wouldn't have affected them much at all. Once they'd got me buried they would have gone back to work. My death would have grieved my mother far away, but probably no one else. What meant so much to me would mean very little to them, at most it would provide material for a ghost story to while away the long winter evenings. What was the point of dying like that.

The Boss was the first to fetch breakfast. He hogged the stove, blowing on his hands. "God, it's cold! What damnable weather!" The old Accountant, gingerly clutching his mess-tin with both hands, padded softly to his pallet to sit down cross-legged. Having taken off his gloves and cap, as if praying to the precious buck-wheat gruel, he proceeded to eat in silence. He never warmed himself by the stove and was afraid to disturb the rest of us by eating noisily. He was so self-effacing, it would have been cruel of me to have upset him by dying.

The Lieutenant had gone to South Fort a couple of days earlier and found the post-office closed, so he was getting ready to make the long trip again. "Those bastards!" he swore. "Cushy desk jobs and they still take time off." He'd forgotten his own days off when holding a desk job. The Editor and the rest were the same as ever, like a woodcut print on a calendar which remains the same day in, day out. It amazed me that they had no idea of my emotional turmoil during the night. Obviously, no matter what emotional crises I went through, whether I died or turned over a new leaf, it would make virtually no impact at all on people so wrapped up in their own affairs. Their senses seemed blunted by their monotonous existence here, so it ought to be very easy for me to quietly start a new life. The prospect exhilarated me. I threw off my quilt, scrambled up, wiped my face with a damp towel and went to the kitchen. . . .

The vast steppe, so bleak yet so magnificent, brought hot tears to my eyes. Give me a little of your majestic spirit! If I had the austerity of a clod of earth, I could stand up and transcend self. The Dead Dog drove his cart slowly, letting the horses amble where they pleased through fields bathed in wintry sunshine. Magpies chattering gaily followed behind to peck at our horse-dung. The hay in the barnyard was golden, the top of each rick glinting in the sun. Thirty *li* away to the east, a train puffed slowly along, its plume of smoke leaving a girdle of mist on the horizon. The borders of this black billowing smoke gradually turned indigo, a beautiful sight beneath the azure sky. The aroma of frozen straw and splendid achnatherum hung in the still air and mingled with the odour of the dust churned up by our cart. Basking in the sun I grew drowsy. People experience the greatest sense of well-being not when wide-awake but when they're half dozing.

My heart had been singing ever since my crisis had passed. Harmony, brightness, purity and joy seemed to dwell in these fields with their birdsong and their sweet-smelling fresh air. Death might be tempting, but life was far more alluring. Consciousness itself was a joy. Suffering and remorse were forms of consciousness too, both were part of the experience of living, and therefore a joy. Sparrows chirped overhead, looking this way and that as they soared on their little wings.

Why, even these small creatures wanted to transcend themselves!

Transcend self! Transcend self!

After supper instead of going to see Mimosa I sat down, leaning against my folded quilt, and took out *Capital* which I had neglected for three weeks or more, only using it as a pillow.

When the Lieutenant had read his registered letter from home, which cheered him up, he politely returned the lantern and turned up the wick for me. Instead of starting to read immediately, I quietly, rather apprehensively, fingered the book's yellow cover. It was my only means of "transcending self". My only way to "heaven". What could I learn from it? Would I be able to assimilate the abstract concepts in it? . . . Though I had never read *Capital*, during political study I'd read a Russian textbook called *Political Economy* which was required reading for cadres. It had struck me as dry and dogmatic, divorced from reality and utterly boring.

Now at least, coming back to *Capital*, my stomach wouldn't interfere with my brain. I opened the book respectfully at "Chapter III. Money or the Circulation of Commodities", and the footnote where I had left off. My room-mates were chatting listlessly. The Boss told the old Accountant a "cure" for grinding his teeth in his sleep — have the whole lot pulled out. Even this sadistic joke failed to raise a laugh. Before long, though, as I started reading, I became oblivious to the sounds around me. Marx used such vivid, graphic images to illustrate economics that, though I didn't fully grasp his meaning, I was gripped by his fluent literary style. Each page had superb passages. His strict logical reasoning was expressed with the evocativeness of poetry. For instance he wrote:

> "In order that a commodity may in practice act effectively as exchange value, it must quit its bodily shape, must transform itself from mere imaginary into real gold, although to the commodity such transubstantiation may be more difficult than to the Hegelian 'concept', the transition from 'necessity' to 'freedom', or to a lobster the casting off of his shell, or to Saint Jerome the putting off of the old Adam."

He went on wittily:

> "If the owner of the iron were to go to the owner of some other commodity offered for exchange, and were to refer to the price of iron as proof that it was already money, he would get the same answer as St. Peter gave in heaven to Dante, when the latter recited the creed —
>
> The weight and purity of the coins
> You offer is more than enough,
> But how can I tell if you have them in your purse?"

It takes genius and magnificent revolutionary spirit to write like this. Marx had the ability to link up and integrate all fields of human knowledge. The more I read the more impressed I was by his grasp of politics, economics, history, art and literature — even poetry! Sometimes the solvent in my mind was unable to dissolve the concentrated crystallization of his knowledge. But I didn't tire of reading. I found the book a fascinating riddle. Whoever solved it would surely make a fortune!

He cited a whole wealth of material, and the footnotes below the text were fascinating. He quoted Shakespeare and Sophocles too as circumstantial evidence of how commodities turned into money. That immediately made the abstract subject dramatic and specific. The adobe room smelling of straw, rat droppings and smoke was suddenly transformed into the stage of a historical play, where commodity-owners and the possessors of money acted their parts to the hilt. By now I had completely forgotten my surroundings.

Marx quoted the views of bourgeois political economists on each subject, sometimes pointing out how they had inherited or developed each other's ideas, not failing to give credit where credit was due. Elsewhere he struck out ruthlessly to demolish their pseudo science wittily and trenchantly. So each page shone with the quintessence of history. Readers could see the progress of human history and thought. And when I read his reference to the memorial Wan-mao-in Chancellor of the Exchequer presented to the Chinese Emperor in 1854, I felt especially stirred. Marx hadn't neglected us either. While writing this great work, creating Marxism, he deliberately included the state system of our old oriental country!

Everyone else at "home" had turned in. The lamplight was dim, I wasn't disturbing anyone. The old Accountant was grinding his teeth; the Lieutenant was snoring loudly; the Editor was talking in his sleep; while I was intoxicated by incontrovertible logical reasoning and encyclopedic knowledge. The ability to express rational ideas in terms of graphic images from real life is a rare gift for any thinker or artist. And Marx was a past master at this. I was starting to read *Capital* seriously as a fine work of literature, in which I admired each sentence. Literature can work miracles in people's minds. Can smash their preconceived ideas and reshape them.

Both art and ideology have the power to intoxicate men. Together they are doubly potent. Though still unable to grasp to the full the subtlety of this wine, it was going to my head. When the crippled storekeeper's rooster crowed — all other roosters had long since been eaten — I had just finished Section 2. How clearly the last page debunked the high-sounding arguments of bourgeois humanists.

Marx wrote:

> This sphere that we are deserting, within whose boundaries the sale and purchase of labour-power goes, is in fact a very Eden of the innate rights of man. There alone rule Freedom, Equality, Property and Bentham. Freedom, because both buyer and seller of a commodity, say of labour-power, are constrained only by their own free will. They contract as free agents, and the agreement they come to is but the form in which they give legal expression to their common will. Equality, because each enters into relation with the other, as with a simple owner of commodities, and they exchange equivalent for equivalent. Property, because each disposes only of what is his own. And Bentham, because each looks only to himself. The only force that brings them together and puts them in relation with each other, is the selfishness, the gain and

the private interests of each. Each looks to himself only, and no one troubles himself about the rest, and just because they do so, do they all, in accordance with the pre-established harmony of things, or under the auspices of an all-shrewd providence, work together to their mutual advantage, for the common weal and in the interest of all.

Marx analysed this so clearly, I was only sorry that I'd read it too late. Amazed, too, that since then so many other people have written reams of articles to expose the hypocrisy of bourgeois logic. Put together they could fill a huge library, yet they aren't up to these few hundred words by Marx. Moreover, when I was being criticized in 1957, no one used this passage of his to shatter my illusions about humanist literature. I resented that. Not the fact that they criticized me, but that it was such ineffective criticism. Their farcical bawling and shouting had simply confused me and made me cynical.

The final paragraph, read in our adobe hut, made me laugh. With a few deft strokes Marx depicted the relationship between capitalists and workers.

On leaving this sphere of simple circulation or of exchange of commodities, which furnishes the "Free-trader Vulgaris" with his views and ideas, and with the standard by which he judges a society based on capital and wages, we think we can perceive a change in the physiognomy of our dramatis personae. He, who before was the money owner, now strides in front as capitalist; the possessor of labour-power follows as his labourer. The one

with an air of importance, smirking, intent on
business; the other, timid and holding back, like
one who is bringing his own hide to market and has
nothing to expect but — a hiding.

After lying down to sleep I kept this picture in mind,
but it underwent a change. The people striding in front
were my uncle, my father and the Morgans whom they
so admired for being "intent on business"; following
behind were all the workers they employed. But in a
flash this picture changed again. Now the workers
were striding in front "with an air of importance, smirking, intent on business", while those who had led the
way trailed after them "timid and holding back, like one
who is bringing his own hide to the market and has
nothing to expect but — a hiding." As for me in my
ragged padded jacket, like a tousled, dirty beggar, I
couldn't walk proudly in front with the other workers,
could only shuffle along between the two contin-
gents. . . .

28

After being so deeply stirred I slept extra soundly. I
woke up as exhilarated as if I had taken a dose of
Benzedrine. And with a sense of superiority vis-à-vis
my room-mates which made me more tolerant of them.

The Boss came back from the kitchen in a foul temper
because the bun given him had a piece missing. While
the rest of us ate on our pallets, he squatted by the stove
examining his bun and cursing the cook. He also fumed
that in future the light should be put out earlier, so as
not to keep others awake. "Half a bun can't make up

for that lost energy. . . ." He grumbled. The rest looked at me, and I knew I was his target. These people wouldn't care if you dashed out at midnight to start a fire, so long as you didn't disturb them.

His criticism had no effect. Though I was there with them in this mundane adobe hut eating a brown buckwheat bun, I was mentally so buoyed up by high ideals that no insults or jeers could hurt me.

When we went to the stable, the head of the carters' team told Team Leader Xie that Hai Xixi had asked for a few days' leave to go to town. Xie's face fell and he pursed his bearded lips but made no comment. Hai's cart was standing there idle, and his horses were enjoying themselves munching on the hay in the trough. Another carter went over to hitch them to his cart, intending to give his own team a rest. Xie glared at him and yelled, "What the hell are you doing? Leave them alone. Let them take it easy for once." Perhaps he thought Hai deserved some time off too. But why should Hai suddenly want to go to town? Didn't he take it easy each evening with Mimosa? I felt disturbed. No matter who falls in love or what form his love takes, no one can look on indifferently when he is crossed in love. Hai's unique personality made me feel concern for him and sympathize with him. Although we were rivals I couldn't shake off the attraction he had for me.

But Mimosa took a much simpler view of things.

When our cart came back that afternoon she was waiting as usual in front of the dunghill. She signalled to me that I should go to her place. I could see that she was smiling but couldn't make out whether her smile was derisive, teasing or kindly.

Being young and inexperienced, my judgements about other people and ideas on love were based on the books I had read. I had supposed that after my loutish behaviour we would both be embarrassed the next time we met. After supper I read for a while but couldn't concentrate. To go or not to go? I fiddled about till darkness fell before setting off to her cottage.

There was no moon that night and it was pitch black and bitterly cold outside. The sky was studded with stars. A typical winter night: bright overhead, black underfoot, as if the freezing air had segregated the light. I hunched my shoulders and had the uneasy feeling that I was in for a beating.

She was sitting sewing on the *kang* as usual — there was no end to her mending. I later discovered that she helped women with big families to mend their husbands' clothes. When I went in she sprang up and smoothed her tunic.

"Why didn't you come last night?" she asked with a smile, imitating my way of talking.

Funny! That mocking question dispelled all my doubts and anxieties. I didn't know whether to laugh or cry. I might have apologized to her, made a clean breast of my feelings, but she was so relaxed that it seemed unnecessary. I began to relax too.

"Didn't you tell me to study hard?" I countered. "I stayed in reading."

"Id-i-ot! Can't you read here?" She pinched my cheek playfully. "Last night I peeked at you through the crack in your door." Giggling, she folded her hands and squatted down. "You looked like a Buddha!"

I flushed. Her playfulness and warmth seemed a little provocative. But she meant nothing of the sort:

there was a childlike innocence about her. I felt more ashamed than ever of having misjudged her. My education and reading had taught me to categorize people. Even the most objective psychologists will classify people according to different types such as phlegmatics or cholerics. And in literature you find even more types: steady, flighty, unrestrained, serious. . . . Now I realized that, apart from Marx's division of people according to their economic status and class, there can be no absolute generalizations about them. Mimosa was herself, a flesh-and-blood woman. One moment steady, the next frivolous, roaring with laughter, then very much in earnest and the last time she had spoken to me in earnest she had nearly made me kill myself out of shame. You can't analyze people rationally as you would analyze events, to understand them you have to rely on intuition as well. This helped me to grasp what Marx meant in his Preface to the First Edition: "I paint the capitalist and the landlord in no sense *couleur de rose*. But there individuals are dealt with only in so far as they are the personifications of economic categories, embodiments of particular class-relations and class-interests." Each specific individual from one and the same economic category and class is a living being who can be "painted *couleur de rose*"; but the economic category which makes him the embodiment of "particular class-relations and class-interests" is something which has to be analyzed rationally. This is where literature differs from economics.

This sudden association of ideas may have been laughable, but it seemed to me that I had obtained a fresh understanding of life. I felt not just relaxed but rather elated.

After I had eaten she pulled out a brand-new felt blanket, telling me that she had sent someone to buy it in South Fort for seven yuan, so that she could make me some trousers and, with what was left over, a little suit for Ershe. Patting it she gloated, "We'll wear woollen clothes too, just like city folk!" She chattered away about the woollen clothes worn by people in her old home. They used a primitive bone teazle to tease sheep wool into knitting yarn. She showed me a "sweater" she had made like this, grayish-white and shapeless as a sack. I blushed at the thought of the rough, coarse wool scratching her skin through her blouse. At the same time I felt a pang of sympathy. For her, wearing wool was a city luxury, a real wool sweater even more so. Such a lovely, kind-hearted woman and she had probably never seen a real wool sweater in her life. She couldn't begin to imagine how I had lived as a child. Maybe that was what had made her pity me. Unlike me, she couldn't understand historical causality.

She unfolded the blanket. It was one of those gray blankets with a red stripe which I had seen stacked in the small shop in South Fort. She measured it, using her thumb and forefinger, her lips moving in a silent calculation. The lamplight lit up her fluttering eyelashes, her bright eyes rapt in thought. Her eyes seemed to make her whole face shine with a captivating, heart-warming radiance. Yet she was a woman who had never worn a sweater, who considered this woollen blanket a luxury! My past way of life and limited experience made it impossible for me to reconcile my ideas of beauty with the beauty in her actual life. It was just as impossible as transplanting a Downy Myrtle to this cold arid soil on the border of the desert.

After supper I said, "I hear Hai Xixi's asked for leave to go to town."

"Who cares where he goes!" She went on calculating, her head bent over the blanket. "He can go wherever he pleases."

It was all so simple! I've been tormenting myself these last days for nothing, I thought. Her attitude to people and to life, though a little crude, was highly practical. The wind in the wasteland blows this way and that; how can you order it about at will?

Intellectuals' attitudes to people and to life, though more sophisticated, are unsound and impractical, unable to adjust to the turbulent course of history. Ever since, I have been grateful to her for silently infusing me with something of the spirit of the wild wind.

29

Every evening after eating our rations from the kitchen I took *Capital* to her place to read — that should have pleased the Boss. She lifted the oil lamp down from the wall and put it on a tin on the stove. "The higher the lamp the more widely it sheds its light," she said. And indeed the room seemed much brighter. Ershe was so well-behaved that apart from begging her mother sometimes to sing she didn't disturb me. Mimosa didn't ask what I was reading or why I wanted to study, nor did she refer to that evening when she had broken away from me and urged me to stick to my books. Apparently she believed that it was a good thing for a man to study, though she couldn't have explained why or given me the same advice as the lecturer in philosophy.

"My grandad was a scholar," she told me. "I remember, when I was small, I kept seeing him reading, holding a great thick book just the way you are." After a while she added, "That good-for-nothing Xixi quit studying to roam about all over the country. I've got no time for that."

That gave me a clue as to why she preferred me to Hai. The way she described her grandfather's book made me guess that it was a Bible or Koran. But there was no trace of religion in her make-up. A frank, lively optimist who's been through it all stops taking a mystical attitude towards life.

I cradled my book under the lamplight. She and Ershe chatted quietly on the *kang*, the shadow of my head falling across them. Ershe seemed to have been infected by the serious atmosphere — she kept her voice down. Sometimes when I stopped to listen to their laughter, I realized what warmth they had given me. This tiny room could hardly contain her unfailing affection. She reminded me of a small delicately fashioned boat sailing over a calm sea in a fairy tale.

Once Ershe was asleep, she knelt on the *kang* to cut out my "citified" woollen pants. The scissors' soft snipping sound was like the patter of a warm drizzle on green bushes. She didn't speak to me, but if I happened to look round she might raise her lovely eyes to smile at me. It was evident from her radiant face that she enjoyed this atmosphere. And this enjoyment dated from her childhood — she thought it right for a woman to have a man studying beside her. Chinese women down the ages have always had this beautiful fantasy.

The woollen trousers were finished in a day. The

gray blanket had three red stripes at each end. Now the three stripes at one end crossed my thighs. Wearing these "citified" pants I looked like a clown in a circus. Ershe clapped her hands at sight of me and gurgled:

"Rag doll! Rag doll!"

"Don't say that! Say 'dad'!" Mimosa slapped her gently, then squatted down again to put the finishing touches to the trousers. Her face was hidden from me. What she'd said set my heart pounding, but she was so volatile, I couldn't be sure exactly what she meant.

"There! A perfect fit!" She stood up, covering her mouth to laugh. "I've made you a cap too."

She told me she'd copied the cap from the old Accountant's and made it out of the blanket remnant. It was the kind worn in Shanghai in winter, and had a red pompom on top.

"Fancy your thinking of this!" I put the cap on, laughing. "I wore a cap like this to go to school as a kid."

That evening I put on these Rag Doll's pants — she was going to unpick my padded suit and wash it. And wearing the cap she'd made me I settled down to read "Part III. The Production of Absolute Surplus-Value". I was warm from tip to toe and my stomach was full. Engels once said that people's prime needs are food, shelter and clothing; only when these needs are met can they devote themselves to politics, science, art and religion. And setting out from this simple fact Marx had discovered the laws of historical development. Laws which applied to macrocosm and microcosm alike. Now I had the mental energy to explore profound problems. When I read the next section of *Capital* I was quite carried away because, although apparently unrelated to me, it enabled me to grasp instantly the way in which I should view my present circumstances and determine my goals in life.

Marx wrote:

> Labour is, in the first place, a process in which both man and Nature participate, and in which man of his own accord starts, regulates and controls the material re-actions between himself and Nature. He opposes himself to Nature as one of her own forces, setting in motion arms and legs, head and hands, the natural forces of his body, in order to appropriate Nature's productions in a form adapted to his own wants. By thus acting on the external world and changing it, he at the same time changes his own nature. He develops his slumbering powers and compels them to act in obedience to his sway.

So in order to remould himself a man must first regulate Nature and his surroundings. Only by doing this can he change himself. In the last four years and more because I had been acting on Nature to change it, I had also changed my own nature. But I had done so unconsciously, in a ridiculous way. The crude, primitive methods I had been forced to resort to had made me crude and primitive myself. Only by consciously using methods conforming to the laws of development to regulate Nature and my social surroundings could I attain my goal. And this could only be achieved through study, by integrating myself with the "wisdom of mankind". The extent to which a man remoulds himself depends on how successful he is in regulating Nature and his social surroundings. To enjoy life and freedom a man must explore them day after day.

So there was no reason for me to despair or to lament my fate. Because wherever you are, life is full of ups and downs. The harder the circumstances, the more ability will be displayed by people with true self-knowledge. I knew from my own experience that people have amazing reserves of strength, with death as the only limit. Unfortunately, while I lacked consciousness, I had only displayed the instinct of self-preservation. Now I was confident that I could develop my dormant powers and transcend self. And this would bring me happiness and fulfilment.

My mind was reeling. Now, suddenly, I saw light. I believe there is some scientific base for the concept of "attaining enlightenment". It represents a sudden qualitative change in the process of reasoning. The realization shook me, brought tears to my eyes. . . .

At this point she tiptoed over and leaned against my back. One hand on my head, she looked over my shoulder as if to see what it was that had stirred me so deeply. But I didn't want her to realize the gulf between us, a gulf that could never be bridged. I feared that might destroy both her and my intoxicating happiness. My present circumstances seemed fantastic: economic concepts and human life, reason and passion, harsh reality and dreams transcending time, poverty and beautiful fantasies, abstract categories of every kind and a lovely flesh-and-blood woman. . . . These merged together, blurred, flickered and disappeared. Yet they were all as authentic as the pebbles at the bottom of a brook, the moon behind scudding clouds, a small bridge in the morning mist.

I slowly took her hand off my head. Its palm was crimson from being immersed in lye, and the calluses were white. Hard work had roughened her hands yet given them strength, warmth and dignity. The lines on her palm, clear and simple, displayed her openness and optimism. I examined them one by one. The heart line ended in a whorl — a dead end — which made my own heart miss a beat. The mental euphoria I'd felt gave way to the tenderness of love, and one of Byron's verses sprang to my mind:

> By those tresses unconfined,
> Woo'd by each Aegean wind;
> By those lids whose jetty fringe
> Kiss thy soft cheeks' blooming tinge:
> By those wild eyes like the roe,
> Can I cease to love thee? No!*

This tenderness rose above the tumult of sexual desire. Like a stream rushing down towards the sea, I had taken one step in transcending self, leaving more room in my heart to store up the desires of youth. My love now was calm yet deeper, like the water in an inlet. With tender affection and a dream-like joy I put her hand to my lips and kissed each finger in turn. Then I placed it over my face. When I let it go I shed a tear on it. My heart was so stirred by her, by love and by my sublimation that I couldn't help blurting out:

"Darling, I love you!"

She was still standing behind me, her full, high breasts resting against my back. She made me take her hand again, and with the other stroked my shoulder.

---

* From *Maid of Athens Ere We Part*. In the original each verse ends with a line of Greek, which has been translated into Chinese as "You are my life, I love you." To retain the rhyme scheme we have used instead a line from Byron's last verse.

When I kissed her fingers her hand had suddenly trembled from fright and bashfulness. I felt that for her this was a new sensation, yet she too was enjoying the happiness of love. Now she pulled her hand away and leaned over my shoulder to press her face against mine. She asked with happy surprise:

"What was that you called me?"

"I called you ... darling."

"That won't do!" She gurgled with laughter.

"What should I call you then?"

"Call me *rourou* (pudgy)." She prodded my temple with one finger.

"Then what will you call me?" I teased.

"I'll call you *gougou* (puppy)."

Though *gougou* was a term of endearment, it was a far cry from my old romantic notions. The form her love took and the terms of endearment she used rather embarrassed me — they seemed so laughable. Though I didn't want her to sense the gap between us, I was only too well aware of it myself.

30

On the surface, the contents of *Capital* had no relevance to my present circumstances. Marx made clear his main theme from the start when he said that the capitalist mode of production presents itself as "an immense accumulation of commodities"; yet here on the edge of the desert there was such a shortage of commodities that we couldn't even buy ourselves woollen pants. In his book universal money had regained the form of its original precious metals; but here potatoes were being bartered for carrots and carrots for watches, while money was a most unreliable symbol of value. . . . Precisely becaue of this, though, the work didn't strike me as dogma. The more I read the better I learned how to think, learned the Marxist world outlook. I was able to equate "commodities", "money" and "capital" with the x,y and z in algebra, and as Marx analyzed and used each concept my brain naturally evolved a new method and pattern of reasoning. Moreover this method of reasoning could be used to analyze anything in the external world. This world outlook and method were not hard to grasp. It depended on faith, on the firm belief that this world outlook and method conformed to the laws of development.

At the same time the concepts in *Capital* weren't strange to me. Born into a bourgeois home I had been brought up by capitalists, one a stockbroker, the other a factory-owner. So as a boy I had often heard my elders, true disciples of the Morgans, discussing the difference between value and exchange value, the circulation of money and the metamorphosis of commodities, money's role in circulation, hoarding and the different functions of universal money. . . . I was ten when I first heard of *Capital*. It was in our elegant sitting-room when an old professor from Sichuan University introduced the book to my father. He said, "To run a factory well and be a successful capitalist, you've got to read *Capital*." Obviously everyone can make use of objective truth. Hadn't Kennedy studied Mao Zedong's strategy of guerrilla warfare? I had learned this a few days earlier on a trip to South Fort to buy salt. The salt was wrapped in a sheet of the *Round-up of Foreign News*, stamped "Not to be passed on".

So to me there was nothing dry or obscure about Marx's book. As I read it various abstract concepts regained their original concrete form; each page was a vivid, graphic slice of life. Each evening in Mimosa's cottage, I devoured this intellectual feast. And as I transcended self I also transcended this rugged region at the edge of the desert. Sometimes when my eyes were tired from reading in that poor light, I would look up at Mimosa. I was beginning to feel estranged from her. Sweet, lovely and honest though she was, she hadn't outgrown her crudity. Seated on the *kang* she watched me with startled, mischievous or merry eyes. The smile lurking in the lines at the corners of her eyes and mouth seemed ready to burst into hearty laughter. Evidently my expression was ludicrous. However, I knew she had no inkling of what I was thinking. And my state of mind perturbed me. She hadn't outgrown her crudity, and I had regained my memories of the past and become an "intellectual", though I still accepted favours from her, so what was our present relationship?

A man can only search his memory for experiences or knowledge to compare with the present. She wasn't, of course, a fallen woman like those I'd read about, but the term "American Hotel" disturbed me with its overtones of dissipation. When she served up a piping hot meal and put my bowl beside me, or when she softly sang those stirring but slightly wanton folksongs to Ershe, I couldn't help thinking of the poems of certain literati, of lines like "a red-sleeved girl burns incense as he studies at night", or "she sings softly as I blow my flute".

Now that I was beginning to "transcend self", my

feeling for her was also beginning to change. As Goethe wrote in *Faust*: "Two souls dwell in my breast." On the one hand, while I read Marx, she wanted to transform my outlook, bringing it in line with that of the working people; on the other, my past experience made me conscious of a gap between them and myself. I was superior to them mentally, on a higher intellectual plane.

31

We had no calendar, there wasn't a single one in the team. There'd once been one in the team office, but we heard that it was stolen before our arrival. By then it was impossible to buy another, as the theft had taken place in June, by which time there were no calendars in the shops. Team Leader Xie told us: "That swine stole 180 days. What a dirty trick!" It was generally believed that the thief had wanted the calendar to roll cigarettes. Xie and the Accountant could only check up on the date when the farm messenger came to our team every two or three days. Each time someone went to the farm headquarters on business, or to shop in South Fort or visit relatives in other teams, Xie reminded him, "Be sure to bring back the date!" "Bringing back the date" became the duty of everybody going out. To see what day of the month it was by the solar and lunar calendar, and how many days there were to go before the next festival. There was no need to look up Sundays, since we never took Sundays off anyway. The day after pay day was always the holiday. Since we had no sense of the week, we often went all the way to South Fort for nothing, as there Sunday was a day of rest.

Last year we had no calendar. And none after New Year either. Probably we'd got used to doing without one. The Cripple went to town before New Year to buy tools and stationery, but forgot to buy a calendar. Team Leader Xie swore at him, "Are you so damned afraid of growing old that you have to stick to last year's calendar? If you'd bought an almanac, hell, you could choose a lucky day to fetch home a bride." The Cripple flushed, his face blotchy. He'd been widowed for several years, and was nearing forty.

And so the time slipped past until one "date-scout" brought back the good news: "The Spring Festival's coming up."

Actually, in those lean years, the farm had no special provisions either for New Year or for the Spring Festival. But the biological clock in each of us made us look forward to both, and the farm-hands all had a festive look on their faces. Besides, as the villagers made such a big thing out of the Spring Festival, each team secretly did what it could, depending on what it was able to produce and the team leader's disposition. The last few days there had been a lot of speculation about how many sheep might be killed, how much mutton each family would get, and who would receive the offal. The offal couldn't be distributed by weight, only thrown in as an extra; so three families might take home the tripe, heart, liver, lights, head and trotters of one sheep to share out between them. But it was so seldom that a sheep was killed, no one could remember from one time to the next whose turn it was now, and no records had been kept. So by the stable, the sheepfold and out in the fields heated discussions took place, more involved and protracted than any United Nations debate. The mood was still lively and cheerful, however. We bachelors didn't get a share in either the mutton or the offal, at most we'd get a couple of ounces of meat ready cooked for us by the kitchen, so we didn't take much notice of the arguing. Besides, most of our group were getting their residence certificates, work permits and grain coupons transferred. The Lieutenant had already left us, and was probably now getting ready to celebrate the festival at home. The Boss, who lived in the provincial capital, had recently been notified of his transfer to a farm in the suburbs, and as soon as our farm okayed it he would go home.

There were still three days to go to the festival. That afternoon a light snow started to fall. Icy snowflakes blew down our necks and wet the handles of our shovels, so that soon our cotton-padded gloves were soaked. Team Leader Xie, as always, looked up at the sky and swore, "Hell!" then yelled, "Knock off!" We'd been shovelling dirt over compost some distance from the village and all started off home at a run.

The snow fell more heavily, but I didn't hurry. The dirt track was already covered over. The sparrows had to flap their wet wings hard to speed back to their leafless thicket, where they slowly preened their plumage, looking up helplessly — like Xie — at the leaden sky.

Snow in the northwest doesn't melt when it reaches the ground. If it falls on your hand you can make out the design of each snowflake, as if carved by some master craftsman in the sky. And even as the flake melts, it still retains this design.

Black clouds had gathered, yet the sky seemed

brighter. A twilight glow hung in the air, and the horizon appeared to have expanded. In the distance the smoke of the train was jet black in contrast to the snow, moving past like a magic brush adding a parallel stroke to the horizon and leading to a far-distant realm of fantasy.

By the time I got back there was no one in front of the stable. Mimosa must have gone straight home. The whole village was shrouded in the stern winter silence. Our place was extra warm, the Editor hadn't gone to work and had stoked up the stove, which was now red hot with sparks flying. And we were in luck. Because of the festival the kitchen had issued us bachelors with half a catty each of real wheat flour. The cook had chopped up carrots, with shallots and salt as seasoning, to make us dumplings.

Since the rest would soon be going their different ways, unlikely ever to meet up again, my room-mates had been on good terms the last few days. The old Accountant looked after me specially well. After fetching back my meal for me from the kitchen, he had put it by the stove to keep warm.

As the others ate they cheerfully described the first thing they meant to do on getting home. The Boss was determined to "have a good meal of mutton with noodles". The Accountant reckoned he could be back in Shanghai by the Lantern Festival, in time to eat sweet dumplings made from glutinous rice flour. The Editor's home was in Lanzhou, where his relatives had found him a job in a workshop run by the neighbourhood committee. He told us about his favourite local dishes. . . .

"Festivals turn our thoughts homewards." I couldn't go home, I didn't have a home to go back to. It was impossible to visit my mother. A hard seat on the train from the provincial capital to Beijing cost over twenty yuan. And I hadn't yet paid Mimosa for the woollen pants she'd made me. Now she was making shoes for me too. I knew she wouldn't take money even if I had it, but that raised the question of just how our relationship was to develop.

I'd been greatly tempted by the idea of marrying Mimosa and settling down here. For a while that had seemed to me an unattainable goal. But now, soberly aware of the gap between us, I had rejected it.

Of course I still went to her place every evening, I almost thought of it as my home. Ershe and I were now the best of friends. I no longer told fairy-tales that only grown-ups could understand, and when I was tired of reading *Capital* I played with her. Out in the cold wind all day frisking in the snow and ice and better nourished than most other children, she was a bit tomboyish but she wasn't rough, she still had a girlish gentleness about her. She liked me to scare her by pulling my cap down so that only my eyes showed. That threw her into fits of laughter.

However, Mimosa had still shown no sign of wanting to marry me or anyone else. When Ershe once again called me Rag Doll, she scolded her and told her to call me "dad". I looked at her carefully. There was no revealing expression on her face, only that distinctive smile of mock indignation. Was she flirting? Conforming to some crude local custom? Perhaps like a wild creature she loved freedom? I couldn't make her out. Sometimes her affection for me perplexed me.

When I woke up at night I often thought of our relationship. Now that I was back to normal, beginning to "transcend self", I couldn't go on accepting her sympathy and living on her bounty. I could stay in this ramshackle adobe hut, sleep on a straw pallet and put up with the old Accountant grinding his teeth. . . . Because once I had tried to integrate with the "wisdom of mankind" and raised my political consciousness by studying Marxism, I seemed to have embarked on a new life. And that impelled me to search for my heart's desire. Yet what this was I was not too clear, because no one, including Marx, had described communist society in detail. So what I desired was simply a richer, fuller life involving greater hardships.

So I could no longer endure living on her bounty and began to feel it shameful, as if her charity vitiated the hardships I was undergoing in my search. What it boiled down to was either I had to break with her, or we must become man and wife.

But could I marry her? Did I love her? In the quiet night I dispassionately analyzed my feelings. At the bottom of my tender, dream-like affection for her was simply gratitude. Simply a reflection of the love I had read about in books. I knew she was quite unaccustomed to my ways of expressing love, and so couldn't understand my love or me. Nothing could bridge the cultural gap between us. . . . In short, much as it upset me, I felt that we were incompatible.

Still, when I'd finished my dumplings I went to Mimosa's place.

Dusk was falling. Flurries of snowflakes whirled everywhere, white and glistening through the grey sky, grey fields, grey village. Instead of falling straight down like rain they fluttered about like insects, making me even more confused.

Her door was wide open. She was standing in the doorway, wearing a scarf as though about to go out. Ershe, bundled up too, a pancake in her hands, was stolidly waiting next to her. Seeing me, Mimosa smiled and stepped aside to invite me in. The first thing I saw was a big dish of dumplings waiting to be boiled — far more than the three of us could eat. I recognized the dish as the one that was usually on our kitchen table.

This increased my misgivings. I frowned, "Where did those come from?"

"Where from? They're a present," she answered casually, quickly knotting her scarf.

"Who from?" I sat on the stool, shoving the dish away.

"Can't anyone who wants to give me a present?" She threw me a sidelong glance and wrinkled her nose, smiling.

"All right," I snapped. "I'm not eating any!" I instantly realized how ridiculous it was to lose my temper. How could I interfere with her life? What was I to her? Nothing! At the same time I thought, "This finishes it. We can't go on."

"All right, all right! If you won't eat them then we'll feed them to the dogs." She spoke as if teasing a child. She seemed incapable of taking anything seriously. How often her banter had swept aside my scruples and doubts. I was no match for her.

"We're in luck!" She winked at me with another smile. "The team's going to kill ten sheep! If they did it in the daytime, most likely the sheepfold would be broken down by people crowding in to get the blood; and if the farm headquarters heard about it they'd haul Xie the Beard over the coals. So Xie the Beard said to kill them at night and take the blood to the kitchen — lucky for your lot! The Cripple's sent for me to help. Don't you think that's a stroke of luck? Wait till I come back and I'll boil you up a sheep's head with chopped tripe. . . . There's rice in the pan, help yourself. Ten old sheep to be killed, skinned and cut up, so that each household gets a share, that could keep me busy till dawn. I'm taking Ershe over there to sleep, they have a warm *kang* there too."

I sat there woodenly. The Cripple must have nicked these dumplings from us to give to her! "American Hotel" I fumed inwardly. "American Hotel!" Though I knew Mimosa was skilled at skinning sheep and cooking, so she always got roped in on occasions like these, I suspected she must have made a "deal" with the storekeeper, for why else should he do her such a favour? She must be a loose woman.

"Go off to work then," I growled, standing up. "I'll go back to my group."

"Why should you?" She widened her lovely eyes in surprise. "Have something to eat, and read for a while. If you don't want to wait up for me, go back and sleep. Lock the door when you leave . . . silly *gougou*!"

She pouted, pinched my cheek fondly yet mockingly, and pushed me on to the *kang*. Then picking up Ershe she made off at top speed.

32

I sat woodenly on the *kang*. The room was bleak without Mimosa and her little daughter, making me realize how much they meant to me. In their absence

the cottage had lost its warmth. What should I do? . . .
She was such an enigma, I didn't know what to think.
I stood up listlessly to light the lamp and took the lid
off the pan. The bowl of rice inside it was still
steaming. After an unhappy meal I started reading.
From the sheepfold came plaintive bleats, they must
have started slaughtering the sheep.

While I was reading the door was flung wide open.
The oil lamp flickered as a husky figure moved inside.

Hai Xixi!

Alarmed, I sprang to my feet. I stared at him in
silence, fully on my guard.

"I know Mimosa's gone to the sheepfold," he said.
"I figured you'd be here, since you weren't at home."
Like Team Leader Xie, he considered someone's sleep-
ing quarters as "home". "I've got something to tell you,
Zhang. Just between the two of us."

His unusually mild tone, not in the least belligerent,
reassured me. He hadn't called on Mimosa for a long
time, and now he looked around as I had during my first
visit. By the dim lamplight I saw confusion in his eyes.

"Sit down then," I said like a host, pointing to the
kang.

"Let's go to my place. I've left it unlocked, I've left
my stuff there." He gave me no explanation of his
earlier aversion to me, nor did he try to allay my fears,
as if we'd been friends all along. Because he let bygones
be bygones I trusted him.

"Okay." I picked up my book. "Let's go."

Following our fight Hai Xixi had gone to the provincial capital and had stayed there till after New Year.
When he got back he drove his cart like a demon again,

not talking to anyone. If he met me or Mimosa he ignored us, as if he'd never known us. And feeling apologetic, natural enough towards a defeated rival, I never mentioned him in Mimosa's presence. Sometimes she spoke about him, but without any special feeling. Why had he come to look for me now? Judging by his lowered head and heavy steps, he had something serious to tell me. I followed, both tense and curious.

It was still snowing. The freezing wind whirled dazzling white snow through the pitch-dark night. By the time we had trudged to the stable our caps and shoulders were covered with snow.

"Come in." He opened a side door and we stepped in one after the other. The little room, not more than seven metres square, had a low ceiling. A bright lantern hung from a pillar in the middle.

We brushed the snow off our caps and clothes. Then he took off his slush-covered boots and seated himself cross-legged on the *kang*. "Come on up," he told me, reaching out for a big black kettle singing on the stove. Having brewed tea he filled two mugs which he had got ready in advance.

"Taste it, honest-to-goodness tea, with brown sugar in it."

I sat opposite him. There was an old tattered quilt on the *kang* and a red-laquered table which had been polished till it shone. The only other things in the room were halters, whips, ropes and straps stacked neatly on the ground.

He kept silent, frowning and smacking his lips as he sipped the tea. The adobe hut was very quiet. All we could hear was the stamping of horses' hooves on the other side of the wall. Presently Hai put his mug down half full. He seemed to be trying to control his feelings. Wiping his mouth with one hand and looking away from me he said:

"Zhang, I'm getting out."

"Getting out? Where to?" Since he was treating me like a close friend I couldn't help feeling concern for him. "Why should you leave?"

"Hell! How can I stay in this dump!" He shrugged this off. "I've got the skill and strength to earn thirty yuan anywhere. Fact is, I never meant to stay here long, it was only after I got to know ... Mimosa...."

He stopped. I had flushed at the mention of her name and could only watch him in silence. The horses were stamping again in the stable next door. His hands on his knees, his elbows outstretched like the wings of an eagle, he stared straight in front of him. It moved me to see this rough, hot-tempered fellow suddenly grow so solemn. Then I thought: Why not give Mimosa to him, they're so well-matched. But immediately I realized my own base motive, my betrayal of Mimosa's love, so I kept quiet.

After a while, he calmed down, turned to me and said, "I've got a sack of soybean, over a hundred catties, which I'm leaving for you and Mimosa. And this table of mine you can have. Come and fetch it tomorrow morning. I'll stow the sack behind the hayrick, the place I showed you. Don't take it in the daytime, come after dark, and don't let anyone see you, understand?"

"Why. . . ." I didn't know whether to accept or not. I knew that he meant well. But his gallantry made me thoroughly ashamed. I didn't want to go on accepting favours.

"Don't worry, it isn't stolen." He misunderstood my

hesitation. "I know you scholars don't eat stolen food. I'll tell you where it comes from. As soon as I got here I sowed a plot of soybeans on the wasteland to the west. Dammit, there's plenty of land lying waste round here. This autumn I harvested a good four hundred catties. Xie the Beard knows about it, but he hasn't told farm headquarters. He's a decent old bastard! That's why I respect him."

They had too high an opinion of me, thinking I didn't eat stolen food. I knew my own weaknesses. I remembered how I'd cheated the old peasant out of his carrots, had got barnyard-millet flour from the kitchen on false pretences, had sponged off of Mimosa.... I did these underhand things while Hai sweated to clear land — that was the big difference between us. So which of us was the better man? I frowned.

"Why don't you take it with you?" I asked with genuine concern.

"No! Wherever I am I won't go without food. I'm not like the two of you, a woman and a scholar. . . ." He pointed at the corner of the *kang*. "See, I've got this big quilt to take."

I saw then that we were sitting on a bare mat, and his quilt was already strapped up in one corner with a white box fastened to it, ready for him to carry off.

"Are you going right away?" I asked in surprise.

"What's the point of waiting?" He gave a snort of laughter. "Do you expect me to go in broad daylight? I'll tell you, I'm not like you, you've got a residence certificate and grain coupons. You can leave whenever you apply for a permit. I'm a drifter, dammit, and I know how to get by. They want me to sweat my guts out in this dump, nothing doing! If I left openly they'd send men to stop me, might even tie me up. Last year ... no, the year before last, they got a whole lot of runaways...."

"Where will you go?"

"Where? China's a big country. I've already been to plenty of places. I tell you," he slapped his chest and declared, "with my skill and strength I'll be welcome anywhere. First I'll spend this festival with my aunt at the foot of the mountain, then make my way to Inner Mongolia. They have farms there too, and better pay! But don't tell anyone."

I nodded. "Don't worry, I won't. But you can't go on like this for ever. Team Leader Xie told me how much you've travelled."

He abruptly lowered his head to stare blankly at the small table, not wanting me to go on. I knew that once this rough, self-confident man had reached a decision no one could change his mind.

The kettle was singing again, the horses next door were whinnying plaintively. We said nothing, and the atmosphere suddenly became oppressive. Hai drained his tea then set down his mug. As if he had drunk liquor, not tea, he shook his head, blinked and rubbed his face with his large hands. Then keeping his voice down, he sang mournfully:

> There's good food and drink in Gansu,
> Yet my face is gaunt as can be;
> I know the reason why:
> My sweetheart's done this to me!

After singing this he slapped his thigh and sighed, "Oh, women fancy young fellows."

He meant that he had lost face, that his pride had

been wounded. His tragic impotence in the face of fate made my heart contract with pity. He could have settled down here and founded a family, but now he was going to drift about again — and I was responsible. I had sabotaged him. I hung my head wretchedly too, as though prepared for a whipping.

After a long silence he heaved a deep sigh and raised one hand as if to brush worries aside. Quickly sobering up, he pulled himself together and filled two mugs from the kettle, then moved closer to me saying:

"Tell me, Young Zhang, between the two of us, what book is that you're always reading? Looks something like a Koran. You know, I watched several times outside her window, and you were always reading. Fact is, I studied the sacred works too as a boy."

Mimosa had never questioned me about this, but it had caught his attention. I was glad of the chance for both of us to relax a little. Patting *Capital* I told him that it wasn't the Koran, it was Karl Marx. He asked what use it was. I told him we could learn the laws of social development from it. We couldn't transcend those laws, but understanding them would enable us to reduce our sufferings, just as understanding the course of the four seasons enabled us to farm in accordance with natural laws. "Social development's like the weather," I said. "Both can be predicted, both are inevitable."

"In-ev-it-able." He cocked his head, narrowing his eyes thoughtfully. "In-ev-it-able. I get you. We have another name for it — the will of Allah."

"That's different. . . ." I started to explain.

"It's the same!" He cut me short and went on decisively. "Allah's will, that's what you call in-ev-it-able.

But then there's the choice a man makes for himself. For instance, I could have studied and become an imam. But I didn't, I chose to cut loose, it was my own decision. If I suffer for doing wrong, that's not Allah's will, I brought it on myself. I can't shift the blame on to Allah. There's Allah's will but we make our own decisions."

This somewhat incoherent speech staggered me. Like the meaningless spell "Open sesame" it could open a heavy stone door. Idealist philosophy and materialist philosophy are quite different, but they do have certain common factors. He had been talking about "individual choice". Though I was born into a class doomed to extinction I still had my freedom of choice. What he'd said helped me to understand a problem that had baffled me in the past: Marxism points out the natural laws of social development, and I believed implicitly in their scientific truth; but then why were we going hungry? This was due to our own mistakes. We were being penalized for not acting in accordance with the objective laws of society — it wasn't Marxism that was to blame! People's temporary mistakes and setbacks can't detract from the validity of Marxism. . . .

While I was sunk in these reflections he went on enthusiastically defining various Muslim religious terms. Maybe as a distraction from his worries, to carry him back to an illusory paradise. As he warmed to the subject his talk became even more far-fetched.

More plaintive bleats were sounding from the sheepfold. How many sleep had they slaughtered? It wasn't far from the stable and the bleats sounded sad and shrill. He suddenly lost interest in what he was saying and hung his head in silence.

The lantern flickered and dimmed. "Hell, it's running out of oil!" He jumped up to turn up the wick, and at once black smoke rose from the clean polished shade. He bent forward to lower the wick, then remembered that he ought to be going, so he drew back his hand and sat down to face me.

"Well, Zhang, you must marry Mimosa!" he blurted out.

"Why. . . ." I was taken aback.

"I can tell you, Mimosa's one of the best," he asserted. "That talk about an 'American Hotel' is nonsense! I know how clever she is. Accepts presents, but won't let anyone take advantage of her. It's true, you should marry her. You'd be living in clover."

"I . . . I haven't thought about it," I stammered.

"You haven't thought about it!" He slapped his knee angrily and glared at me. "You swine! You think she's not fit to marry a scholar? I'll tell you something. Once I looked through her back window when she was bathing. Oh, what breasts, what a figure. . . ."

He was always taking me by surprise. I couldn't help bursting out laughing too. But I knew he meant it, he was genuinely concerned for me. And he had confirmed that, in this team at least, Mimosa had a clean record. At the same time I realized why she had broken off so abruptly when talking about him that day. She must have seen his outrageous behaviour. After that however much he courted her she always called him "useless trash". Now I knew the reason.

"Well?" he asked finally. "What other plans do you have? You can't sit for the imperial examinations. All your book learning is useless if no one will hire you.

She's a handy needlewoman and cook, can work in the fields as well. I'm afraid she'd be wasted on you! ..."

Bleating sounded again from the sheepfold, and he said he had to go. Having gulped down his tea, he picked up the kettle and made me help him shoulder his load.

"Can you carry such a heavy weight?" I asked dubiously.

"No problem! Thirty *li* to the foot of the hills, that's not far." He swung the heavy bedding-roll and, without saying goodbye or shaking my hand, told me to put out the light and lock the door before going to feed the horses. He turned then and squeezed out through the narrow door, to plunge into the darkness and the snow.

As I left the stable, the world was a mass of swirling snow. . . .

Mimosa was still in the sheepfold. I went "home" to sleep.

33

I burrowed down into my ragged quilt, but was still awake when Team Leader Xie called through our window:

"Zhang Yonglin, Zhang Yonglin! Young Zhang, Young Zhang. . . ."

This urgent summons made my heart sink for fear that something had happened to Hai Xixi. Pretending to be asleep, I wondered how to answer his questions. Meanwhile he kept on calling, "Young Zhang, Zhang Yonglin. . . ."

The old Accountant nudged me. "The team leader wants you, Young Zhang."

I got up slowly and yawned, "What is it?"

"Hurry up, come to a meeting in the office."

I didn't think Hai's escape could have been discovered so soon. Probably the meeting was to discuss the allotment of the mutton, and maybe we bachelors would get a share too. I threw on my clothes and hurried over to the office.

All the heads of different groups were there, each holding a hand-rolled cigarette. They'd filled the room with smoke. In the middle of the table was a basket of tobacco leaves grown in the team, supplied free of charge to the group leaders during meetings. "Give me a paper, would you?" I rolled a cigarette too and started puffing away like the rest of them.

Presently Team Leader Xie came in with a sack and plonked himself down, panting, in front of the table. The ceiling lantern lit up his blood-stained hands, making me stare in surprise and nearly drop my cigarette, for the scene reminded me of one of Sherlock Holmes' cases. The thought of Hai and Mimosa made me sit rigid.

Luckily all Xie said was, "That damn Hai Xixi's taken off!" While feeding his horses Dead Dog had noticed that Hai's door was locked — hell, I shouldn't have locked it! When he looked in through the window with his lantern, "The *kang* was completely bare." So he'd gone to the sheepfold to report this to Xie. Xie swore that we had to go and drag the bastard back. "He can damn well run away after the ploughing's done!" He ordered us group leaders to head out in different directions, issuing instructions like an army commander. As

I was thinly dressed, he told me to take the east highway to the little railway station thirty *li* away to intercept Hai there. He added, "There's a stove there, you can warm yourself up. When I've seen to things in the sheepfold I'll come and join you."

Only then did it dawn on me that the blood on his hands was sheep blood. And he'd omitted to send anyone by the path to the foot of the hills. I relaxed. Then he bucked me up even more by opening his sack to issue each of us with two frozen buckwheat buns. "You'll have a hard search, so here are some extra rations," he explained.

After the meeting the group leaders left the office. "Hell, what's the use of searching in all this snow," they grumbled. "Better go home and turn in." Sure enough, they all headed home.

I had to go to the station, since Xie was going to join me there.

The snow was falling thick and fast. North, south, east and west, everything was a blurred flurry of white. The snow stung my eyes, I could hardly keep them open. I could easily get lost in such hellish weather. I began to wonder why Hai had chosen a night like this to take off. Then I realized how astute he was. Hadn't the group leaders all gone home to sleep?

I plodded along the highway. Luckily it was bordered by willows and by walking between them I couldn't lose my way. I pulled my wollen cap down over my eyes, and at once my face felt the warmth of Mimosa's concern for me.

I thought over Hai's parting proposal and though in two minds about it, was touched by his unselfish friendship. I realized that goodness, sympathy, pity and all the human virtues had not been driven out, as I had imagined, by hunger and cruel beatings. No, the harder conditions were, the more remarkable these virtues seemed. Was it really true that when fate dragged me from my ivory tower, it had nothing good in store for me? Wasn't it precisely under these tough conditions that I had enjoyed the most precious warmth and friendship?

I felt very, very fortunate. What time was it now? It must be after midnight. The only sounds to be heard were the soft swish of the snow and my steady breathing. The snowy night was so still you felt your soul might take flight. Ahead, between the willows, a small bridge came into sight, its back humped to bear heavy loads. Just over two months ago, I suddenly recalled, Hai had driven his cart over it, fetching us from the labour camp to the farm, and sitting proudly on his shaft had sung that stirring folk song. He must have been thinking of Mimosa then, impatient to get back to her. But now a great change had taken place, and so quickly! He had been defeated in love and was running away while I, his successful rival, was shamelessly chasing him. As I thought of Hai with the heavy load on his back trudging painfully through the snow to the foot of the hills, my happiness ebbed away, for it was only too evident that it was founded on his bad luck. I couldn't help remembering his comment on that verse:

> Moon obscured, wild geese fly high
> As the Hunnish chief flees by night.
> We give chase with light cavalry,
> Snow shrouding our bows and swords.

In Lu Lun's depiction of the heroism of the Tang general, Hai had detected the grief of the khan. No wonder then that his observation had been so unlike standard literary criticism. Today, over a thousand years later when we were living in one big family of different nationalities, why should we object to his view? On the surface he might seem headstrong and crude but he was actually a solid, warm-hearted character with all the fine qualities of our ethnic minorities.

These good farm-hands had shown me sympathy, friendship and unselfish concern, always thinking the best of me. But how had I repaid them? I'd brought them nothing but grief.

I paused for a moment on the little bridge, my head lowered to watch the snow fall into the darkness beneath it. I reproached myself bitterly for having caused others such unhappiness. Yet the man I had wronged had not only forgiven me, he had done all he could for me, done me a kindness at parting. My remorse was like bitterness cut into my heart. Ah, Hai Xixi, Hai Xixi, dear friend, how can I repay you?

34

The station was really tiny. When I saw the red signal-light by the track I groped my way to it. There was no platform, but an adobe hut about the size of a police box stood beside the railway tracks. The piled-up snow on the roof made it look like a solitary mushroom in that vast expanse of white. Inside it was pitch dark without a glimmer of light. But as Xie had said there was a stove made out of a petrol drum, now nearly burnt out. I brushed off the snow on my clothes, found a poker, swept it over the floor and managed to find a small heap of coal in one corner. When I had stoked it up and the fire was burning well, I sat down on a bench. I took off my shabby padded shoes, scraped off the slush on them, and with the top of one shoe swept clean the stove top to toast my buns and dry my shoes there together.

Soon flames were flickering out from the front of the stove, their red light brightening the little room. I roasted my feet on the lower part of the stove until soon I was warm all over. As I turned over the buns I surveyed my surroundings. The four walls were daubed with sketches made by passengers waiting for trains, like a primitive hunters' cave in Africa. I was surprised not to see a ticket window, then remembered the Editor telling us that this wasn't a station but a halt, where slow trains simply pulled up for a minute. The slow train wouldn't be here till 4 a.m.

I waited. Munching on a bun I thought of Hai Xixi. By now if all had gone well he should have reached his aunt's place. With all my heart I wished him a good Spring Festival and a happy future.

I dozed off before the warm fire. It must have been some time before I heard steps crunching through the snow. Team Leader Xie threw open the door and came in.

"Dammit, what a big snowfall!" He stamped and patted his clothes and cap, craning his neck like a tortoise with a coughing fit. "So you're still here eh? Well, better here than outside. . . . Those fellows will be having a devil of a time searching in this snow!"

He didn't know that "those fellows" had gone home

to sleep. I felt rather sorry for him, but admired his responsible attitude and appreciated the consideration he'd shown me.

I made him sit down beside me, and offered him my second bun. He held it up to examine it and remarked that it was well toasted but didn't eat it, just put it back on the stove. He said they had boiled up some sheep bone soup in the sheepfold, and added buckwheat buns to make a mush — two bowls for each of the helpers. Knowing that Mimosa and Ershe would have had their share warmed my heart.

"Team leader," I asked, "do you think you'll manage to catch Hai Xixi?"

"Not a chance! He's a clever devil, there's no catching him." He wiped his nose, his eyes fixed on the fire.

"If you know you can't catch him, why make us all chase him?" I asked in surprise.

"Ah," he sighed. "If we didn't, headquarters would bawl us out. 'Someone makes off and you don't lift a finger, Old Xie — what are we feeding you for?' They'd give me a telling off. I'll wait here for the four o'clock train, then take it to headquarters to report."

He told me that this station lay 30 *li* east of our team, and the farm headquarters was 20 *li* to the south. The next railway station was just 2 *li*'s walk from it. He'd got everything well worked out, had made a show of chasing after Hai Xixi and could take this convenient train to headquarters.

"Has he done anything wrong, that the higher-ups insist on catching him?" I asked in bewilderment.

"What the hell has he done wrong? He's too capable, the scoundrel, so everybody wants to hang on to him. You don't know, you've just seen him carting, but he can plough and hoe or turn his hand to building. Where else can we find another good worker like him?"

So what Hai had told me was no empty boast. "In that case, if you caught him, what would you do to him?" I wanted to know.

"What would we do to him? Nothing. Just make him promise not to run off again. He hasn't robbed anyone."

Xie had rested his elbows on one side of the stove and his face glowed crimson. The skin of his cheeks was flabby, and the firelight showed up the wrinkles he had acquired working out of doors for years. He must have had bad trachoma, for his eyes kept on watering. I imagined he was much younger than he looked, but now, just as when he'd first talked to me alone, his expression was that of a kindly old man. I was very touched and, in my eagerness to team up with Hai Xixi, I nearly told Xie to fetch him back from his aunt's place. But I thought better of it. I mustn't let Hai down. I asked:

"Where do you think he's heading?"

"Where? To Inner Mongolia I bet. But he has an aunt too at the foot of the hills, so he'll have gone there for New Year."

I gave an inward start. Apparently it was deliberate that he'd sent no one by that path to the foot of the hills.

"Ah!" He wiped his watering eyes, not really upset but looking as though he was. "Even if we dragged him back we couldn't keep him. I know that bastard, with no wife or family he won't stay put very long. Drag him back today and he'll be off tomorrow. Who can keep him? He only stayed with us because of a woman."

I dared not say a word, suspecting that he knew how things stood with us. Head lowered I turned over my buckwheat bun, now toasted brown.

The snow must have stopped, we no longer heard its soft swishing sound outside. The crackling of the low-grade coal in the stove added to the air of tension.

"Well." He suddenly turned towards me. "Young Zhang, take my advice and marry Mimosa."

This was the second time I'd received that advice this evening, from two different men. Guessing at his train of thought, I was too flustered to say anything.

"Mimosa's an able woman," he went on. "She may carry on with men, but what's wrong with that? A woman bringing up a child on 18 yuan a month in hard times like these — what do you expect her to do? If you marry her, she'll settle down properly."

I wanted to yell at him: Mimosa doesn't carry on with men! But after four years in a labour camp and still working under surveillance, I hadn't the courage to argue with Team Leader Xie. I kept my head lowered in silence.

"Don't ditch her," he continued presently. "Lots of girls get taken in when they're young, but later make decent wives. And don't listen to that talk about an 'American Hotel'. For months she was going steady with Hai Xixi, but then for some reason or other she turned against him. The two of you seem to me to be cut out for each other. You're a good worker, the right age for her. You can have children by her. Why not settle down on this farm? Life's easier for two than for single people. We'll soon be over these hard times, and things will start looking up. I hear that this month

the Central Committee called a big meeting in Beijing.*
Seems the policies of the last few years are to be changed. Once life improves, you can make a go of it anywhere, can't you? Why must you run back to town like
the rest of your group? ... The point is, you've got your
life ahead of you. What's past is over and done with."

He hadn't lectured me, had carefully avoided the
touchy subject of my class origin and my mistakes, and
had even told me inside information about the Central
Committee. It was a long time since a Party cadre had
spoken so kindly to me. He was very much my senior,
the red firelight made his tired face seem old before its
time, gave him a look of fatherly compassion. No matter how rough or uneducated a man is, if he has genuine
feeling and sound common sense, he has a natural
dignity. On this quiet night, by the baking stove in this
small cave-like room, the gap between us was bridged
by his kindly concern. Tears welled in my eyes and in
the crimson firelight fell like drops of blood on to the
stove.

After a glance at me he said no more. Putting his
hands up his sleeves he leaned back slightly against the
stove and went to sleep.

35

The train was a combined passenger and freight train.
The dark green passenger coach was pitch dark, without a light; the huge tarpaulins over the unidentifiable
goods on the freight cars were covered with grimy snow.
The antiquated engine seemed to be wheezing with

---

* A meeting of 7,000 people convened in January, 1962.

asthma as it chugged to a halt. As soon as Team Leader Xie had boarded it, it chugged off again, vanishing in a cloud of white steam. When the steam dispersed everything was desolate again. The snow had stopped, even the patter of swirling flakes. The whole world was still: above was blue sky and below, the vast white plain. Leaving the mushroom-shaped hut I crossed the railway and made for the willow-flanked highway.

I moved steadily ahead, my heart at peace. Tonight manual labourers and the world had all of a sudden entranced me. Reality had surpassed my fantasies. People's hearts could be so noble! Headstrong behaviour, crude speech and ragged clothes could not detract from their radiance.

As I walked along thinking, it struck me that in the Chinese and western literature on which we had been brought up there had been no characters like these: humble, crude manual labourers with their own moral code, yet intelligent and capable of the finest feelings. Fate had given me the chance to discover these rough diamonds, and I must remember each and everyone of them.

As it began to grow light, a stretch of molten silver appeared on the horizon. A willow bough beside the road snapped under the weight of the snow, and crystal powder danced in the air like falling pear blossom petals. All around me silver bells seemed to be tinkling as if I were wandering through fairyland. The loveliness took my breath away and exhilarated me, making me suddenly feel particularly sensitive. I realized that however hard a man studies the Marxist classics, even if he is able to recite them by heart, if he doesn't love ordinary people and thinks himself superior to crude uneducated workers, then he is no Marxist. Don't capitalists also study *Capital*? Didn't Kennedy study Chairman Mao's guerrilla tactics? Working people don't exist in the abstract, they are workers like Mimosa, Team Leader Xie and Hai Xixi, though they may fall far short of the grandeur of literary characters.

Stirred by this sudden insight, I strode on towards the little village tucked away in the snowy plain. I wasn't cold, my blood was racing. My love was waiting for me there, the dear one with whom I would spend my life. It occurred to me that if I married her I could change my bourgeois blood, and let the fresh blood of workers flow in my children's veins.

By the time I reached the village it was broad daylight. But there were still no footprints in the snow, the farm-hands were still in bed. I went straight to Mimosa's door.

She had probably not been back long from the sheepfold, having just cleaned the sheep's head and offal given to her. On the floor stood earthenware basins and pots. Something in the pan was steaming. The place reeked of mutton. Ershe was sound asleep on the *kang*. Mimosa's hair was tousled, her face tired as she busied herself cleaning up. But when she saw me her eyes flashed with joy. She scolded:

"Why did you go off on that wild goose chase? All the others went home to have a good sleep."

Her indifference to what had become of Hai Xixi displeased me. I wanted my wife to have some sympathy. I retorted, "How could I not go? Team Leader Xie sent me."

"How . . . how?" she mocked. "If you'd caught up with him, could you have dragged him back?"

"Of course I could," I said sharply. "Don't you know what a good fellow Hai Xixi is?"

"I never said he wasn't!" After a pause her face clouded. "You, you have no thought for me."

"How can you say that?" I protested. "Do you know what Hai Xixi said to me when he left?"

"How should I know?" She sounded on her guard. Then she burst out giggling. "How should I know?"

How could I propose to her? To her nothing was ever serious or sacred. Maybe I don't understand women. I always found her harder to fathom than Hai Xixi or Team Leader Xie.

"He, he advised me . . . to marry you."

I stammered this out. But I knew at once that this wasn't the stirring poetic, romantic proposal I'd had in mind on the way. It was as dry and insipid as dregs of beancurd. It couldn't move her and it left even me quite cold.

"Why can't he mind his own business!" Though she wasn't too angry, she did put on a sarcastic smile. I was appalled. Had I made a mistake, didn't she love me?

Since I'd blurted this out I had to go on. "At the station Team Leader Xie suggested it too. Said life's easier for two than for single people. . . ."

"So he's butting in as well!" She sprang to her feet, her back stiff as a poker. After dumping the basins on the stove she snapped, "Other people have no right to meddle! I know my own mind."

My ludicrous proposal had been a complete fiasco. Life had just unfolded a new vista before me, but now it suddenly switched back to the old harsh, prosaic reality. Had all her goodness to me stemmed from love, or was it just a flighty woman's idea of fun? I stood irresolutely by the door. Should I up and leave? Or stay here to clear up what she meant?

Just then we heard the Cripple approaching outside. She hastily pushed me aside and bolted the door, then nestled up to me, sticking out her tongue and smiling mischievously as she waited for the storekeeper to knock.

"Mimosa, Mimosa." He tried the door then called again huskily, "Mimosa, Mimosa. . . ."

After a pause she answered lazily, "Who is it?" She looked up at me and smiled, wrinkling her nose.

"It's me, Mimosa."

"I've gone to bed," she drawled. Her voice was the opposite of her expression. "I'm worn out. If you've got more work for me, wait till I've had a sleep."

"Oh, there's nothing that needs doing. Get up, on the third pillar to the west in the sheepfold I've hidden some offal for you. Go and get it." He offered her this as if begging for a favour.

"All right then." She pulled another face at me. "I'll go in a while."

He still didn't want to leave and shuffled around outside. I had felt very tense during this exchange. The last time she and I had still been keeping a distance, but now she was in my arms, fooling the storekeeper while she fiddled with the buttons on my jacket. Though I'd often taken risks to scrounge food, when there was much more danger of being discovered, I'd never felt so confused. I shivered. She went on pulling faces, but I couldn't smile, I wasn't in the least amused. At last the Cripple limped away, and outside silence fell again.

She crowed with laughter, turning in my arms to

face me. "He's still after me, the fool! I'll get that offal in a bit. Why waste it."

I sighed. Life's splendour had faded, leaving it squalid and ugly.

"Look at you, half frozen." She stroked my hands, then put them round her waist and tucked them under her jacket. "I'll soon warm you up."

I could feel the warmth of her body through her thin blouse. Though her soft, resilient waist was in my grasp, her nearness failed to arouse me. I was afraid of another misunderstanding. Which should I believe in, her coldness just now or her present tenderness?

"Stupid puppy, so dense!" She looked up at me. "Why talk about life being easier for a pair than for single people? Have you thought that, if we married, you'd have to cut firewood, fetch water and help with housework? Once we had a baby, you'd have to wash nappies too. You'd be so run off your feet cooking and cleaning, you wouldn't have time to comb your hair. Your eighteen yuan isn't enough to keep you, let alone a baby too. Wouldn't that be the end of your coming here to eat, then wiping your mouth and studying? You're really a stupid *gougou*!"

It dawned on me then that her plan was to sacrifice herself for me for love. But what could she see in me to make this sacrifice worthwhile? The world, mankind and these uneducated manual workers regained their lustre in my eyes. I realized that the reason I couldn't understand her was because I'd never sacrificed myself for anyone I loved.

I was too involved with myself. Even my desire to "transcend self" was for egoistical reasons. That was the greatest difference between us.

I held her close, feeling that now I really loved her, that it wasn't simply just gratitude.

I murmured eagerly, "Let's get married, Mimosa! If other people can manage, so can we. Why not let me share your burden?"

"Why . . . why!" she feigned anger, pushing me away a little and fixing me with flashing eyes. "I don't want you to be like other men, all wrapped up in their homes, never getting anywhere. You're a scholar, you must study. So long as you study I don't mind slaving away till I'm blue in the face. What burdens of mine could you share? If we married, would those idiots go on sending me things? See, I didn't lift a finger, but there's sheep offal there for me. Just wait to eat it, silly *gougou*, that's the way. . . ."

She wanted me to study, but had never explained to me why. Apparently she thought studying was my vocation, just as a cat's vocation is to catch mice. The idea amused me, but I had to admit that it was realistic. That's how women's minds work, I thought to myself.

But I certainly thought it shameful to depend on a woman's charm to live in comfort and study. That would be stooping too low. "No!" I repeated. "No, let's get married, I can't let you go on like this. We've got to get married."

"Silly *gougou*," she retorted, "I haven't said I won't marry you, I've been meaning to all along, didn't I make that clear? As soon as things start to improve we'll go and register, and leave everyone else standing there gaping."

"No," I insisted. "I can't let you go on fooling people."

"Who's fooling whom? Silly *gougou*! Just think, do

they buy that stuff? If I didn't take it they'd hog it themselves anyway. I tell you the only straight cadre in this team is Xie the Beard. Even the cooks are crooked."

Her ingenious, realistic, cool-headed analysis threw me off balance. What moral principles was I supposed to abide by? It hadn't occurred to her that if we tided over hard times her way I'd lose my masculine self-respect. She saw this as a justifiable expedient whereas I, who had regained my strength owing to her expedient and had started studying again, now felt ashamed and felt that it wasn't right.

"No!" I persisted. "I don't want you going on like this. We'll get married. Team Leader Xie has approved it, we'll get registered straight away."

"Don't you trust me? Are you afraid I'll run off with somebody else?" She sounded unusually serious. She'd misinterpreted my eagerness to get married. Nestling up to me again, she stood on tiptoe and pressed her cheek against mine. "Well then," she went on softly, "take me now. Take me now if you want to."

She was exhausted after her busy night. There were dark circles under her lovely eyes.

She was offering herself to me purely out of love. That made me unbearably happy. This overwhelming happiness, which welled up in my heart like a string chorus, was not sexual desire nor ordinary love, but a chaste exalted passion. Carnal love makes one want to possess the loved one; pure love wants only love itself. Men created god in their own image, and in so doing they must have felt this passion. I kissed her devotedly, then gently released her.

"No," I told her. "We'll wait till we're married."

"All right." She moved away, looked up at me and

declared, "Don't you worry! If they cut off my head, I'd still follow you dripping with blood!"

"If they cut off my head, I'd still follow you dripping with blood!" What solemn, poetic pledge could compare with this wild and passionate declaration to express true, eternal love?

Ah, life, your hardships and loveliness make me tremble!

36

I slept till noon, when I was woken up by one of the group leaders. It was the grim-faced farm-hand who'd taken us out to work when we first arrived. He told me that Team Leader Xie wanted him to take me and my bedding by donkey cart to farm headquarters. Probably they'd be busy over the Spring Festival and had sent for me to help out for a few days.

I scrambled up and quickly rolled up my bedding. When I went to Mimosa's place for the shoes she had made me, I found her fast asleep. Never mind, I could wear them when I came back. I'd make do with my old ones for the time being. The group leader also gave me four buckwheat buns which Xie had told him to fetch from the kitchen for me to eat on the way. The two of us got on the cart and jogged off towards headquarters.

That was the first time I had been there. The place wasn't much bigger than our team, it had a few rows of brick and tiled houses, a mill and a fairly big shop. I saw a tractor station too, with two petrol drums lying in the snow outside. The group leader dropped me off in front of an office, saying, "Here you are, take your bedding inside."

There were five men there, apparently farm-hands drafted from different teams, some sitting on chairs, some squatting beside their luggage. No one greeted me, they were deep in their own thoughts. The atmosphere suddenly struck me as oppressive and I looked anxiously out of the window, but the group leader had already driven away.

Presently a cadre came in with a sheet of paper, followed by a youngster who looked like a driver. Frowning, he checked the names on his list then told the driver:

"All right, they're all here, take them off."

We followed the driver out with our bedding rolls. He stopped beside a tractor. Clapping his greasy gloves, he sized us up one after another, then asked:

"Which of you is the 'rightist' who taught at the provincial cadre school?"

I stepped forward. "I am, but that was years ago."

"I know." He grinned. "Sit in the cabin. The rest of you, look sharp and get on the trailer."

The other five jumped up, cursing as they cleared off the foot of snow on it. I stuffed my quilt behind my seat. When we were all set and the driver had checked the coupling, he cranked up the engine then climbed aboard and drove off.

The tractor headed down a dirt road to the west. All around was snow and ice, the branches of the roadside trees were like crystal tassels. Sunlight straggled through the dense clouds, dappling the silver plain with gold. Magpies and crows circled round us searching for food. The going was hard, we kept skidding. The young man had to concentrate on driving. He looked about my age, with the beginnings of a moustache, a rather short nose and bright eyes.

When we reached a more level stretch, he leaned back in his seat and glanced at me. "My old man knows you," he remarked. "He studied in the cadre school, you taught him."

"Oh." I didn't ask who his father was — what was the point? The past was over and done with. And to what fate was the tractor taking me now on this vast mist-shrouded plain?

"Know where we're going?" he asked, turning the wheel.

"No," I said. "I was about to ask."

"Ah." He sighed and answered sympathetically, "I've got to take you to that team at the foot of the hills. You've probably heard of it. It's for hard cases. Your lot are considered trouble-makers. You weren't on the list to begin with, but this morning someone came from your team to get his residence registration transferred — a skinny old fellow who's going to move to the provincial capital. You must know him, you were room-mates. He told the personnel section that last night one of your team ran away, someone who hung around with you every evening, who went to get you just before he took off. You must have been in cahoots. They looked up your file, found you had a bad class origin and are still called a 'rightist'; so they decided to add your name to the list. I saw them do it. That bearded team leader of yours came and kicked up a row, swearing that you weren't involved and vouching for you; but they bawled him out for his carelessness for letting a skilled worker run away and for protecting a 'rightist' who'd been denounced in the press, told him to go back and write a self-criticism. This farm of ours, you know, has a shake-up before each festival, as if they expect baddies to make trouble then. Before New Year I took four men to this team, today six more. . . . You'll have to watch your step there, or you'll get flayed alive."

Strangely enough, this came as no surprise. I didn't panic. After all I was still on the same farm as Mimosa, so we would be meeting again before too long. I was furious with the Boss, though, for taking this last swipe at me. People can be extraordinarily good but they can be extraordinarily vicious too. That is why they have created ghosts and monsters as well as gods. My anger outweighed my longing for Mimosa and put me on my guard. I fixed my eyes on the vast snowy plain where sunlight was breaking through the clouds like flashing swords thrusting at the foot of the hills. The sight was somehow familiar, as if I'd seen it in a dream. Now I was in good health and had a certain grasp of Marxism, so that wherever I went I could cope with whatever fate had in store.

The tractor was rocking. Once more the young driver concentrated on the road. I suddenly remembered that I hadn't told Mimosa about the *kang* table and the sack of soybeans Hai Xixi had left for her. Someone might steal the table, but I was the only one who knew where the sack was hidden. Once the snow melted and the weather turned warm, the soybeans would start sprouting.

The youngster had been right. In this team at the foot of the hills we weren't allowed to ask for leave or see anybody but immediate family. Two months later, a farm-hand who had stayed in on sick leave told me in secret that "a good-looking young woman" had come that day to see me, bringing a bundle. She was cross-examined at length by the team leader, who made her take her bundle back with her. That day I'd been carrying rocks for ten hours to the canal. I was so exhausted that apart from regretting that she'd come all that way for nothing I fell sound asleep without even stopping to think about her.

Soon after that we heard that there must be no let-up in class struggle, and I was sentenced to three years of surveillance for my "counter-revolutionary writing". During the movement for "socialist education" I was sentenced to three more years of labour reform for "trying to reverse the verdict on my case". Returning to the farm after that I was just in time for the "cultural revolution" and was made a "counter-revolutionary revisionist" under mass dictatorship. In 1970 I was imprisoned in the farm's lock-up. As it wasn't under the security bureau or run according to modern prison regulations, it was simply a Chinese version of the Spanish Inquisition.

In 1968, when I went back to the farm from the labour camp, I learned that while I was under surveillance Mimosa had remained unmarried. After I was sent to the labour camp, she took Ershe to the county town to join her brother, and not long after that accompanied his family to Qinghai. Apparently her brother was said to be in some trouble too.

In 1971, we prisoners in the farm lock-up were not even allowed to read Chairman Mao's works, for fear that if we studied them we might learn tactics to struggle with the farm authorities. One day I was sent to build a stove in the staff-room of the primary school. As the teachers were all at class, I looked round eagerly for books, but the only book there apart from the students' compositions was an encyclopedia. I looked up "Mimosa", and this is what I found.

> Plant name. Latin name Albizzia julibrissin. Also called "silk tree". This is one of the leguminosae of the sub-order mimosa. It is a deciduous tree, the leaves folding together at night. It blossoms in summer and has a pink flower. Its small sickle-shaped leaves are edible. Grown mainly in central China, it likes sun, can stand drought and will grow in poor soil. Its reddish-brown wood can be used to make furniture and sleepers. The bark can be made into glue. The dried bark, used in Chinese medicine, is thought to "promote joy, assuage sorrow, brighten the eye and give the desire of the heart". In the treatment of disease it promotes blood circulation and is regarded as a tonic, vulnerary and sedative. A gummy extract from it is used as a plaster for carbuncles and swellings, and as a retentive in fractures and sprains.

Why, this was a description of my Mimosa! Didn't she love sun, and wasn't she able to stand drought and grow in poor soil?

But that night I couldn't sleep — she failed to cure my insomnia. I kept seeing mimosas before me until finally they merged into a sea of green.

37

A whole twenty years had passed. A fifth of a century! My country and I had won through hard times, had paid the price demanded from us by history. Once more it was a snowy spring as I drove back to the farm in a Toyota with the heads of the provincial cultural department and film studio. We had brought the feature film based on one of my novels, and were going to show it to express our thanks for the farm's co-operation. After the film the farm's director and Party secretary saw us back to our well-equipped hostel. When I asked the director where Team Leader Xie was, he had never heard of him. Xie had probably left long before his own transfer here in 1978.

But late that night I slipped out of our hostel. There was hazy moonlight, the night air was icy. Not wanting to disturb the driver, I set off on foot to my old team.

The pure white snow, as pure and white as ever, had covered the whole team where I had lived. The night was peaceful, dreamlike, except for the barking of dogs by a sheepfold. As I stood on the bridge, shadowy scenes from the past came to my mind. I could hear her singing a sweet, lilting, passionate folk song!

> Golden hills, silver hills,
> On sandalwood we lie;
> We two can never part
> Till twelve Yellow Rivers run dry!

I saw her approaching me with a smile. Floating through the air, leaving no footprints in the snow. Still lovely, healthy, merry and radiant. Coming up to me with the laugh I remembered so well, she declared:

"If you chop off my head I'll still follow you, dripping with blood!"

. . . But the night was hushed. The world was shrouded in snow. There was no one in sight and not a sound could be heard. . . . My eyes, so long dry, filled with tears over memories of the distant past, tears as icy cold as the water from an old well. Yes, if men lose their memories they lose themselves. Though my life here had been so hard, this was where I had started to understand life's beauty. Mimosa, Team Leader Xie, Hai Xixi. . . . Though we had lost touch, these ordinary farm workers had inspired me, had helped to make me a new man.

In June 1983, I attended an important conference in Beijing. As an army band played our rousing national anthem and I stood up solemnly with heads of the Party and state and delegates from all walks of life in different parts of the country, those familiar faces suddenly flashed through my mind. I thought: Our national anthem isn't just being played for the revolutionary veterans who fought to build up our republic, not just for those who laid down their lives to safeguard its territory and make it strong. It's also for those ordinary workers who, ever since Liberation, have consciously or unconsciously kept close to our Party, supporting it with all their might, till we have finally found the right road to take. They are real "mimosa trees" growing all over our land. Their bark may be rough, but with their luxuriant branches they have made this dear land of ours more beautiful.

I am an intellectual born in a bourgeois family and given a feudal and bourgeois education. Yet today I have the honour of attending this historic conference to discuss affairs of state in the Great Hall of the People. I must always remember those ordinary working people who gave me material and moral support when I was on the edge of an abyss, so that I sought for the truth in Marxism and, during those most difficult years, had faith in our country as well as in our Party. They took me by the arm, set me on the road leading to this red carpet in this Great Hall.

I salute the lovely, sacred mimosa trees growing over the whole length and breadth of our land!

September to November 1983
Xiqiao, Yinchuan

Translated by Gladys Yang

Bitter Springs

HEY, don't doze off. The thing I fear most on the road is people next to me falling asleep. Dozing's contagious.

Have a cigarette. You don't smoke? How can somebody who writes for a living not smoke? Anyway, I do. City drivers aren't supposed to smoke on the job but here it doesn't matter. At any rate, sitting in a cab by yourself all the time gets too depressing. It's not like back east. Here you can go for hundreds of miles without seeing a village or any sign of life, on and on, until you just can't keep your eyes open any longer.

Take a look, either side of us is desert. That's the Gobi. You probably used to think the Gobi was flat and yellow, but it's not. It's just these fist-sized rocks as far as you can see. After the Gobi you start getting up into the mountains. They're not like the ones you see in movies either — they've all got flat tops like iron nails. We have to go along a place called Dry Gully to get into the mountains. What a name! It's so dry that if you cry your tears are gone before they have a chance to fall; there's no grass, no trees, not even any birds or ants, it's just like being on the moon. You'll see it in a bit. After driving in that for a while, how could anyone not fall asleep? Anyway, I'm lucky to have a reporter along with me this time — we can talk.

Have you travelled a lot? Until you got to Xinjiang you probably didn't realize the country was so big. The Uighurs always say that in Xinjiang even beggars have to go round on a donkey because if they don't they'll starve to death before they get to the next village. Of course, that was in the old days, but it gives you a good idea.

I like having company when I'm driving. Whenever I see people walking along the road, I always slow down and see if they want a lift. Out here, in this empty desert with those mountains looming up ahead and this heavy sky, when I see people puffing along all alone I feel sorry for them. I sort of admire them too. In a truck you don't realize it, but if you walked you'd know how rough it is to shuffle along step by step on a road like this.

If I've got someone with me, then we're company for one another. We long distance drivers spend more time with machines than we do with people. If you pass someone you know on the road you don't even have time to smile before you've both whizzed by one another. It's better working with animals. When I was a kid I used to drive a donkey cart — they're cranky animals but they're still living creatures and if you're feeling in low spirits you can always talk to them. They always seem as though they can understand you, twitching those floppy ears. But a truck isn't an animal — if it was alive, it'd be a lot of trouble. When you've been driving for a while, you get to feeling an odd kind of loneliness. That's why when they get to a station and stop drivers like to have a good laugh and a swear. Why do they swear? They just want to practise talking. People have a need to be together.

A few years back we used to have a company chief who absolutely forbade us from giving people lifts, said it was dangerous. But then he used to take cigarettes and liquor for carrying people's goods on the side and ended up being given the boot.

Giving people lifts is no small thing. Somebody signals you, you stop, he gets on and just in that tiny moment he thinks to himself that there are still a lot of good people about. And when you see his smiling face, it makes you feel better, you drive with a bit more energy and don't get sleepy. I'm not much of a talker, just so long as I've got somebody along with me then I don't get to feeling too lonely. I'm talking more than usual with you today. I like talking with educated people.

How did I get to Xinjiang? That's a long story. Actually, you could say I was a returned educated youth. You can tell from my accent that I'm from Henan. I got to lower middle school back in my home country. Had a lot of hopes in those days. When I saw soldiers in films I wanted to be one, or if I saw doctors I'd want to be a doctor, or if I read a book I'd think about being a writer. Anyway, whatever I thought, I never expected I'd be a long distance driver. When I was in my third year at middle school I wrote a poem on our blackboard bulletin which had a couple of lines which went something like, "My hopes are like a ribbon of stars, glittering across my forehead." Not bad, you say? Now, don't make fun of me, I was only seventeen then. My teacher said that a village youngster with ambitions like that ought to go far.

Who'd ever have thought that in 1960 things would have been so tough at home that my mum and dad wouldn't have enough to eat, so this promising "village youngster" had to give up school and get back to look after them. But three people at home was too many. I was an only son, and the two of them sat down and cried and said to me, "Child, you'd better leave and try and make a go of it somewhere else. You've got nine years' schooling, you'll definitely be able to earn a living." We Henanese are survivors you know, from all the way back we've moved where we had to to make a living. If there's been some kind of natural disaster at home then we take off to another province. Well anyway, just then we got a letter from someone in our village who'd gone to Xinjiang saying it was a good place to live. You could get work and enough to eat. I was reminded of a song we learned at school called "Our Xinjiang Is a Fine Place", so I decided to come here.

Those days they were strict about vagrants. We waited for a moonless night for me to leave home. My dad went with me for a couple of miles to the end of the commune land but then he couldn't go on any longer and squatted by the side of the road wheezing. I took out a couple of cornmeal pancakes my mum had stuck in my bundle and slipped them inside his jacket. "You go on back," I told him. "I know the way, I've got a map. When I get there and get a job I'll send you back some money."

Young people don't feel so attached to home — even if they go without food they're still strong and want to flap their wings and fly away. So I didn't even shed a tear, nor did I really have the least idea what my parents must have been feeling then. That's the sort of thing you come to understand more as you get older. Now, whenever I try and think of the last few words my dad and mother said to me, or even what they looked like the last time I saw them, all I can see is that image of my father squatting by the roadside. It used to be that when I drove alone at night that image would always appear in front of me, always in my headlights just by the side of the road. It seemed to be stuck to my windscreen like a traffic permit — it went with me everywhere, nothing would make it go away.

Now and again I forgive myself and think if it'd been my mum who came with me that night then the two of us would've said more to one another. My dad was a tight-lipped old farmer and I wasn't much of one for talking either. Sons are never as close to their fathers anyway I guess, but they'd brought me up for eighteen years and when we had to say goodbye I didn't even have a grateful word to say to them. . . .

Well anyway, on with my story. . . .

That's how I got to Xinjiang. In those days the railway line only came as far as Weiya. It's not a bad-looking town now but then it was just a bunch of broken down old mud houses stuck on the desert. People just pitched tents all round the houses one after the other, several rows deep. Since Weiya was the terminus, everybody coming to Xinjiang piled off there. The buses kept on going west and the trains kept bringing people from out east. They were all shapes and sizes and ages. There'd often be a few thousand of them living in those tents, trampling the snow down until it was just messy slush.

What kind of people were they? Well, some of them were transferred here officially, university graduates assigned to work here, people who came with factories which moved here, but most of them were "illegal vagrants", what they later called "drifters". Now they give us a pretty fancy name — "voluntary pioneers". I guess you could say that that was a kind of rehabilitation in itself. To be frank, those vagrants or voluntary pioneers have a lot to do with Xinjiang's being so much better off today. I know a lot of them who've become outstanding workers and professionals, engineers, and production and construction corps leaders.

We drifters got on pretty well, in fact when we got together you'd think we'd known one another all our lives. Just a sentence or two and you'd have a good picture of somebody's background. The tents were originally just for production corps and factory recruiters and the recruiters were looking for unemployed drifters like me. Weiya was really like a big market in those days, noisy and crowded, as busy as Nanjing Road in Shanghai. You'd get recruiters shouting, "Hey, come on over here! We'll give you good salaries, plenty of grain, you can't afford to pass it up!" or "Hey, this way, we've got all the milk you can drink, apples as big as your head. Miss this one and you won't be able to do anything about it later!"; or they'd shout things like, "Hey, we don't want any of you corn-eating yokels over here. Bumpkins brought up in barns and suckers who can't stand the feel of money better not head this way!" They all made it sound as though if you signed up with them you'd eat the best, live in a big house and have your pockets bulging with money.

On the train, I was worried that without papers I wouldn't be able to get work. But when I got to Weiya, one of the old hands told me that if you didn't have a commune change of residence certificate, a voter registration card would do; if you didn't have that then a letter from a friend or relative in Xinjiang would be all right. The places that needed people most, the ones with the noisiest recruiters, had the toughest work in the poorest places. As long as you weren't missing an arm or a leg and had eyes, ears and a nose, they didn't need to see anything else!

The guy who told me this was in his forties and always used to wear a greasy old padded jacket. He said he knew a little about medicine and wanted to find the right sort of job, so he hadn't signed up with just any of the recruiters. Since he seemed to have a little education, I took out my lower middle school diploma and gave it to him. I remember how his eyes lit up and he said to me, "Hey, you're a real treasure. With this, the very least they ought to give you is an office job. Don't go to any of those talking recruiters." Then he pointed over at one of the tents and told me to look for work there.

Not surprisingly it was a little quieter round that one. It had a sign on the front flap which said "Xinjiang Education Department, Weiya Office". The people inside were a lot better mannered, not like the fast-talking barkers. Inside the tent they had a petrol drum stove and a bare wooden bench with a row of job applicants sitting there. The man in charge of registering people was fat, I remember. Those days fat people were a rarity so he made quite an impression on me. Not all of the applicants there had papers either. If you didn't have any certificates, then the fat man would give you an oral exam. The questions were to find out what level of education the applicant had and he asked things like "How many continents and oceans are there?" and "What type of country is the People's Republic of China?" or "Who discovered the periodic table of elements?" and "What does 'Confucius said: Is it not a pleasure having learnt something to try it out at due intervals' mean?" I listened to him and found that I could answer all of them. The fat man was from Shaanxi and seemed well educated and friendly. When he got to me, I handed over my diploma. He looked really pleased and just asked me when I'd arrived, how many there were in my family and whether or not I'd come alone. Then he quickly wrote my name in a registration book and told me to turn up early the next morning to go to Urumqi.

When I came out of that tent, I was beside myself with excitement. I just spread my wings and soared. Being an administrator would have been better maybe, but being a teacher wasn't bad. I remembered a Soviet film called *Village Schoolmistress* which I'd seen twice as a kid and which had made a strong impression on me. Since the main character in the film was a woman I can't say I'd completely identified with her, but now, with that kind of prospect opening up before me I remembered how I used to want to be a teacher. I thought of how when I got old I'd be just like that schoolmistress — white hair, glasses, surrounded by scientists, writers, army officers, all former students of mine. . . .

Just as I was letting myself get all carried away I suddenly ran into two young girls. They were about the same age as me and were dressed a bit like students. Both of them had braids. They'd noticed me while I was talking to that other drifter and came over to have a word. I could tell from their accents that they were from Henan and it turned out to be a place less than fifty kilometres from my commune. They asked me if I'd found a job. I told them I had, and a good one too, and just spouted out everything that had happened, bragging about how the fat man had been so impressed with me that he hadn't even bothered to give me an exam. They looked miserable and told me they hadn't found anything and couldn't really do manual labour. I believed them too. They were thin and sallow, not like these healthy teenagers you get today. Anyway, I just casually blurted out that they should go to the same place I did and see if they could get jobs as teachers.

That night I put up at one of the local inns. I don't know whether it was a state place or one privately run by a Uighur. It had two long brick *kang* with a hollow brick wall for heating running in between, but the wall was icy cold when I touched it. I remember the place was three yuan a night and there wasn't any bedding at all. It was so crowded you had to wedge yourself in as best you could.

I discovered there that some of the others had changed jobs a lot — wherever the going was good, that's where they went. These old hands would squat on the *kang*, backs against that wall and talk about their experiences, rolling cigarettes and smoking all the while. Listening to them, it seemed there wasn't a place in Xinjiang they hadn't been to. You know, reporter, in those days Xinjiang was really wide-open, not like back east where you've got to have a pile of permits every time you take a step. Xinjiang really used to be the most backward place in the country and the changes here over the last thirty years have a lot to do with their more open labour policy.

Anyway, to get back to what I was saying, when I got up next morning I thought to myself that since I was going to be a teacher from then on I'd better try and make a good impression on my first day, so I spent thirty *fen* on a small basin of fresh water and had a wash. When I got to that tent, the other new employees were already getting on the truck one by one. The fat man was standing next to it counting them. But as soon as he saw me, he scowled and said, "Get out of here. You seemed an honest sort, but you were up to no good. We don't want you here, find yourself some other place!"

I was really shocked. "What do you mean?" I said.

"What do you mean?" he mimicked my accent. "What sort of young man drags two girls all over the place with him? What's going on? When I asked you yesterday, you told me you came here alone. What a liar!"

I tried to stick up for myself. "I didn't come with those two girls. If you don't believe me, give me a test."

"Test what?" He just threw up his hands. "They all say they've got middle school educations, but if you ask them the simplest arithmetic they can't answer, or they think Gorky was a Chinese. Absolute nonsense!"

Intellectuals are always stubborn and this fat man more than most. Maybe those two girls had used my name, lied to him, made him angry. Anyway I could see he wasn't going to back down, whatever I said.

The truck started up and I just stood there alone. The fat man swivelled around in the cab, pushed the door open and shouted to me, "Young man, if you want to be a teacher, decent behaviour is the first requirement. If you don't have that, it doesn't matter how much education you've got."

So I'd got all excited for nothing, my dreams of becoming a teacher were shattered and all of those scientists, writers and army officers vanished. The fat man vanished too and the tyres of their truck spattered me with slush. I was totally down in the dumps and turned to go, but just then I saw those two girls standing timidly beside a tent watching me.

"What did you do! It's all your. . . ." I remember I started to give them a real tongue-lashing.

They stood huddled together, looking down and said, "We had to . . . we didn't even get through primary school and when the fat man wanted to test us we told him not to bother since we'd been at school with you. We told him we all graduated at the same time and that you brought us here. But we didn't expect. . . ."

I could see they were on the verge of tears and that they knew they were in the wrong. When people are drowning they grasp at straws, they hadn't deliberately meant to harm me. So I didn't say anything more and just started off to the recruiters' tents.

"Hey," one of the girls shouted. "Quick, take us with you. We come from the same place and we trust you. We'll go wherever you go."

"Forget it," I told them. "Whether you trust me or not, if people see me hanging around with two young girls they'll get the wrong idea. Didn't you see the way that fat man shouted at me? Isn't that enough?"

Then the two of them started to cry, "Well, what can we do? We're out of money, we don't know a soul here. We can't even get back. . . ."

As soon as I saw the tears falling, I just couldn't hold out. Anyway, we did come from the same part of the world so I told them, "Okay, don't cry. While we're all out of work we can stick together, I've still got a few clothes I can sell."

Like I said, I was an only child and so although my family were poor peasants, I never lacked for clothes. During that couple of years when the peasants did so well, my parents bought me a lot— they really wanted me to look good — and sent me off to school.

When I think about it, if the country had gone on the way it was in '56 I'd probably have been a university teacher by now.

I was saying that then Weiya was just like one great big market place. The recruiters would be standing in front of those tents shouting and then all round you'd get people selling things. They'd sell whatever they'd brought with them, some of them even sold black market grain coupons. Of course, they were all drifters like me, since who'd need to be doing that if they already had a job? You didn't have to set up a stall or hawk your wares, you just stood holding whatever it was and people would come over to see what you had. I took out my warmer weather clothes, a pair of blue twill trousers and a new white cotton shirt, and sold those for ten yuan. Money wasn't worth that much in the 60s — a bowl of tea was thirty *fen*. Three people eating for a day managed to eat their way through that trousers and shirt of mine.

That night I went back to the inn but the two girls didn't have any idea where they'd sleep. The next day the two of them came to me with their eyes all red and puffy and said, "We're really sorry, we mucked up your job and now we're using up your money and we feel even worse. We've talked it over, and we decided to go and sign up at the manual labour place. It's about all we can do."

Well, I could hardly even look after myself, never mind anyone else, so if they'd decided to go off and do that all I could say was, "All right, go on the two of you. But try and get the lighter work and conserve your strength. . . . At any rate, it's got to be better than back home. At least you'll get something to eat."

They went off to sign up and that afternoon they got on a truck to leave. I sold another shirt and went over and gave them each a couple of yuan. The barkers were still standing there shouting, "Hey, come on with us, all the milk you can drink . . ." and the two of them just sat up there on the truck sobbing their hearts out. I couldn't help feeling totally miserable as I stood there — it was as if they really were my classmates and we really had come together to this strange new life in Xinjiang.

We drivers get all over the region. A few years later I happened to be in Korla and there was a truck ahead of me unloading pears. I realized that I knew the woman carrying baskets but it took me a while to finally work out that it was one of those two girls. She was a lot stronger and fatter and I would guess had married and had a kid. I watched her for a while but I didn't have the nerve to talk to her.

After the two girls left, I stayed on in Weiya and evenings I'd get together with the other drifters. You know, those people were a good-hearted lot. Despite all the hard times they'd been through they were always pretty kind about anyone else's problems. When everyone heard what had happened to me and they'd all handed round that middle school diploma, they came up with all sorts of advice and finally pushed me into going to Hami, where they said I could get a job in accounting.

Being an accountant would be all right too, I thought to myself. I'd learned how to use an abacus at middle school. I decided to head for Hami.

In those days the Weiya buses were always packed to

the gills and there was no way you could get yourself a westbound ticket in less than a week. I only had a few yuan left and no more clothes to sell and couldn't wait that long. So I did what the drifters advised me to do, and went to try and hitch a ride on one of the goods trucks.

The parking lot was to the west of the tent city. It was all criss-crossed with tyre marks and the snow was spattered with oil; there were vehicles parked all over the place — I'd reckon there must have been a good hundred of them. Some of the drivers looked all right enough but others looked pretty fierce. I hung around for ages that morning too shy to talk to any of them. I remember the sun climbing high up in the sky. I just stood there timidly as the trucks moved out one by one. But then I suddenly heard someone who drove a fuel truck speaking my local dialect, so I moved over in his direction as though I was interested in watching him fix his engine.

After a bit, the guy he'd been talking to left and the driver finished his repairs. He closed the hood, turned round and suddenly saw me. "Hey, young fellow, get me that bucket of water over there, would you," he said.

I took him the water and said, "Mister, where are you going?"

This driver had a kind face and smiled as soon as he heard my accent, "Hm, seems like we're from the same neck of the woods. Where're you headed?"

I told him I wanted to go to Hami. He said he was going to Urumqi and could take me along.

After putting water in the tank, he jumped down from the bumper and told me to hurry up and get my suitcase. I just held up my bundle and said everything I owned in the world was in that. I remember the way he laughed and patted my head. "Come on," he said. "Let's go!"

I guess you could say that this driver was my sort of "master". As we went along, I told him all about the situation back home. He asked me what I was doing going to Hami and what relatives I had there, so I told him exactly what I had in mind and even gave him my diploma to look at. He said to me that I shouldn't look down on manual labour, that the world had been built by human labour and that it was really the most noble sort of work. He'd started driving back home in '47 after joining the army and had come to Xinjiang in '49. They'd wanted him to take an office job, but he wasn't interested and went back to driving after leaving the service. The two of us seemed to see eye to eye on everything and before we even got to Hami, he'd decided to take me on as an apprentice.

So in the end I didn't get out at Hami and the two of us just went straight on to Urumqi together.

Now he's retired and spends all his time gardening. I go over to his place a lot. He told me not to bother bringing him any presents unless I ran across good plants. You see that orchid behind you? I bought it yesterday from a trader in from the Northeast. Cost me fifty yuan. I'm taking it to him tomorrow, he's really going to be pleased.

Are you fed up with listening to all this? I know you reporters write about VIPs and heroes and the like. I've never done anything important in my life, it's all been pretty ordinary. I've been commended and won awards and that kind of thing but that was all just in the company, they didn't even put it in the *Xinjiang Daily*. I know you don't write about the sorts of things I've been talking about, no newspaper would publish it. Just thought I'd try and keep you amused for a while.

Sit tight, we start heading up into the mountains after that next bend.

Anyway, from then on I started driving. I think life is sort of like moving tyres, spinning round fast; good times are like when you step on the gas, bad times like being stuck in the mud — you spin round and round but you can't get out. Well, all the same, twenty years has gone by in a flash. Of course, I've changed my actual vehicle a lot during that time. The very first one I had was a Soviet truck. After that I drove one of our Liberations, then a Czech Skoda and even a Romanian truck. This Japanese Hino I just started driving recently.

The age of a car has nothing to do with time but with how much mileage it's put in. I think it's the same with people. Some people live fifty or sixty years without running into bad times or trouble and you could say that they stay pretty young. Others have a rough time right from the start, by the time they're thirty or forty they've been through so much they're already old. You know, Mr Reporter, it's the people who've known bad times who can give you something to write about. Take me for example, I've been to the Soviet Union, Afghanistan, even to Pakistan. I nearly lost my life in accidents a few times when we were building roads in Pakistan. I can tell you, piloting a spaceship would be easier than driving in foreign mountains with no proper roads. In Xinjiang too in those days, who'd ever heard of a good road? It was always either like driving on a washboard or just straight desert. Crying wouldn't help you much either if you got caught in a storm and stuck somewhere out on the road. In winter, when the snows came, the roads just turned into rivers of ice, so hard nothing could crack it. When you got up to three or four thousand metres, you were taking your life in your hands every inch of the way and if you made a mistake then you and the truck would just go plunging straight down the mountainside.

The second spring I was here my mum and dad died, working at an irrigation site. I got a letter from my uncle saying that just before my mother went she kept calling out my pet name. Afterwards they found two money orders I'd sent her in her pocket. She'd never even gone to the post office to cash them — there wasn't any grain in the shops or the market anyway — so I'd sent her money for nothing. My uncle used it to buy her a flimsy coffin and fix up my father's grave. In '64 I scraped together enough to go back and their graves were already covered with grass. The willow trees planted that year were as thick as your arm.

While I was there, I went out to have a look at the road I took the night I left home and the place my father had sat, but it had all changed; now it's a wide road, all gravelled, and the place where my father was would be in the centre with tractors going up and down it. The old master driver put it nicely — he said that vehicles always had to move forward, that you always had to keep your eyes on the road, it's okay to check the rearview mirror now and again, but if you do it all the time then you'll turn the car over. So I decided to come back here and go on driving.

All the same, I didn't have anyone left in the world and I felt sort of lonely all the time. We drivers don't actually get a chance to see that much of one another, you're always pulling out when someone else is checking in. I hardly ever got time to spend the odd day or two with the old driver. Then the "cultural revolution" started and even old friends wouldn't tell one another what they really thought, nobody trusted anyone else. If you met a stranger, you had to give them a good once-over and work out first of all whether they were class enemies and what their class background was. You couldn't say what you thought to somebody you just met, like now. But people still aren't as close as they were as during those tough times in the 60s. What do you think makes people most miserable? For me, the worst thing is when you can't say what you really feel. When people get up in the morning, they put on their underwear, then their clothes, then a padded coat and finally they wrap themselves up in an invisible suit of armour before going out. Everybody's huddled inside their own suit of armour, so even though there might be a lot of people working in a company, they never really get to know one another.

In those days, I always kept things pretty much to myself. One day my old master said to me, "You ought to think about getting married, you know. You're already in your late twenties. If you had a home and someone to look after you, then maybe your spirits would pick up a bit." I thought about it and realized he was right, so I decided to fix up a wedding.

Finding a girlfriend in Xinjiang isn't easy. There're a lot more men than women and the chances for meeting a girl are few and far between. But luckily we go

all over the place and not long after that a lot of our
company drivers met up in a Dabancheng canteen; they
got to talking and one of them suddenly shouted out,
"I've got it! Right under our very noses too. There's a
girl right here in Dabancheng who's just come in from
northern Shaanxi — I'll go and see about her for you."
The others all started ribbing me about it and one of
them started singing a Kazakh song:

> You Dabancheng girls have long, long braids
> And lovely sparkling eyes,
> If you want to marry, then please don't marry
> Anyone else but me. . . .

The singing got me all worked up. All right, I
thought, let's give it a try.

The girl they had in mind was from Mizhi County.
They'd had really bad harvests in that region so she
was like me in the 60s and had left home because there
wasn't enough food to go round. They say in Shaanxi
"a Mizhi girl makes a happy man", like the Uighurs
say, "Dabancheng girls are as pretty as flowers." She'd
just turned twenty and had a primary school education.
She wasn't bad-looking, and although her braids weren't
that long, she did have large, pretty eyes. Her aunt
used to sell tea at a roadside stall and they had a tough
life. The aunt didn't ask for much, just that the girl
got a residence permit and grain coupons. I could tell
from the way the woman spoke that she and the girl
didn't get along, and that all she wanted was to see the
back of her as quickly as possible.

It was all fairly easy to arrange. A few of us talked
it over and then went and settled the matter with the
aunt.

When I got back, my old master was very opposed to the whole business. He shook his head and said to me, "How can you be so casual about this? You hardly know anything about her. You're talking about something that's for the rest of your life. Don't be in such a rush, I'll come up with someone for you." I said to him that I'd been around a lot in the last few years and met a lot of people and wasn't that inexperienced. The girl was serious, not the flighty type, and I'd made up my mind. To tell you the truth, I'd never even thought of getting married all those years, I'd just sort of pushed on day by day. So when the old driver brought it up it triggered something off, and suddenly it seemed the most important thing in the world. I wanted to go through with it as soon as I could, so I didn't listen to him and went ahead and married her.

You're still pretty young, are you married? No? Well, I'll tell you a thing or two about marriage. I've married twice, so I guess you could say I know a little about it.

When two people live a fairly uneventful life together day after day, without any difficulties to really test the strength of their feelings, then you have to look at the ordinary things, at the housework, the cooking, that sort of thing, and at their facial expressions, to get some idea of what they're really feeling. It's nothing to do with education — you have to rely entirely on feelings, or as you intellectuals would say, on a kind of "intuition". If a woman really cares for you, then you can feel the warmth of her hand even if she gives you a slap across the face: if she doesn't, then she can hold you in her arms all day long and you can still feel the iciness in her heart. You know, in the outside world, people can put on false faces and get honours for themselves, but it's at home, living together, day in and day out, sharing the same bed, that the real feelings can't be hidden. With some couples, it doesn't matter if they're always squabbling. If you just carefully watch the looks they exchange, you can see that they could still be a loving couple. Other couples treat one another with every possible courtesy, but they never share the same dreams.

This Shaanxi girl was good, very hard working and a good housewife, and she never spent time gossiping with the neighbours, never caused any trouble. She kept a very careful record of how the housekeeping money was spent every month. Whenever I got home from work there would always be a hot meal waiting for me on the table, my clothes were always cleaned and mended without my saying a word. As for affection, however, there wasn't an ounce of that.

Here in Xinjiang, we tend to get married first and fall in love later. We think affection is something that can develop after you get married.

I'm sure I don't have to remind you how chaotic everything was in those days. It was pointless thinking of trying to do anything for the country, all you could do was throw yourself into fixing up your house. I made a lot of furniture, Czech-style, Polish-style, varnished and polished it till it gleamed. I made a sofa and a standard lamp too. I'd saved a bit of money while I was working in Pakistan, and my monthly salary was enough for the two of us.

But her attitude towards me was like a servant to a master, perhaps not even that. Even servants used to have a joke with their masters now and again, but

she never cracked a smile. Nor did she take any pride
in the furniture I made, never even sat on that sofa.
She wouldn't wear any of the clothes I bought for her
either. I came to realize that this wasn't to economize,
but to deliberately keep her distance from me. If I
had time off, or when I'd come home from work and
the two of us would be together, she'd either fuss about
doing things she didn't have to do or just sit there like
a martyr, off in a corner by herself on a little stool.
She'd just stare off into space and keep on heaving
great big sighs. If I tried to drag her out to see a film,
she wouldn't even turn round, she'd just say, "What's
there to see? They always have the same old films!"
That was more or less true, so we'd just chat. But she
only talked about things to do with the housekeeping
and never said anything affectionate or anything that
didn't concern domestic matters. I don't care whether
you laugh at me, reporter, but I think a husband and
wife should be affectionate to one another. But she
was absolutely blank. I got more and more depressed
and upset.

Even when she slept next to me she never took off
that invisible suit of armour. Can you imagine how that
gets to you? Was I blind, pockmarked or disabled or
something? I was twenty-eight years old and thought
I wasn't *that* bad-looking nor that cranky, nor had I
done anything really bad in my life. So what was the
reason? It didn't seem to be in keeping with her natural
sort of character either. I used to sit and brood about
it all day long, actually I couldn't get it off my mind.
You know, trouble in a marriage is a lot more unbearable than political or financial trouble. If you get
knocked about politically but have a happy marriage,

then there's still some consolation when you get back home; you can be poor, but if you've got a good woman you can still be happy. But with this kind of wife, it was even worse than being a bachelor. To tell you the truth, that's when I started smoking — drinking too — not past the three gram limit, mind you, I still had my driving to do.

So we went on like that for half a year. After a bit, I noticed that whenever the neighbourhood women saw me coming, they always looked as though they felt sorry for me, as though there was something on their minds. Just after we got married, they'd always stop me when I came home from work and have a few jokes. Those old biddies liked to rattle on about whatever scandal they could find. But I noticed that when they talked to me they were always kind of hesitant and never mentioned my wife at all. I began to wonder why. Although the two of us weren't exactly affectionate, we didn't squabble either!

Then one day our company had to make deliveries to Yili and we stayed overnight at the Oasis Hotel. A few of us got together and bought some kebabs and a couple of bottles of the local liquor and sat around talking and drinking. We'd got through half the drink and everyone was feeling merry when the driver who'd sung that Kazakh song started up again, this time singing a Shaanxi ballad:

I come from a family, quite well known,
In Mizhi County, Thirty-*Li* Village,
This Fourth Sister's found herself a Third Brother,
Who's become my dear, dear one.
Third Brother's in the army, down in the valley,

Fourth Sister's blue, working in the fields.
How I long to go down and see him,
But I'm afraid that people will laugh.

Then everyone started saying how Shaanxi girls were the prettiest and most loyal in the country and how once they'd got themselves tied up with someone it was for life. A few of them started teasing me because my wife was a Mizhi girl. Then in the middle of everything a young guy who'd had a bit too much said to me, "You'd better be careful, your woman's Third Brother isn't you, it's someone else. . . ."

The whole place went silent as soon as he'd said it, and the other drivers shot him filthy looks. He knew he'd spoken out of turn and just leaned over and ate his kebabs without saying another word.

There was obviously something in what he'd said. I was distracted and couldn't pay much attention to the others' fooling about. After a while, this young guy got up to go to the bathroom and I followed him out.

Out in the corridor I grabbed him by the arm and said, "What did you mean by that? Don't be afraid, I won't hold it against you."

He went red and just sort of mumbled, "I didn't mean anything, I was only joking. . . ."

Just then one of the older drivers appeared and said, "Since it's come out, we'd better all talk about it and not leave him in the dark. Come on, let's go back inside."

So those drivers told me what everybody else already knew. Three months back a guy from northern Shaanxi had arrived looking for her. The neighbours didn't know who he was but they used to hear them crying and whispering together in the house. Our company's living quarters are set out in rows, about a hundred families or so, not set off from one another, and you can't hide anything much from anybody else. A lot of the drivers' family members didn't work and the women would spend their time visiting one another catching up on all the gossip. They did a good job too — police detectives were no match for them — so before long they'd put together a fair amount of information: This young guy was from the same village as my wife, had just finished doing his military service and had made the trip specially to find her. They obviously meant something to each other. He'd got himself taken on as a temporary stoker in the animal products company across from our compound. He used to go to my place a lot when I wasn't home and apparently the two of them would close the door and sit whispering to one another.

"Now don't get too worked up and jump to conclusions," the drivers said. "We didn't mention it before because the two of you seemed to be doing okay, and if we'd made a mistake we would've messed things up between you. You're a broody sort too, and we were afraid if we were mistaken we'd stir up big trouble."

I listened to them with a lump in my throat and fighting back tears. "I'm grateful for your concern — actually you should've told me earlier. Things haven't been what they seemed between us anyway, I've had a pretty miserable half year. . . ." I said.

When I told them what it had been like, they all got really annoyed. Some of them said we ought to catch the guy and beat him up and then pack him off home. A few of the others thought that was letting him off too lightly, and that we ought to turn him in to the police. The older ones said we should just keep it to ourselves and once we'd got rid of him everything would all be all right, she could have a baby and perhaps she'd settle down a bit.

My head started to spin like a kaleidoscope — all sorts of ideas of a way out took shape in my head — evil, kind, cruel, generous — in the end, I couldn't make up my mind.

So when I got home, I kept an even closer eye on her. But she was the same as always, careful about money, neat and tidy. I wanted to get at her but I couldn't find a reason; I wanted to get the thing out into the open, but I couldn't somehow find a way of bringing it up.

Then we had to have an overhaul and I stayed home for a few days. After it was finished I was just about to set off when I discovered there was something wrong with the gear box, it was making a grinding noise. The mechanics were pretty sloppy then, they never fixed anything properly and they often messed up perfectly good vehicles, so we drivers had to do a lot ourselves. So that day I didn't go out and instead spent the morning working on the truck.

At lunchtime I headed home, carrying one of the mechanics' wrenches with me. When I walked in the door, I found her together with that young guy.

She was sitting on the bed, and he was sitting next to her on a stool. They were hanging their heads and had long faces as though they were trying to think of a way out of something. When they saw me, they jumped up. He looked absolutely panic-stricken, but she seemed quite calm and quickly moved in between the two of us, not so much to shield the guy as to give me a look which said, "Well, what are you going to do about it? If you lay a hand on him you'll have to deal with me too!"

To be quite honest, when my head'd been spinning I'd wanted to grab the pair of them and beat them up, but when it came to the crunch all I could do was shake all over. He took advantage of my hesitation, slipped out from behind her and made off. She went over to the bed and sat down, grim determination written all over her face.

I asked her again and again, "Who was that guy?"

At first she didn't say a thing, then slowly tears started falling from those big eyes, splashing down onto her clothes. She didn't lower her head, turn her face, or say a word, she just sat there weeping.

I'm a softie and I can't stand to see people cry. As soon as she started, my anger cooled down. I tossed the wrench into a corner and threw myself down on the sofa. I just wanted her to lie to me, say he was her brother, or someone from her village, and leave it at that. The older drivers had been right, we'd get rid of him, and then we could have a child and be like everybody else.

But she didn't lie to me, she just kept on crying and didn't say a word. I put my head in my hands and just sat there. I looked round at the new furniture, at that fashionable sofa and standard lamp and slowly it dawned on me that there was nothing between the two of us. All that highly varnished furniture was just like ice and it seemed to send out a chilling kind of light. What was it all worth? So we'd have a child, then what? I'd seen plenty of drivers who had a whole pack of kids at home but who drank themselves silly because husband and wife were unhappy and looked elsewhere. Driving's a good job, the money's good, you don't get political worries and all that, so why do some of them drink like fish? If you look into it, you'll almost always discover it's because of problems at home.

Since she wouldn't talk, I went out to look for him. Whatever, I had to get to the bottom of it. I didn't have anything to eat — who could eat at a time like that — and left.

The guy lived in a little place next to the animal products factory. It consisted of two adobe walls fitted against the chimney and managed to be sort of triangular and crescent shaped at the same time. Since it got steam from the chimney it was quite warm. It was certainly a new kind of building.

He was no coward. He saw me pushing open the cardboard door, and as though he'd known I'd go looking for him, he very politely indicated I should almost sit down and then poured some tea. You can't hit a man with a smiling face, so what was I supposed to do? Nor can you start knocking someone about the moment you walk in, so in the end all I could do was sit and listen to what he had to say.

He told me that the two of them had grown up in the same village, collected firewood in the mountains together, gone to school together and that when they were in their teens they'd decided to marry. Both their families had given their consent. He'd then gone into the army and they were going to marry when he came out. But during that time there was a famine, her father died and the family couldn't cope so she had to come to Xinjiang to live with her aunt. That aunt knew all about this, but since I had a good job, earned good money, and could arrange a residence permit, she'd pushed the girl into marrying me. The girl, seeing her aunt wouldn't budge and with her boy-friend so far away, didn't know what to do. She finally gave in and married me. But, she told him, she'd never for one second stopped longing for him.

"We're both young and I'll tell you straight," he said to me. "I came to get her to divorce you, to take her with me, whether here working in Xinjiang or back home — but in the three months I've been here I can see that Xinjiang is a good place to live. Although she doesn't love you she says you're a good person and she doesn't want to hurt you, but she's caught in the middle. Lately I've come round to thinking that since the three of us are in this fix, I'll stand aside. But I do want to say this — first, we haven't been up to any-thing behind your back, second, I was engaged to her first even though you married her, and we were together for eighteen years or so while you've only lived with her half a year. You didn't love one another when you got married and even now how much do you care for each other? We got engaged because we were in love, I thought of her every single day those three years I was in the army, so if you want me just to take off and forget about her, I can't. If you can understand this, then you'll forgive me. If you can't, then hit me, but I'll have to fight back, because I haven't done anything wrong, and I still feel I haven't acted unreasonably!"

Well, he more or less went on in that vein and while he was talking he took out all the things she'd made specially for him, a sash, embroidered slippers, a little pouch, to prove her affection for him. I guess they are the sorts of keepsakes Shaanxi girls give. As I listened to him and looked at all those nice things, my heart ached — she'd never made anything for me. But I remembered she'd said I was a good person and I felt a bit better — she'd said what she really felt about me to someone else. I hadn't been wrong about her, she was no flighty girl all right, but a serious young woman who had deep feelings. The trouble was, her feelings weren't for me.

But I still hadn't cooled down completely and said to him, "You told me you didn't get up to anything behind my back, so why did you run off like that when you saw me?"

He went red and replied, "Because you had a big wrench in your hand, and I thought that in your state you might bash me with it!"

"So you ran, but weren't you afraid I'd hit her? And you still say you love her!"

He looked down and mumbled, "I was standing just outside the door. . . ."

As we were talking, she suddenly burst in, probably thinking the two of us were having a fight. Seeing us calmly sitting there, she relaxed a little, but then leaned against the chimney and started crying. This time she did make a noise, a heart-breaking sob.

The two of us didn't speak and all you could hear in that little hut was the sound of her sobbing. As I listened, I suddenly thought of those two girls in Weiya. What would have happened if they'd found themselves in the same situation? I guess like her they wouldn't have resisted that much either, and just married anyone to get by, to keep body and soul together. What had she done wrong? Nothing really. I don't know why, but just then, while my brain was spinning round, all I could think of was that scene in Weiya.

After a long, long pause I finally said, "Come on, it's no use crying over spilt milk. It's all clear now. You can only be with one of us. You'd better make up your mind now, which one is it going to be?"

She kept crying and didn't say anything. It seemed that she was using up a lifetime's tears. After a bit, the other guy, choking on his words, mumbled her pet name and said to her, "You should stay with him. Now that I'm here I can see you've got a good life, I can relax a bit. The two of us weren't meant to be, it was all for nothing, let's just leave past things past."

As he said this she started crying even louder, sobbing uncontrollably. Don't you think that just about said it all? How could I torment her any longer. My heart went out to her and I just felt bad that it was me who was out of luck.

"Well, I can understand her attitude," I said. "If she stays with me, she'll be unhappy, I'll be unhappy and you'll be unhappy. I'm the same as the two of you, drifted here from back east. I've seen a lot of this kind of thing come about, all because of troubles back at home. But China's a big place, if you put your mind to it, you can do anything, and the two of you can live a good life here. You should be together."

After I'd finished talking, she stopped crying and seemed a little calmer. Although just at that moment I felt as though a great burden had been lifted, when I thought of how I'd never have her love, thought of being alone, I felt wronged again and wretched and couldn't help crying. So the three of us sat in that little hut and cried and cried.

She and I very quickly got a divorce. There was all kinds of talk, but I turned a deaf ear. This thing was happening to me, I was the one who had to make the decision. After she'd packed up her things and was about to leave that afternoon, she suddenly seemed reluctant to go, made supper for me one last time and then said quietly, "I could stay one more night here."

That was the only time she ever said anything affectionate to me. I knew what she meant. Only a country girl would express her gratitude that way. But it was only gratitude and nothing more. "No, you go," I told her. "I'm more interested in affection. You two be happy, don't lose one another again. Although we won't be man and wife, we'll still be friends. If you need anything, just let me know. . . ."

They were a capable pair. Since private businesses have been allowed, the two of them set up a stall selling snacks, mostly Shaanxi style. Seems to me they do a better business than the Uighur kebab stalls, and now they've saved several thousand. Of course I've eaten plenty of their food. They know when I've checked back in and send something over. Now, we two couples see a fair amount of one another. Whenever my wife comes to Urumqi, she wants to have their buckwheat dumplings. You ought to go and try some, they're pretty good! Their stall is just by Hundred Flowers Village.

Right, I've wandered a bit from the subject, I'll go on with my story.

When my master got home from a meeting back east and found out what had happened, he got his wife to make a special meal and invited me over. "I wasn't wrong about you," he said to me, "picking you up on the road and making you my apprentice. You did the right thing, you did what you should have done!"

I drank a couple of glasses of alcohol and started getting miserable. I dont know, I just felt as if I'd been wronged. My old master said, "Don't feel so bad about it. She was someone else's to begin with, she was never yours — you just gave her back to somebody, that's all. If you think she was yours to begin with and you let someone else have her, then you're wrong."

I said, "That's not what I was thinking. I just feel that I had good intentions and that I didn't get anything in return."

"Then you're even more wrong," he replied. "If you have good intentions just so you can get something back, then your intentions aren't good to begin with. Being a human being isn't like doing business."

He was right. When he took on this aimless drifter as his apprentice, did he think I would give him anything in return? A driver isn't like somebody who works in a factory, you finish your apprenticeship and then you're gone. My master has a lot of apprentices, they're spread all over Xinjiang; some of them still come to see him when they come through Urumqi, some of them finish their apprenticeship, spread their wings and fly away and you never see them again. He doesn't mind whether they visit or not, it's up to them. Thinking about what he said, I felt calmer.

But, my reporter friend, I tell you, once you've been married it's not the same. Before, no matter how she treated me, when I'd come back from a run, there'd always be hot food on the table and my clothes were clean, I felt good and I looked good. After she left, I didn't know what to do with myself and felt all empty inside, sort of apathetic, out of it. Do you know what the life of a long distance trucker is like? All year round, rain or shine, you're always out on the road. You spend more nights in inns than you do at home. Today you share a room with this bunch of people, tomorrow with another bunch. The blankets are filthy, it doesn't matter which end you put over your head, it'll still stink of smelly feet. Drivers with families have something to look forward to; it doesn't matter what you go through out on the road, because after you check back in you can go home. But me, I go home, the pot's cold, the stove is cold, if I want a hot meal I have to go out to a restaurant. On the road I often see drivers stop and buy things like garlic and peppers and eggs from the peasants by the roadside. I feel sort of envious. Look at him, he's a man with a family. If I buy something good, fresh vegetables or whatever, I haven't got anyone to give them to.

Did I feel regrets then? It wasn't a question of regret. Sometimes I'd check in, come back and see the two of them outside in the yard in front of the boiler house making adobe bricks. They'd be dripping with sweat and smiling and look over and wave at me. It made me feel a kind of warmth and a certain sadness, can't really say what it was, but it wasn't regret.

As time went by, as the days passed, it all faded away, I got used to the idea. We drivers, we have something, we get to see a lot of the world and at the same time, being in Xinjiang is good. When spring comes and you drive along the banks of Lake Sayram, look at the blue, blue water, the swans which have just flown back or the slopes all covered with kirghiz grass and irises and the straight pagoda pines in the valleys, it takes the pain away. In summer, when you drive with your windows rolled down for the first time and let the mountain air in, you get filled with a kind of hope and energy. . . .

Oh, we've come to the top of the mountain, it's time to go down. Going uphill is easy, it's going down that's hard. . . . But don't worry, I know this road. . . .

Do you want to hear more? How did I get married a second time? Okay, just so long as you don't nod off. It's sort of interesting, it was a time when I wasn't thinking about marriage at all. . . .

Two years later, I was driving along this route. That day, the wind was blowing hard, the dust and gravel were kicking up against the glass, you couldn't see a thing for five metres around you. I'd just passed Kumishi and was heading into Elm Valley, the sun was already down behind the mountains. On either side of Elm Valley are cliffs, with a stream running down the middle. There are elm trees along the banks of the stream. Don't know how long they've been there, but they're huge, with crooked branches and knots all over them. Every single one of them is a weird shape. The tops of the trees were swaying back and forth like they were drunk. But the wind wasn't blowing so badly there, there was water and some trees and the visibility was much better.

I was gliding along with the wind. In the distance, I saw a woman wearing a grey scarf, holding a child, sitting by the side of the road. She seemed to be wearing a cotton padded overcoat, the child wrapped inside of it, looking too fat to move. You couldn't tell how old she was. She had two bags next to her. I thought she wanted a ride, so I slowed down a little. But when

I drove up to her she didn't wave at me, she just glanced inside the cab.

I drove on past. But that look was like a blinding flash which had burst in my face and imprinted an image of her expression. What was in that glance? Suspicion, fear, hope, expectation? I'd already gone past a little way, but I just didn't feel right about it. It was like she was a load that had fallen off my truck — if I didn't give her a ride, I couldn't drive on.

I stopped the truck and opened the door. What a wind there was! It almost blew the door off. I held on to my hat and ran over to her. "Where do you want to go?" I asked her.

She said she was headed for Bitter Springs. "Then what are you waiting for?" I said. "Get in."

She shrank back from me, looking me over. It was only then I noticed she was a Shanghai educated youth. She wasn't wearing an ordinary cotton padded overcoat, but a dark grey parka, and her face was half covered by a brushed wool scarf. The child she was holding was about four. His soft white face was frozen blue and he was nestled in his mother's parka, staring at me with big, frightened eyes.

A gust of wind blew into the valley and whistled through the trees. I didn't have my overcoat on and was shivering with cold and urged her to get in the truck. She was still hesitant and clutched the child even closer, like I wanted to grab her.

I knew why she wouldn't get in the truck. My reporter friend, I'll be frank about it, there are some bad drivers, they take lone women hitchhikers along for a while and then look for a place in the mountains or desert, saying the engine has broken down and they can't go on any further. A woman is helpless, there's nothing she can do except let him take advantage of her, satisfy his lust. Then there's the kind of driver who likes to pick up young girls or married women. They really don't have anything as bad as that in mind, they just want to tease or flirt. Shanghai educated youth are pretty sharp. When they come back to southern Xinjiang after visiting home they usually get off the train at Daheyan to save money and then hitch a ride the rest of the way. If it's a couple or a group, they always get the women to stand at the side of the road to flag down a truck. Once it stops, the men climb out of their hiding place in the ditch. That will tell you what Shanghai educated youth think of us drivers. She must have been waiting for a bus or a truck driven by an older guy. Or one with other women in it. She didn't trust a lone young driver like me.

The wind started to blow even harder and the sun had completely disappeared behind the mountains. I remember the swaying trees were a screen of pitch black. If she let my truck go by, she would have been hard put to find another. I pulled my driver's license out of my uniform pocket, waved it in front of her and said, "If you don't trust me, take my driver's license as security. The last bus has gone past already and even if you wait for another truck, they won't necessarily give you a ride. Anyway, there aren't any behind me, I know. Even if you don't care about yourself, you ought to care about the child. Look how frozen he is, come on, get in the truck."

She didn't take my license. She threw a worried glance at the child, looked me over again and finally stood up with a sort of helpless expression. I helped her carry her bags and quickly put them into the cab.

I've given rides to plenty of people and lots of three, four and five year olds. They never sit still at that age. If they're not touching the gears, then they're playing with the dashboard or shouting at the top of their lungs out the window. It was strange though, because this child didn't make a sound. He lay in his mother's arms, and didn't move a muscle. After a while, the sky got dark. Xinjiang is like that, it gets dark all of a sudden. The child began to cough badly. She got upset and started stroking him. She kept turning him over and over, wrapping him up more and more tightly. I took my foot off the accelerator and listened. The child was wheezing badly. I reached over and touched him. His forehead was burning.

"God, that's bad," I said. "That child is sick!"

The mother didn't answer, she just suddenly started to quietly cry.

The child wheezing and the mother crying, I hurried up and stepped on the gas. Ahead of us, the lights of Ushitala winked from the mountain pass. Ushitala is a tiny place, just a few houses. We usually stop there on overnight runs. But I didn't stop, I just kept right on through.

"Stop! Stop!" she yelled and shouted, banging on the door.

"Don't worry," I told her. "We've got to find a hospital right away. I know Ushitala better than you do, there isn't even a barefoot doctor here."

She was crying and shouting and pulling on my arm. "It doesn't matter! It doesn't matter! I want you to stop, I want you to stop!"

My arm was caught in her grip and I had to drive with one hand. There was a curve up ahead of us. I remember saying nervously, "Don't worry, I'm telling you don't worry. I'm not a bad person, really, I'm not. . . ."

"No! No!" she shouted, frightened. "Where are you taking me? I beg you, stop! Please, stop! . . ."

We were almost at the curve. One side of it was mountain and on the other was a drop. It was no laughing matter. I struggled to pull my arm away from her, but she just wouldn't let go, as if by pulling my arm she could make the vehicle stop. Finally I roared at her, "You think I don't want to stop at Ushitala? If you're not tired I am! I want to take you to Yanqi to find a hospital. . . . Please, let go of me, let go of me. . . . Look, I'll show you something!"

The woman probably saw the danger ahead of us in the headlights, and loosened her grip. I made the turn smoothly and pulled out a white porcelain mug from underneath my seat. Trembling I said, "See, this is my prize. . . . I told you I wasn't a bad person. Don't worry, you hold on tight to your child . . . but I beg you, please don't make so much trouble."

My action must have been pretty funny. What could a white porcelain mug prove? It only had the word "award" painted on it in red letters. Almost everybody has one, it doesn't prove anything at all. I don't know whether the porcelain mug actually did anything or whether this educated youth just gave up, but she finally calmed down and hugged the coughing child and let me drive on to Yanqi without any further trouble.

I don't have to tell you what hospitals were like in

those days. It would have been easier to fish a needle out of the ocean than to get a doctor in the middle of the night. I drove back and forth through the empty streets of Yanqi, trying at one hospital and two clinics. The lights were on in all of them but there was nobody on duty. We shouted till we were hoarse but no one answered and we ended up wasting a good hour.

"Damn it! Let's go!" I got back into the cab angrily. "To Korla! I know a doctor there."

Just then the child's breathing weakened and his forehead got boiling hot. He was shaking, already in a coma. Tears rolled down the woman's face, I remember how the blue light of the roadside lamps was reflected in them. She was at her wit's end and all she could do was listen to my directions.

I stepped on the gas and raced on to Korla. Along the way, all I could hear was the wind shrieking through the cracks and the road seemed to stand up and fall into our faces. Black shadows flashed by on either side of us. There was no other traffic, and no one stopped me from driving at top speed. I'd never driven so fast, all I could feel was the front wheels bouncing as if they would fly off any minute. I couldn't think about smoking, my hands were wet from gripping the wheel. All I was afraid of was that it would slip out of my hands.

We passed Bosten Lake and came to the banks of the Konqi River, the water in the truck's radiator was boiling and the truck hissed like a tuckered out horse. I jumped out and said, "Don't be afraid, don't be afraid, we're almost at Korla," took out a hammer and smashed a piece of ice and put the pieces on top of the radiator.

I'd stopped the truck in the middle of the night in this deserted place and the woman seemed scared again. She sat in the cab hugging the child to her. I didn't turn off the headlights and did all my work as far away from her as I could. When I got back in the truck, she seemed to let out a sigh of relief and asked me in a trusting tone of voice for the first time, "Can we find a doctor in Korla?"

I told her we could.

My friend, once you've got someone's trust, it gives you a certain kind of strength to push on and get something done. I thought to myself that even if that doctor was hiding under his bed, I'd drag him out.

It was dawn when we got to Korla. I didn't drive to the hospital but went straight to the doctor's house and knocked on the door.

"Who's there? Who's there?" he asked grumpily after we'd knocked for a while.

"It's me!" I shouted. "Have you forgotten? . . ."

This doctor was from Sichuan. Last year, when he got back from a home visit loaded down with trunks and baskets and furniture, he was stuck in the middle of Daheyan and couldn't find transport. The weather was turning and he was in a complete flap, all worried. I was the one who helped him get everything home. He was very, very grateful and insisted on giving me something, but I didn't accept anything. He said if I ever ran into any trouble, he would help, no question. So this time I took him up on it.

He opened the door and asked in a sleepy voice, "Whose child is this? Is it yours?"

I looked back at the woman sitting in the truck and said, "Yes, it's mine. Hurry up."

He woke up, pulled himself together and started looking for the duty doctor at the hospital, a nurse and the pharmacist, and put mother and son into a hospital room.

There was nothing else for me to do. I drove the truck over to Hostel 2, drained out the water, found a room and took a nap. As soon as it was light outside I was on the road to Aksu.

A week later, on my way back from Kashi, I thought to myself, even if it's none of my business, I should at least go back and thank the doctor. I went to his house with fifty *jin* of that famous Aksu rice.

The minute that short little doctor saw me he shook his finger at me and laughed. "What on earth were you doing? That woman from Shanghai said she doesn't know you and yet you claimed to be the kid's father. You didn't tell me the truth. I couldn't even get a decent night's sleep."

I kept saying sorry and asked how the child was.

The doctor laughed, "Your kid is fine, he can leave the hospital tomorrow."

I unloaded the truck and in the evening didn't have anything to do. I listened to the people in the hostel playing the *huqin* violin and singing from the revolutionary model operas. My thoughts were like the notes from that *huqin*, constantly going off key, never settling down. All right, I thought, go and see the child.

I took two tins of food and walked into the hospital room. I saw her sitting next to the child's bed. The child was lying there gesticulating and babbling away happily. Now I could see her properly. She was at most twenty-six or twenty-seven, with big eyes, a pale complexion and had a sort of sadness about her. When she bent over to tend to the child, I noticed she was a gentle and kind woman, completely different from that night when she seemed almost crazy, grabbing my arm.

She looked up and saw me standing by the bed and her eyes suddenly shone. She said with some embarrassment, "I can never apologize enough for that night. I . . . I've been through the worst and it got to me."

"Forget it," I said. "How's the child?"

"He had acute pneumonia. The doctor said if we'd come any later, it would have been too late. That night, thanks to you. . . ."

Her expression was filled with gratitude, her eyes moist. I felt embarrassed and lowered my head to play with the child.

The little boy had obviously grown up in Shanghai. He spoke with a Shanghai accent and had fine, light skin just like his mother. After we'd played for a while I asked him, "What do you want to be when you grow up?"

The child said, slowly and clearly, "My — mama — wants — me — to — be — a — driver — like — uncle — when — I — grow — up!"

My nose felt as though I'd just sniffed vinegar, my eyes were suddenly full of tears. I turned my head to stop them from falling and pretended to laugh out loud. The child's words meant more to me than any award or praise. It seemed like there was a soft tender little hand stroking my heart, forcing all of the words into my throat, stuck there so I couldn't say anything.

The child hooked his little finger round mine and

asked this and that. I just answered whatever came to mind, feeling a growing sense of responsibility towards him as I did so, as though he were my own son. What would happen to him in the future? Coming from a big city on the Huangpu River could he ever get used to this Gobi Desert where water is more treasured than oil? I know what life is like for Shanghai educated youth. The first group of them who came to southern Xinjiang came here in our truck convoy. They were all about seventeen or eighteen. They raised a red flag on top on the truck, singing and laughing, and when they saw the alkaline patches on the ground, they said it even snowed in summer here. The following year, some of them went home for a visit and sat in my truck crying. After seven or eight years, "educated youth" weren't young anymore, like this woman, they'd become "old bags" in everyone's eyes. But they still had to live in huts dug into the earth, eat salted vegetables and drink water from cisterns. . . .

Then, well, it's the sort of stuff I don't really have to say, you reporters should know it better than I do. At that time, I never thought there could even be a "gang of four", much less that there could be a fall of the "gang of four". I thought things would just go on the way they had and you could more or less predict what the child's life would be like.

"Weren't you going to Bitter Springs?" I said to her. "I'll take you there tomorrow."

She blushed and looked down, "Is it on your way?" she said. "How could we trouble you any further? . . ."

"Don't worry about whether it's on my way or not," I told her. "Tomorrow you just get everything ready and wait for me."

The truth of the matter was that that small fellow had hooked his little finger round my heart. I wanted to go with him to see his father, make friends with his father, so that if someday they ran into trouble I could help out a little.

The next day I switched loads with another driver so he would take some Bosten Lake reed mats back to Urumqi and I would take a load of fertilizer south to Yuli.

By the time I got to the hospital they'd got their things together. She was wrapped in that thick brushed wool scarf, smiling, her eyes sparkling. The child held out his hands wanting me to carry him. I picked him up and he turned and said to the nurse, "Goodbye auntie." What a bright sunny day that was! It was the happiest day of my life, like I'd just come to fetch my wife and my newborn son to take them home.

On the road, the child was even more lively. He was just like other children, touching the gearshift, feeling the dashboard; he'd never ridden in a big truck before and everything was new to him. He never stopped asking questions. It was the first time my small cab had ever been so full of life and I was like the child, it was the first time I discovered that these things I touched every day were actually so interesting. That day, the engine ran on happily as if it was singing! The hard seat felt especially springy, one little bump and my head could touch the roof.

Some time after ten o'clock we reached Qunke. After unloading the fertilizer, I bought a few buns, got back in the cab, and said:

"Come on, let's get going to Bitter Springs!"

I don't know if you've ever been on that road. It

drops down gradually into the Tarim Basin and then to the edge of the Taklamakan Desert. A lot of it's often covered with sand. In fact, you can only tell it's a road from the tracks left by other trucks. A lot of the place names in the area have this "Springs" ending, but don't think there's a lot of water in these parts though. Quite the opposite. They choose those names because water is so precious.

So you can imagine, the further you go along on this road, the more barren it gets. At the start you can still see scattered poplars and willows, then after a while, when the winds start to blow, all you can see outside the window is yellow sand, and it's like the truck is in a cloud, and you can't see a thing.

We went slower and slower, and the child got bored and fell asleep in his mother's arms. The smile on her face disappeared.

"Come on, let's make him comfortable," I said.

I stopped the truck and made a bed for him in the space behind the seats. Sleeping in there would be just like sleeping in a cradle. He snored away quietly behind me, his little puffs of breath tickling the back of my neck. I can't tell you how nice that was.

There was only our little truck crawling along like a tiny insect in the middle of that endless yellow sand. Outside, there seemed to be some sort of invisible force, making everyone inside feel closer to one another. As we were going along, she gave a quiet sigh, and said:

"Look, this was where I wanted to go."

True enough, it wasn't much of a place to look at. I asked her, "What about his father? Is he coming to Tikanlik to fetch you?"

It was a long time before she answered and then finally she said, "He doesn't have a father."

"Oh!" I was a little surprised, unexpectedly a little happy. "Then . . . what happened?"

She gave me a wan sort of smile, frowned and said, "My family doesn't know anything about this . . . but I've always wanted to tell somebody. Not saying anything, it feels like it's suffocating me. . . ."

She was from a capitalist family. In '64 when she graduated from middle school, everyone at the school came beating drums and gongs in a parade to send the students off at the train station. She'd come to Xinjiang resolved to remould herself and build up the border region. She was a teacher when she first arrived. But in '67 a group of rebels took over their set-up and she was sent down to the company to do manual work. Afterwards of course, she got discriminated against more and more. One day, one of these rebels who'd become the company commander suddenly decided she was all right. He told her to take a gun and come up with him to the grassland to hunt gazelle, which would improve the company's diet. The company had people out hunting every week and only the militiamen with a good family background were qualified to carry guns. At the time she was overjoyed, since she thought she'd been "re-educated" by the poor peasants. She went with this "little commander" away from the company and ended up being raped by him under a grove of willow trees. Not long afterwards, she realized she was pregnant, but she couldn't report it to anyone and couldn't get an abortion. All she could do was go back to Shanghai and have the baby. So her parents wouldn't get too upset, she lied and told them she'd gotten married in Xinjiang. She left the child with her family until recently. Her parents were not having an easy time. The "criticize Lin Biao and Confucius" campaign and the "Red Typhoon" hit Shanghai, her parents were evicted from their home and sent to the countryside to do manual labour. She didn't want to add to their burden and went and brought the child back to Xinjiang.

"I want to bring him up," she said. "He hasn't committed any crime. . . . My schoolmates all advised me not to bring him back, but I had to. I've already suffered all kinds of hardships and as far as I'm concerned there isn't anything worse that can happen."

"Where's that villain now?" I asked angrily, only just realizing why she'd been so timid that night.

She gave a bitter laugh. "He got himself transferred to another unit as head of the security section."

Life is like that, you can tell your secrets to someone you don't know, to a stranger, just like I have today. She told me matter-of-factly, without any emotion, as if she was talking about someone else. She was telling me all of this, but more than that she was telling herself, she wasn't trying to get my sympathy or beg me for even more help, she was just going over her past in order to deal with even bigger, more difficult problems. Her tone of voice said as much.

I looked over at her. She was deep in thought. Not like that night when her eyes were filled with tears. I believed she could do what she said she would. In her eyes, there wasn't anything else now that could be more difficult to handle.

Because of this, because I couldn't help feeling a certain admiration and sympathy for her, I asked with concern, "Why don't you genuinely get married?"

She told me there were no more young single men from Shanghai in her area and that she didn't want to marry someone from anywhere else although other Shanghai girls had done so. She said if she married anyone else, she'd never be able to get back to Shanghai.

So I said to her, "I'm from back east too. In my experience, how you get along in life doesn't depend on where you are but on who you're with."

She chuckled a little and said, "That's a cliché."

"There's a saying in Pakistan," I replied. " 'Run at the sight of a cat is a rat's cliché, but as far as the rat goes, it's a truism.' There are a lot of clichés that are truisms for people too." She looked at me and gave a little sigh, "What you said may be true, but there's a gap between truisms and reality."

Fortunately, we had an empty truck, so by the time the sun set over the desert, we'd reached Bitter Springs. It's an oasis, the scenery is nice and the soil is fertile, but it's been ruined by the kind of people who treated her so badly. The group of Shanghai educated youth who came to meet her all had a bellyful of complaints. One particularly scruffy fellow they called the "American soldier" patted me on the shoulder and said, "Thank you, sir! If we were in Shanghai we'd invite you to the Laozhengxing or if you like Western food, the Hongfangzi. But here. . . ." He threw up his hands to show that there was nothing he could do.

I knew if I stayed I'd only make them feel uncomfortable — there was nothing much to eat and nowhere to stay; she'd just got back and needed to put everything in order. "I'm going back to Tikanlik," I said, "I have something to do there, I won't trouble you."

The child ran over to me, took my hand and shouted, "You stay here too, I won't let you go!"

I squatted down, patted him on the head and said, "Uncle has to go off and take another load. There's a lot of stuff waiting for me to carry. You be a good boy and stay here with Mama."

He tilted his head to one side and thought and then asked, "Are you coming back?" "I'll be back," I said. "Is Uncle going to drive his truck back?" "Yes, I'll drive my truck back." "Promise?" "Promise."

She was standing next to the child. I stood up, saying to him and repeating to her, "I'll be back."

Back in Urumqi, that image of her and the child was always in my mind, no matter what, I couldn't get rid of it. I was lost, as if I'd left my heart in Bitter Springs. After my old driving teacher came back I went to his house and told him the whole story and how I felt. "All right!" He banged the table. "If you don't go after her, who are you going to go after?"

I bought a load of special holiday food and went out and bought a lot of toy cars, then hitched a ride on a friend's truck and on New Year's Eve reached Tikanlik. Against the wind and snow, I walked to Bitter Springs and pushed open the door of her "home", just as all those Shanghai people were eating their New Year's Eve dinner. . . .

Later on she'd ask me, "Why did you fall in love with me?"

"I always think love is something you can't explain," I'd reply. "I like *pingju* opera, but there's one line in *Liu Qiao'er* that I've never liked. It goes something like, 'I love him, he can write, he can add, he can work, when he comes home he can be my teacher.' How can you analyse love so objectively, how can you weigh it up like that? To tell you the truth, I've been married before. . . .'" I'd told her everything about my relationship with that northern Shaanxi girl. I said, "Objectively speaking, no matter how you look at it, I was a better bet than that northern Shaanxi fellow in every way. But that girl just didn't love me, she'd rather suffer hardships with him. Living in a hut that wasn't even a hut, a cave that wasn't a cave. Making adobe bricks in the summer sun till the skin burnt off their faces and making matchboxes in the winter till their fingers cracked. Why? It puzzled me, I couldn't understand it. Now I do — it's love! I feel about you the way that northern Shaanxi girl felt about her lad. And you're asking me to tell you why. . . ."

She listened, her eyes red and then nodded and said, "I guess I understand. . . ."

Okay, ahead is the place you wanted to go. Where do you want to get off? . . . It doesn't matter, I'll take you to the door. . . .

Now? Oh now, everything's fine. She's the vice principal of Bitter Springs Middle School. Me? They show me a little consideration and let me just drive this one route. Every winter and summer vacation they come to Urumqi.

I get home once a week. The child is already at middle school, but he doesn't want to be a driver any more. He wants to be a writer, says he wants to write about me and his mother. I told him, "Your mother and I aren't heroes, and anyway there are lots of things that just can't be written about. If you write about them, people will criticize you and say you've written about the darker side of life." He said, "But Dad, you don't understand, the essence of literature is truth. And you and Mama are real people!" Well, my reporter friend, I don't know whether that little fellow's right or not!

The year before last her father got rehabilitated and got his back salary. If she hadn't married me she could've moved back to Shanghai. Once I drank too much and got a little tipsy and said to her, "See, you regret it all now, don't you? If you hadn't married me you could have gone back to Shanghai, couldn't you?"

She didn't say anything at the time, but that night she lay next to me in bed and sobbed and said, "What did you mean? Weren't you the one who said, 'How you get along in life doesn't depend on where you are but who you're with'? Why should I want to go back to Shanghai? You're underestimating me." I knew I'd been a little too heavy with the joke and cajoled her for a long time before I could get her to smile. Since then, I've never drunk more than I should. . . .

Ah, Bitter Springs. When I think of all the people I've met in my life, I'd say it's not only this woman who's drunk bitter water who's a treasure — all those who've suffered, who've drunk bitter water, are our country's treasures, all of them have hearts of gold. Don't you agree, reporter?

Translated by Rui An

A Herdsman's Story

IT had never occurred to Xu Lingjun that he would ever meet his father again.

Now, he was talking with him in a luxuriously furnished room on the seventh floor of a smart hotel. Here, outside the window, there was only a sheet of blue sky dotted with a few floating clouds. But there, far away on his farm on the loess plateau, the scene was entirely different with stretch after stretch of green and yellow fields, broad and flourishing. Sitting in this room, wreathed in mist-like smoke from his father's pipe, he found himself flying up and up above the clouds and everything before him transformed into an unfathomable illusion. Yet, the familiar, almost coffee-like fragrance of his father's tobacco, the one with the Red Indian chief on the label, which he'd known from early childhood, proved to him that he was not in some fairyland in the sky but very firmly in the real world.

"Let bygones be bygones," his father said, waving his hand. Ever since obtaining his bachelor's degree at Harvard in the 30s, he'd kept the airs of his student days. Now, sitting on a sofa cross-legged in his fine suit, he continued, "The moment I set foot on the mainland, I learned the current political term 'look forward'. So you'd better get ready to go abroad."

All at once, Xu felt a sort of nameless depression

brought on by his father's appearance as well as by the room's decoration. He said to himself, "It's true that bygones are bygones, but how could I possibly forget all that's happened?"

Thirty years ago, on an autumn day much like this, Xu, clutching a note addressed by his mother, had found his way to a western-style villa on Joffre Road in the French Concession of Shanghai. The yellow leaves looked even more withered after the shower and raindrops dripped relentlessly from the parasol trees outside the barbed-wire-topped wall. The iron gate of the villa had been painted an intimidating gray. Only after repeated pressings of the bell did a small hatch in the gate open and the doorkeeper appear. It was the man who often sent letters to his father and the two recognized one another. Presently, the boy was ushered along a cement path flanked by two rows of ilex trees and soon arrived at the sitting room of a two-storey building.

Of course, his father had been much younger then. Wearing a cream-coloured woollen vest, he was smoking his pipe, his head bent, one elbow resting on the mantelpiece. On the sofa in front of the fireplace sat the woman Xu's mother cursed and damned all day long.

"Is this your son?" Xu heard her ask his father. "Doesn't he look like you! Come over here, child!"

Motionless, Xu shot her a glance. He had seen, he remembered now, a pair of shining eyes and heavily rouged lips.

"What's the matter?" Father looked up.

"Mum is ill. She wants you to come back right away."

"She is always sick," Father growled, leaving the fireplace and pacing to and fro furiously on the green-and-white-striped carpet. Xu fixed his stare on his father's step, trying to hold back his tears.

"Tell your mother I'll be back soon." His father finally stopped in front of him. His mother had heard this time and again over the telephone and Xu knew that it was not to be relied upon. Timid but obstinate, he ventured again, "Mum wants you to go home right now."

"I know, I know. . . ." With that, Father placed a hand on the boy's shoulder, and encouraged him gently towards the door. "You go ahead and take my car. I'll come along in a while. If your mother's condition takes a turn for the worse, urge her to go to hospital first." Leading his son into the front hall, he patted the boy's head affectionately and suddenly continued in a low voice, "If only you were a bit more grown up, you'd know that your mother is a difficult woman to get along with, she's so . . . so. . . ."

Looking up, Xu saw how weak and bitter his father was and felt sorry for him.

But no sooner had the automobile in which Xu sat started along the leaf-carpeted street in the French Concession than the tears coursed down his cheeks and a wave of humiliation, self-pity and loneliness suddenly seized him. He felt that nobody else except he alone was really to be pitied. In truth, he got little affection from his mother. Her fingers touched mahjong more often than they did his hair. And neither had he ever received much guidance from his father. Whenever he did come home, he invariably looked gloomy and bored, and then usually the endless quarrelling would break out between the two of them.

As his father had said, if he had been a bit more grown up, he would have been able to understand. In fact, even at the age of eleven, the boy had long had a vague sense of things anyway. What his mother wanted was her husband's affection, while his father wanted badly to discard such an ill-tempered wife. And neither of them had ever needed him. Xu was fully aware of the fact that he was nothing more than the product of an arranged marriage between a student returned from the United States and a young woman from a landlord family.

That night, as usual, his father didn't come home. Before long, it was learned that he had left China with his mistress, and eventually his mother died in a German-run hospital.

It was at that time that the People's Liberation Army entered Shanghai.

And now, thirty years had passed. After all of these unprecedentedly eventful and changing years, his father had suddenly turned up, claiming to want his son to go abroad with him. All of this seemed mysterious and inconceivable. He could hardly believe that his own father was now sitting in front of him, and neither could he believe that it was really he himself who sat opposite.

When Miss Song, his father's secretary, opened the wardrobe door, he happened to catch a glimpse of several suitcases pasted with colourful labels from hotels in Los Angeles, Tokyo, Bangkok and Hong Kong, as well as the oval trademark of Universal Airlines. The small wardrobe symbolized a whole new world. For Xu Lingjun, however, coming here all the way from his farm had meant travelling by bus and train for two full days after being notified only three days previously. Squashed into a corner of the sofa, his gray artificial leather handbag, regarded as quite fashionable on the farm, now looked crumpled and pitiful in this magnificent room. On the top of the bag was a knitted nylon pouch containing his tooth-brush, towel and several tea-brewed eggs that he hadn't finished on the road. The crushed and dried eggs, which seemed strangely out of place here, re-minded him of the evening of his departure when Xiuzhi, his wife, asked him to take some more for his father. Thinking of this, Xu couldn't help but smile bitterly.

The day before yesterday, Xiuzhi had insisted on taking Qingqing, their five-year-old daughter, to see him off at the county's bus station. It was the first time he had left the farm since their marriage and this trip had thus become a grand occasion in his small family.

"Daddy, where's Beijing?" asked Qingqing.

"It's in the northeast of our country."

"Is Beijing much bigger than a county town?"

"Yes, of course."

"And are there irises in Beijing?"

"No, there are no such flowers there."

"Are there any oleasters?" she persisted.

"Oh, no. There are no such wild fruits."

"Oh, what a pity!" Qingqing heaved a long grown-up sigh. Cupping her chin in her hands, she appeared thoroughly disappointed. To her, all good places ought to have both irises and oleasters.

"You silly girl!" Old Zhao, the cart driver, teased. "Beijing is a very big place. But this time, your daddy might go very, very far away. Why, he might even go abroad with your grandpa. Isn't that right, Teacher Xu?"

Xiuzhi, crouched behind the driver, gave her husband a gentle smile but said nothing. In the same way that Qingqing couldn't envisage the size of Beijing, she couldn't imagine that he would ever go to other countries.

The horse cart bumped along the dirt road. On the north side of the road stretched a neatly tended field, on the south, pasture land extended far off into the morning mist, off to where he used to tend horses. This place had a magnetic quality all its own and so, looking at the grass or at a particular tree, endless memories would well up in his mind. And this morning especially, he found everything on this grassland more precious and attractive than ever.

Knowing that a big oleaster tree stood directly behind a nearby trio of poplars, he hopped off the cart and returned shortly with some fresh fruit which everyone promptly set about eating. Oleasters were a local wild fruit with a bitter-sweet flavour and grew mostly in the northwest. They had served as his staple diet during the famine years in the 60s and it had been a long time since he ate them last. Now, tasting them again, he was seized with nostalgia. No wonder Qingqing had wanted to know whether there was such fruit in Beijing or not.

"Her grandpa has probably never tasted them," Xiuzhi remarked smiling, spitting out the pit. It was the most she had ever exercised her imagination to try and picture what her father-in-law from afar would be like.

As a matter of fact, it was not difficult to imagine, for father and son bore such a close resemblance to one another that Xiuzhi could easily have recognized her father-in-law had she just run across him in the street. Both had long and narrow eyes, straight noses and full lips, and even their gestures betrayed their common blood. The father, however, did not look his age. Instead of being wan and sallow, his complexion was as brown as his son's, having been tanned on the beaches of Los Angeles and Hong Kong. He still paid great attention to his appearance. His hair, though silver, was always neatly combed and his fingernails well-manicured despite the age spots which had long since appeared on his hands. Around the exquisite coffee cup on the side-table lay scattered the Three B brand pipe, a tobacco bag made of Moroccan sheepskin, a gilt lighter and a diamond-inlaid necktie pin.

It seemed highly unlikely that he would enjoy eating oleasters!

2

"Why, how strange, you even get the latest songs here!" exclaimed Miss Song in fluent Chinese. Tall and well-proportioned, her long, black hair bound with a scarlet satin ribbon, she was enveloped in a delicate jasmine fragrance.

"Look, Director Xu, how familiar Beijing people are with disco dancing. It's even more frenetic than in Hong Kong. I guess they're really modernized now!"

"Surely it's hard to withstand the temptation to

enjoy yourself." With that, Director Xu smiled enig-
matically like an ancient sage. "They don't think of
themselves as ascetics any more."

Directly after supper, Father and Miss Song took
him to the ballroom. He would never have imagined
such a place even in Beijing. When he was a child he
had been taken by his parents to the famous dance
halls of Shanghai, places with names like the "D.D.S.",
the "Paramount", "The French Night Club" and so
on, and it seemed now that he was revisiting these once
familiar haunts again. However, seeing the effeminate
men and masculine women loitering like ghosts in the
pale ghastly-white light, he felt at once extremely uneasy, and like someone in an audience suddenly
dragged on to the stage to act, failed to enter into his
role. His glimpse in the hotel restaurant just a moment ago of numerous elaborate dishes which had only
been pecked at increased his strong sense of disgust.
On his farm, people were used to putting the leftovers
into a lunch box, which they brought along whenever
they went to the county town to have a meal in a state
restaurant.

All of a sudden, the music sounded again in the
main hall and several couples began to dance frantically.
Instead of linking arms, they leaned first forwards then
backwards, teasing each other face to face, just like
cock-fighting. And this was how they got rid of their
excess energy! It reminded him of the peasants who
were now labouring barefoot in the hot rice-paddies.
Swinging their arms from right to left and vice versa,
they would lean over to cut the rice. Sometimes they
raised their heads, shouting in hoarse voices to the
peasant standing in the distance, two buckets at either

end of his shoulder pole: "Hey, hello! Water, water! . . ." How good it would be if he could lie down under the shade of a tree near the irrigation ditch with its muddy yellow water, and inhale the fragrance of rice straw and alfalfa on the breeze. . . .

"Can you dance, Mr Xu?" asked Miss Song standing next to him, jolting him out of his pleasant reverie. Turning around, he glanced at her: She too had shining eyes and heavily rouged lips.

"Oh, no, I can't," he replied absent-mindedly, smiling. He could graze horses, till land with a plough, cut rice and winnow wheat. . . . Why should he learn to dance like this?

"Don't put him on the spot!" his father said to Miss Song with a grin. "Look, Manager Wang is coming to ask you to dance."

A handsome young man in a gray suit approached them and after he'd made a low bow to Miss Song, the young couple left for the dance floor.

"Was there something else you still wanted to think about?" Father demanded, lighting his pipe again. "Of course, you know better than I do, it's easy to get a visa at the moment but no one knows what may happen in the future."

"There's still something here I can't bear to leave." Turning around, he looked directly into his father's eyes.

"Including all those bitter experiences?" his father asked sombrely.

"Yes, precisely because of those, this happiness is all the more precious to us."

His father shrugged his shoulders and gave him a puzzled stare.

A wave of melancholy swept over him. It was then that he realized that his father belonged to a world utterly unfamiliar and incomprehensible to him. Their physical resemblance could never balance their spiritual estrangement. They stared at each other in the same way, but neither could see into the deep reservoir of the other's experience.

"Is it that . . . that you still hold a grudge against me?" He lowered his head.

"Oh, no, not at all!" The son waved his hand, using a gesture of his father's. "As you've said, 'Let bygones be bygones.' No, it's something else entirely. . . ."

By then, the music had changed, the light in the hall seemed to have become even more dim than before, and he could no longer make out the shadows of people moving about on the dance floor. Lowering his head again, his father constantly mopped his brow with his right hand, and the expression of weakness and bitterness once again appeared on his face.

"It's true that what's past is past. Still, the bitterness remains when one recalls. . . ." The old man heaved a sigh and went on, "But, I've missed you very much, and now. . . ."

"Yes, I believe you." His father's low-pitched murmur and the pensive music in the background moved him. "And at times I've missed you too."

"Honestly?" His father raised his head.

Yes he had. He remembered in particular an autumn night twenty years earlier. Streaming through lattice paper torn by a heavy rain, the moonlight fell on a group of shabbily-dressed herdsmen lying in the earthen shed. On the ground next to the wall was Xu Lingjun. Shivering all over with the cold, he suddenly rose from the damp rice straw. Outside, the muddy ground, lit brightly by the moon, glistened like pieces of broken glass. There were puddles everywhere and the air stank. Finally, he found a stable, which, with the heat given off by the horses' manure, was comparatively warm and dry. Horses, mules and donkeys were chewing hay. Finding a vacant trough, he climbed on to it, and lay down at once.

The stable was dimly lit by a small sliver of light reflected on to one of its earthen walls and each of the animals had its head lowered over its trough as though paying homage to the moon. He suddenly felt extremely sad. The whole scene somehow symbolized his complete solitude. Abandoned by people, he was now forced to associate with horses and cattle.

He wept bitterly and curled up on the narrow trough, remembering how in his life he'd tried to defend himself from pressures from all directions. At first, he had been forsaken by his own father and later on, after his mother's death, his uncle had taken away all of her things, leaving him alone. He had been obliged to move into his school dormitory and to study on a people's grant. It had been the Communist Party that had taken him in and a people's school that had brought him up.

In those bright days during the 50s, though sensitive and reticent as a result of his early years, Xu gradually became absorbed in collective life and, like most middle school students at the time, he cherished a beautiful dream. And before long after his graduation it had come true. Wearing a dark blue uniform, notebook tucked under his arm and carrying some chalk, he had entered the classroom as a primary school teacher. From then on, he had a new direction in life, a direction of his own.

But not long afterwards the leaders at the school had to fulfil the quota of Rightists set by their superiors and he was suddenly put in the same category as his father. In his past, the bourgeoisie had forsaken him, leaving him nothing but the "immovable estate" of his heritage, and now others forsook him, labelling him a Rightist. In the end he had been deserted by all and banished to this remote farm to be reeducated through labour.

Having eaten its hay, one of the horses walked along beside the wooden trough towards him. Standing as close as its lead would reach, it stretched out its head and he felt a gust of hot breath on his face. Opening his eyes, he saw its brown head nuzzling out grain next to him. It slowly became aware of his presence but instead of being startled, the animal sniffed with its moist nose and brushed across his face with its soft velvet muzzle. Moved greatly by this soothing gesture, he embraced its long, haggard head and wept bitterly, his tears rolling down its brown mane. Then, kneeling on the trough, he carefully scraped together the scattered grains and placed them in a pile before his animal companion.

And Father, where were you then?

3

Now, he had finally come back.

It wasn't a dream. His father was lying on a bed in the next room and he was sleeping on a soft spring bed. Feeling the mattress, Xu Lingjun thought how different it was from that hard wooden trough. Over the carpet, sofa and bed spread many small squares, reflections of the moonlight pouring through the curtain. In that hazy moonlight, the day's impressions surfaced clearly in his mind and over and over again he saw how completely incapable he was of adapting himself to everything here. His father had come back, but they were now strangers to one another. His return had only evoked bitter memories and disturbed his calm mind.

Although it was already autumn the room seemed hot and close. He lifted the woollen blanket, sat up and propped himself against the headboard. Then, switching on the bedside lamp, he indifferently scrutinized the whole room until his gaze at last fell on his own body. As he stared at the muscular arms, the veined calves, the splayed toes of his two large feet and at his calloused palms and heels, he recalled the conversation with his father that afternoon.

Soon after finishing his coffee, Father had let Miss Song go, and had then started to tell his son about recent developments in his company, about the ineptness of Lingjun's half-brothers and his own longing for his native land.

". . . At last, with you by my side, I may have a bit of consolation," he said with a smile. "What happened thirty years ago has upset me more and more. I know that family origin is much stressed here and that as a result your life wouldn't have been an easy one. I even thought that you might not still be alive. But I have been concerned about you all along. Every now and then I'd see you as you were when you were small, especially how you lay in the arms of your wet nurse the day your grandpa held a huge feast in Nanjing. I remember it as clearly as if it had just happened yesterday. There were so many guests from Shanghai that day. You know, you were the first grandson in the family. . . ."

And now, in the soft light from the green-shaded bedside lamp, he suddenly experienced a strange sensation, looking at his own strong physique. Hearing the story of his own childhood for the first time from his father made him sharply contrast his life in the past with his life now. He suddenly discovered the real cause of the estrangement between his father and himself. This boy who was the first son of the eldest branch of a wealthy family held in high regard by the Shanghai magnates and their wives had now become a veritable labourer! And mixed into this transformation process had been so much bitterness as well as so much joyful hard work.

Because of his homelessness, it was arranged that Xu Lingjun should become a herdsman on the farm after his release from education through labour.

In the early morning, when the sun had just risen over the poplar grove and the silver dewdrops were still glistening on the grass, he would unbolt the stable and in a great rush, horses and cattle would tumble out, vying with each other in racing to the pasture. Startled, the larks and pheasants would flee from the thick grass with cries of alarm. Flapping their wings, they skimmed over the herd, darting towards the poplar woods like arrows. Mounted on his horse, he galloped along the well-trampled path as though throwing himself into the very bosom of nature itself.

There was a large swamp overgrown with reeds and

scattered at random amongst them, the horses and cattle began to graze, with only the sporadic noise of their breathing and splashing breaking the silence. Lying on the earthen slope, the young herdsman used to stare up at the sky, at the snow-white clouds which seemed as changeable as life itself. By then, sweeping across the tips of the grass and the swamp's surface, a light breeze gently brushed over his whole body and he felt lulled by the fresh air laden with the mixed aroma of moist earth and horses' sweat. In this contented state, he would catch the odour of his own sweat and realize how closely his own life had been tied to that of nature. It was a state that would arouse in him an endless series of reveries, as if he himself had melted entirely into this wilderness wind. He existed everywhere, yet lost his own individual nature. As a result, his dejection disappeared instantly, both his sadness as well as his bitterness at his unlucky fate, and in their place emerged a love for life and a love for nature.

At noon, their bellies full and round, the horses paced out of the thick reeds one after the other, some quivering their manes, others switching their tails to drive away the gadfly and botfly. Then, gathering around closely, they would look at him with their big, kind eyes. Sometimes, No. 7, a white piebald, would stealthily skirt round several companions to play tricks on lame No. 100. Not to be outdone, the latter would turn and give the former a good kick with its game leg. Quickly dodging aside, No. 7 would circle the herd with its head raised high, silver drops of water flying in all directions. Whenever that happened, Xu Lingjun would pick up his long whip and shout at them fiercely. Promptly pricking up their ears, the other horses and cattle would turn about to shoot reproachful stares at the troublemaker. And finally contrite, like a mischievous upbraided schoolboy, No. 7 would stand in the knee-deep water, quietly moistening its muzzle. Seeing this, the young herdsman felt that although he was living among animals, he had simply become a fairy-tale prince surrounded by a host of spirits.

Under the scorching sun, the cloud shadow moved slowly along the foot of the distant hill. Waterfowl, prompted by the swamp's warmth, began to cry out among the reeds. The place was not only vast, it was beautiful. Here, even the abstract idea of a "motherland" took on definition and became concrete. He felt satisfied and at peace. Life was, after all, beautiful. Both nature and labour had offered him things he couldn't get within classroom walls.

At times, there would be a rain shower in the pasture. At first, it appeared in the form of a screen of black threads suspended over the hill slopes in the far distance and then, buffeted by the wind, would draw nearer and nearer. In a twinkling, the rain would pour down and the whole grassland would be totally enveloped in a white mist. As the shower approached, Xu Lingjun had to drive his flock to the strip of forest for cover. Long whip in hand, he would get on his horse and gallop round the scattered herd, hollering loudly at them. In moments like those, he felt a sense of vitality and strength, no longer insignificant and useless. And it was through this hard battle against the wind, then rain and the mosquitoes and gnats that he gradually restored his faith in life.

Only when it rained could herdsmen from different teams get together under the small canopy which, built as a shelter, looked just like a tiny boat anchored in a vast sea of mist. It was cool and wet beneath the canopy, and generally permeated with the strong scent of low-grade tobacco. Listening attentively to his friends' merry conversations and bawdy jokes, he would now and then be taken aback by the fact that they didn't invest their labour and their lives with so many complex emotions. He was delighted at this new understanding. Honest and simple, these herdsmen were happy, though their lives were hard. He began to admire them.

"They say that you're a Rightist. What does that actually mean then?" An old herdsman of about sixty or so asked one day.

"It means. . . ." He hesitated, hanging his head in shame. "A Rightist is one who has made a mistake in the past."

"No, not at all," put in a herdsman from the Seventh Team. "The Rightists are those who spoke the truth in 1957. That year, the intellectuals were under attack." Frank and outspoken by nature, he was fond of making jokes, and people had nicknamed him "Glib Tongue".

"Why is speaking the truth regarded as 'making a mistake'? If all of us fail to speak the truth, everything will be in a mess." The old herdsman kept on smoking his pipe and continued, "Well, in my opinion, one is better off as a labourer than as a cadre. Look, I'll soon turn seventy, yet I'm still neither hard of hearing, nor dim-sighted, nor stooped, and my teeth are good. Why, I can even still eat roasted soya-beans —"

"And precisely because of that, you'll be a labourer again in the next life!" Glib Tongue interrupted him laughing.

"Well, none the worse for that!" the old herdsman retorted earnestly. "Anyway, without our labouring day and night, the cadres wouldn't be able to keep their positions and the intellectuals couldn't go on with their reading and writing. . . ."

This simple, frank and sometimes sporadic kind of dialogue would occasionally arouse strong emotions in him. Just like seeing a rainbow after a shower, he felt refreshed. It made him long for a return to the simple and honest life, to take pleasure from the present as they did.

Over the course of his long-term physical labour, he became used to a fixed way of life and this new pattern stubbornly moulded him in its own image. As time passed, everything that had gone before eventually seemed like a dim dream, or like a story about someone else he'd read in a book. At the same time, his memory was divided into two separate parts by this new way of life so entirely different from that of the past. As a result, his former big city life grew more and more illusory and only the events of the present were real and true. In the end he had been converted into one who was not only fit but also able to live on this terrain. He had become a herdsman both in name and in reality.

In the early years of the "cultural revolution", people all forgot about his past, but then someone recalled that he had originally been classed as a Rightist and it was felt necessary to parade him through the streets. Just at that critical point, however, having consulted one another under the canopy, the herdsmen of all the different teams declared unanimously that there was no more good grazing in this pasture, and, after orally notifying the administrative office of the farm, they all decided to move on to another pasture on the hill slopes. Of course, Xu Lingjun had to go with them. Once up into the hills, one couldn't return home for at least two or three months. None of the "revolutionary clique", therefore, was inclined to follow suit. In this way, Xu Lingjun put his simple baggage on the back of a horse and rode away together with them, finally leaving the chaos behind. As soon as they set foot on the highway, all the herdsmen shouted cheerfully: "Hell! Now, we've more or less gone up into the hills. Who cares whose mother's going to marry whom?" Whistling loudly, they brandished their long whips to urge on the horses and cattle, raising a cloud of yellow dust as they went. In the distance ahead he could see a grazing area on the slope, glistening in the sunshine like a vast piece of green jadeite. . . . That day remained etched in Xu Lingjun's mind, something he treasured for ever with a special affection.

His memories were a mixture of the bitterness and happiness experienced in different stages and aspects of his life. But he felt that, without the bitter times as a contrast, his happiness now would surely be a pallid and valueless thing.

Then in spring last year, he had suddenly been summoned back to the administrative office from the pastures on the slope. Anxious and fearful, he entered the office of the farm's political department. Having read a document to him, Deputy Head Dong then informed him that it had been wrong to label him a

Rightist in 1957 and that, as well as having his name entirely cleared, it would soon be arranged for him to be a teacher again at the farm-run school. A newly hatched fly was buzzing to and fro in the office, landing now on the wall, now on the filing cabinet. Carefully following the fly's every move, Deputy Head Dong picked up a magazine, itching to swat it. "Well, you can go and get your transfer order from Secretary Pang next door. Report for duty at the school tomorrow." Finally, the fly landed on his desk, but craftily fled before the magazine was slapped down. Greatly disappointed, Deputy Head Dong sank back into his armchair again. After a while, he advised sombrely, "Listen, from now on you must work hard and don't make any more mistakes."

Xu Lingjun was completely taken aback by this unexpected event, almost numbed, as if hit by an electric current. It was hard to grasp the significance of this correction in the political life of the country as well as the radical change it would make to his own life in the future. In fact, he hadn't even dared think of such a day. Nevertheless a great happiness began to seize him. The emotion filtered through his body like alcohol, making him dizzy. At first, he felt a dryness in his throat, then trembled slightly all over and at last burst into sobs, tears running unrestrainedly down his cheeks. Even Deputy Head Dong, who always affected a solemn manner, was deeply moved by the scene, and quickly stretched out a hand to him. Not until this moment, with Deputy Head Dong's hand grasping his own, had he begun to have even a dim hope for his future.

And, once again he entered the classroom in a dark

blue uniform, notebook under his arm and chalk in hand, resuming finally the radiant dream he had cherished twenty years ago. This was not a well-off farm. The children were all dressed in rags and the classroom permanently filled with the intermingled smells of sweat, dust and hay. Sitting motionless behind rough desks with their eyes wide open, the pupils all stared at the newcomer, wondering why this herdsman had suddenly become a teacher. But soon, they placed their trust in him. He didn't think he was making any special contribution, and dared not even imagine that he was serving the socialist cause and the "four modernizations" of his country, which he thought of as marvellous deeds accomplished only by heroes. He thought that what he did was nothing more than conscientiously fulfilling his duty. But even so, he was respected by all his pupils. On the morning he left for Beijing, he noticed that these pupils, standing in twos and threes on either side of the path they took to school every day, fixed their eyes on the horse cart. Probably they too had heard that, having found his rich father, he would soon go abroad. Controlling a desire to express reluctance at his departure, they watched the cart move off until it rolled across the stone bridge, through the poplar woods and finally disappeared at the far end of an uncultivated field.

Sometimes, herdsmen from other teams would come to call on him from more than ten *li* away. The old herdsman was already over eighty, yet he still moved smartly. Sitting on the brick *kang*, he would pick up a Chinese dictionary and caress it, saying, "How clever he is. He fully deserves to be called a scholar. Look, what a thick book. It would probably take a whole lifetime to read it all!"

"No, it's a dictionary, which you use for looking up new words," Glib Tongue explained to his older companion. "How foolish you are! The longer you live, the more muddle-headed you become!"

"That's true. Here I am over eighty, and still illiterate. Whenever I go to see a film, I can't even make out what the title is, and can only see figures moving around on the screen."

"Well, whatever we do we must learn to read. A few days back, while I was preparing medicine for my cattle, I nearly fed them something that was for external use only," said Glib Tongue. "Well, Xu, you are one of us. Now, we're too old to learn any more, so we'll leave the education of our children in your good hands."

"Good!" the old herdsman took up the cue. "If, Xu, you succeed in teaching my grandsons to read thick books like this, it shows that you really care about your poor friends who have shared the same lot with you on the grassland."

The simple words drove home to him the value of his work, gave him further hope for the future. From all of them he had again smelt the odour of horses' sweat, the flavour of grass and hay as well as the breath of nature itself, something he felt he knew, something quite different from the depression he'd experienced with his father and Miss Song.

In the eyes of these herdsmen, in the eyes of his pupils and of the old colleagues who once again worked together with him, he had seen his own worth. Was there anything more precious and pleasing than this?

4

In the morning, he and Miss Song accompanied his father along Wangfujing Street and he found himself unused any more to city life. Here, unlike the countryside, the ground was covered with asphalt or tarmac, not moist and spongy to the step. People streamed along the street, noisy but apathetic. Engulfed in this great commotion, he felt a tension which soon exhausted him.

In the arts and crafts store, the father wrote a cheque for six hundred yuan and ordered an exquisite blue and white porcelain dinner service from the famous Jingdezhen kilns. In a porcelain shop, the son picked up an earthenware jar for two yuan. The delicate little pot with its brown and yellow antique-style decoration could almost pass as a relic excavated from a Han tomb. He had never seen such things in his little county town in the northwest. Xiuzhi had often praised the pickles from her home town and had long wanted a really fine pot. The one she had now had been brought by someone from Shaanxi and for it she had traded five pairs of cloth shoe soles, which had taken her several nights to make. But it was ugly now, its surface laced with white salt stains.

"Your wife must be a real beauty!" said Miss Song coquettishly when they got back to the hotel. "Your love for her is admirable. It makes a person jealous!" She wore a new red-and-black-striped silk blouse underneath her light purple cardigan and a thin gray wool skirt. In the hot autumn sun, her jasmine perfume was even more pungent.

"Well, marriage is a kind of bond and duty after

all." Slowly stirring his coffee, Father heaved a sigh, and then picked over the words carefully as if savouring the meaning. Perhaps he was thinking of his own case. "Whether you love your wife or not, you must keep your promise to the very end of your life or you'll feel guilt, anguish and remorse. I want you to go abroad, but not alone. You must bring your wife and daughter too."

"Would you tell us about your romance?" Miss Song said. "Your love affair must have been rather special. I'm sure there will have been lots of young women running after a handsome man like you!"

"My love affair?" He smiled apologetically. "I didn't even know my wife when I married her, let alone have a courtship."

"Oh?" Miss Song feigned an exaggerated surprise while his father shrugged his shoulders doubtfully.

He wanted to tell them how he and Xiuzhi had married. But their abnormal marriage had been overshadowed by a national disaster, a humiliation for the whole nation. He was ambivalent about whether or not he should tell them the whole story in case they made fun of what he regarded as sacred. Unable to decide, he silently sipped the coffee. There was sweetness in the bitter drink. Sweetness blended with bitterness. Only a mixture of the two could produce such a special, exciting aroma. Father and Miss Song might be able to appreciate its particular taste, but would they be able to understand the meaning of his complex life? In those chaotic years, marriage, like everything else, had been thrown off course. Theirs had been more like a blind combination. Both Xiuzhi and he had found it absurd and had never anticipated the unexpected happiness which befell them. So, the more difficult the circumstances then, the more precious this happiness was now. Whenever they recalled their abnormal marriage, mixed feelings of grief and warmth rose in their hearts, something incomprehensible to anyone but themselves.

It all started one spring afternoon in 1972. As usual, after watering the horses and bolting the corral, he returned to his small hut. He had hardly put down his whip when Glib Tongue broke into the room.

"Hey, Old Xu, want a wife?" he declared. "You just say the word and I'll send her here tonight!"

"Send her here then," he said smiling, thinking it was a joke.

"Great! No going back on your word! The woman's got her certificate to prove she's single. As for you, I've had a word with the farm leader. He said as long as you had no objections, he would give you your certificate at once so I'll go and pick it up for you and give it to the admin people on my way back. Then I'll bring the girl here and we'll have the wedding tonight!"

It was just getting dark and he was sitting on a stool reading when he heard children outside chorus: "Old Xu's wife's coming! Old Xu's wife's coming!" The door was thrown open and in dashed Glib Tongue as he had that afternoon.

"It's all settled and done! I won't drink a drop of your wine but at least offer me some water! Hard work, you know. I almost ran my legs off this afternoon going thirty *li* and back." With that, he ladled some cold water from a pot and gulped it down. Drying his whiskered lips, he heaved a long sigh of relief.

"Hey!" he cried out. "Why don't you come in? This is your home now! Let me introduce the two of you. This is the Old Xu I mentioned. His full name's Xu Lingjun. A nice fellow except he's a little poor. But nowadays, the poorer he is, the more honour he gets!"

Only then did he notice a strange girl standing at the head of a group of children outside the door. She wore a gray, badly creased tunic and held a white bundle in her hand. She scrutinized the dusty, sooty hut coldly as if she really was preparing to live in it.

"What's going on?" He was shocked. "What kind of a joke is this?"

"Why, it's not a joke at all!" Glib Tongue fished out some paper, and slapped the edge of the brick bed. "All the documents're here! It's official. Understand? I told the man in the political department that you were out grazing horses and had asked me to get all the necessary documents together. If you go back on your word, you'll put me in a fix. Do you hear me, Old Xu?"

"What are we going to do?" he asked Glib Tongue, throwing his hands in the air. The girl walked in and quietly sat down on the small stool he had just vacated. She seemed perfectly at ease, as though their conversation had nothing to do with her.

"What's to be done? It's a matter between husband and wife now. How can you ask me?" Glib Tongue placed all of the "official documents" on the brick bed. "Now then, have a happy life together. Next year you'll have a nice chubby baby. You must give me a special treat then." He went to the door and waved his hands, shooing the children away as though they were little chicks. "What's there to look at? If you haven't seen your parents' wedding ceremony, you can at least ask them about it. Now clear off, all of you!"

With that, Glib Tongue took his leave.

In the dim yellow light, he stealthily sized up the girl. Not very pretty, she had a small retroussé nose surrounded by tiny freckles, a head of lustreless brown hair, and looked haggard and wan. He felt sorry for her and poured out a glass of water. "Have a drink, you've walked a long way. . . ."

She looked up and her eyes met his earnest stare. Silently she gulped the water down. Her appearance improved as her strength returned. Moving over to the brick bed she folded up the quilts. Then she took a pair of trousers and smoothed out the worn patch at the knee on her lap, untied a little white bundle she had brought with her, picked a piece of blue cloth, a needle and some thread and began sewing, her head lowered. Her movements were deft and unhurried. She seemed to have a refined vitality which manifested itself in her movements rather than in her appearance. And then this wretched looking girl made the hut spotless with a little tidying here and there. She seemed to be playing a piano with the quilts, the cotton-padded mattress and the clothes as keys. To him it seemed as if there was music in this shabby little hut.

Then suddenly, he remembered the brown horse and his heart ached. He felt that not only had he known her but that he'd been waiting for her all these years. Seized by a sudden wave of passion, he unthinkingly sat down beside her on the edge of the bed. He covered his face with his hands, afraid to let himself believe that happiness had at last come to him, worried that this unexpected joy might only bring him new misfortunes. His hands still covering his eyes, he relished this strange new feeling. The girl stopped her sewing. Her intuition told her that this was a man you could rely on all your life. She did not see him as a total stranger at all and placed a hand on his slightly hunched shoulder. So the two sat on the cloth-covered edge of the brick bed and talked till dawn.

Xiuzhi was from Sichuan. In those years, the people in a province known for its abundance could not get enough to eat, not even sweet potatoes, and starving peasants had to leave their homes to save their lives. Girls who could marry themselves off to someone in another place fared better. Once a girl got settled outside, then she would introduce other girls in her village as wives there too. In this way groups of girls left home with their possessions in little bundles, went beyond Yangping Pass, crossed the Qinling Mountains, and travelled through countless railroad tunnels, short and long, in the direction of Shaanxi, of Gansu, of Qinghai, Ningxia and Xinjiang. If the parents could afford it they would buy their daughter a train ticket. Otherwise the girl had to slip surreptitiously on to a train and try to travel unnoticed, stop by stop. In her little bundle would be some patched clothes, a small round mirror and a comb. Armed with these few small things, she gambled with her youth, perhaps even her life. She might win happiness or she might lose completely.

At the farms in this district, this kind of marriage was popularly known as an "eight-*fen* marriage".* Younger men and older bachelors too poor to buy

---

* Eight *fen* is the postage for a letter.

wedding presents for local girls would turn to those from Sichuan. The Sichuan women here would, if asked, offer a name almost as if they had a catalogue of unmarried girls. Then a letter would be posted. Based on this summons, a girl would arrive and a marriage would take place. Xiuzhi was one of these. Originally, she had come to marry a tractor driver in the Seventh Production Team. But unfortunately, after hitchhiking with identification issued by her village authorities, she arrived to find he had died in an accident three days earlier. She did not go to the crematorium. It was not necessary since she had never set eyes on him. And she was too shy to go to the go-between because she knew the woman was in dire straits too, with a disabled husband and a small child. All she could do was sit in front of the corral of the Seventh Team, gazing blankly at her shadow as it described a slow arc on the ground around her.

Glib Tongue had learned of all this at noon when he had gone, kettle in hand, to fetch some hot water at the corral. Leaving his horses behind, he went from door to door trying to find a way out for the girl. Now there were only three single men left in the team and all three came to the corral to have a look at her, but thought her too scrawny and too small. Finally Glib Tongue remembered Xu Lingjun, then already thirty-five or thirty-six.

And so he had got married. That had been his romance!

"Old Xu's got married!" It had been quite an event in the village. Even those who were engrossed in factional feuds temporarily forgot their squabbling and came to congratulate him, a man impartial to disputes, a man who was harmless and worked hard. Human beings are human beings after all, and the villagers felt warmed themselves by offering their warmth to others, realizing their humanity had not been entirely lost during those turbulent years. Someone gave him a cauldron, others several catties of rice, cloth coupons and so on. A young vet started a collection, and each household offered fifty *fen*, to be used for starting a family. The leading body of the farm decided that he should be given a three-day honeymoon just like any-one else. Even in those dark days the villagers had all been very kind.

So with those charitable donations as a foundation, they started a new life.

Xiuzhi was optimistic and hard-working. With only two years' schooling behind her, she couldn't, of course, express her feelings in a cultured way. But after seeing the film *Lenin in 1918* at the village square the day after her arrival, she repeated a line spoken by Lenin's bodyguard, "There'll be bread, and milk too," and soon this became her pet saying, always causing her to giggle. Her eyebrows were thin, her eyes were small and when she smiled they turned virtually into slits like crescent moons. With her dimpled cheeks as well, she had a charm of her own.

While Xu Lingjun grazed the horses during the day, she made adobe bricks in the scorching noon sun. Afterwards, she carted the bricks back and began to build a wall around her hut. And so on a land of 9,600,000 square kilometres, she marked out eighteen square metres for herself. "At home," she said, "there are always trees in front of each house. You can't see the sky for their branches." So she rooted out two bowl-thick poplar trees from the field and, with surprising strength, dragged them back and planted them on either side of her little courtyard. When the walls were completed she began raising poultry. And as well as the chickens, ducks and geese, she kept rabbits and doves, a pastime which earned her the nickname "Commander of Three Armies". But what made her most unhappy at this state-owned farm was that pig-raising was not allowed. In bed at night she often told Xu Lingjun how she had dreamed of having her own fat pigs.

This remote farm was like a stagnant pond and the leaders were slow about carrying out policies, correct or incorrect, from above. Though there was the risk of being crushed as a "remnant of capitalism", Xiuzhi, like hardy grass growing through the cracks in a rock, stuck to her own ideas and the number of small animals grew rapidly, as though from the hands of a magician. "There'll be bread, and milk too." And sure enough, after one year's hard work, their life was much improved. Despite their meagre wages, they had all that they needed. Xiuzhi had the tenacity even to go against the social current. On her way back from the fields every evening, she carried Qingqing on her back, followed by a crowd of chickens, ducks and geese, while doves perched on her shoulders. Then firewood would be burning merrily in the stove beneath a cauldron of water. Like a Thousand-armed Buddha, she could put everything in its rightful order.

This woman, raised on sweet potatoes, had not only brought him a warm hearth but also had made him strike roots in this land. They nourished the roots with their own labour and their union strengthened his affection for the land, enabling him to see more clearly that a life of work was simple, pure and just. He was suffused with a happiness he had sought so many years before.

And then the day came when Deputy Head Dong announced that his name and reputation had been officially cleared, and he was given five hundred yuan as compensation in accordance with the policies of the financial office. When he told his wife what had happened, she was delighted and her face lit up. Having wiped her hands on her apron, she started to count the brand-new notes.

"Hey, Xiuzhi, from now on we're just as equal as anyone else," he shouted cheerfully in the direction of the little kitchen while washing his face. "Did you hear me, Xiuzhi? What are you doing in there?"

"I've counted this several times but I just can't work it out! What a pile!"

"*Aiya*! You're really. . . . What does the money matter? What's worth celebrating is that I'm politically exonerated!"

"What do you mean by 'politically exonerated'? To me, you're still yourself. They said you were a Rightist in the past. Now after all this time they say it was a mistake. But if that's true, why on earth should they warn you not to make a mistake again? Heaven only knows what they're doing! Who should be careful not to make mistakes again? We'll still live the way we always have. Now we've got money, we'll have a peaceful life. Don't disturb me, let me count it again."

True, Xiuzhi, who was fifteen years younger, had never thought of the two of them as inferior. She was simple, honest and provincial. What was a Rightist?

The question had never entered her small head. All she knew was that her husband was a good man, an honest man, and that was enough for her. Often when working together with the other women she would say, "Qingqing's father's really just a simple and honest man. He wouldn't make a sound even if you kicked him, and he'd move at the same pace if he had a wolf chasing him. It's a sin to bully somebody like him. Whoever has will have to pay for it in the next life!"

It was true that she liked money and was quite frugal and the five hundred yuan delighted her enormously. Her hands trembled, her eyes were brimming with tears of joy. But when she learned that his father was in business abroad, she said nothing about money, instead asking him to take the old man some tea-brewed eggs. She often said to her seven-year-old daughter, "You can only feel at ease if you spend money you've earned yourself. When I buy salt, I know that it's with money I've earned selling eggs. When I buy chilli, I know that it's with money I earned harvesting rice. When I buy you exercise books, I know I earned the money from working overtime threshing and winnowing. . . ." She had no abstract theories, no profound philosophies, but her simple, clear words made the small girl understand that work was a noble thing. Only the rewards of one's own labour could make a person feel good. It would be a humiliation to earn money through exploitation or through dependence on others.

Xiuzhi could not sing. When Qingqing was one month old, the three of them climbed on to a truck and went to the county seat to have a photo taken in the county's only studio. On the streets of that little

town, an ice lolly vendor sang out, "Lo — lly — Lo
— lly —" and that had become her lullaby. While
rocking her baby, she would sing, softly imitating the
northwest accent, "Lo — lly — Lo — lly —" This monotonous, remote, sweet singing not only hypnotized
Qingqing but also soothed her husband who, sitting
beside them reading, felt a simple, fundamental kind
of happiness.

There were lolly vendors at Wangfujing too. But
they never sang, sitting instead behind counters with
long faces. It was dull, uninteresting. He missed her
sweet lullabies, her pet sayings, her optimistic smile.

He could not stay here. He must go back. There
were friends who had helped him when he was in difficulty and who now needed his help. There was the
land which he had watered with his own sweat, which
even now seemed to glisten in the fields after harvest.
There was his beloved wife and daughter. His whole
world was there, even the very roots of his existence.

5

And now he was back at last, back to the familiar
little county town. The county's only asphalt road
stretched in front of the bus terminal still covered with
a thin layer of brownish dust which, when the wind
blew, whirled around the small stores, the bank and
the post office. The cotton fluffer across the road was
still working monotonously as though it had not
stopped once since he left. The bus terminal entrance
was crowded with peasants selling sweet rice, fried
pancakes and sunflower seeds. Flanking either side of

the terminal were dilapidated old houses, on some of which the original engraved lintels could still be seen. The new theatre, still under construction, was enveloped now in scaffolding, on which bricklayers moved about busily.

Getting off the bus he felt as if he had been dropped from a parachute. Now, at last, he was back on solid ground. He loved everything about the place, even its flaws, just as in his own life he now cherished even the bitter memories of the past.

He thumbed a ride on a horse cart and reached his village at dusk. Over the hills to the west, the setting sun cast its oblique rays, bathing the village and its inhabitants in a rosy glow. Xiuzhi's two poplars towered over their house, quiet and still, as if looking at him from the very depths of their souls.

The horses and cattle were tramping home. As they crossed the dirt road they halted, eyes wide, as if recognizing him. Only when the cart was far off in the distance did they turn their heads and continue on their journey, languidly heading for their barns.

A wave of warmth rose within him. He thought again of the conversation with his father before leaving. That evening, the two men had sat in armchairs, face to face. The despondent old man, wearing silk pajamas, was hunched over and smoking.

"Leaving so soon?" he asked.

"Yes. The school's preparing the mid-term examination."

After a brief silence, he said again, "I'm so happy to have seen you." Despite his attempts to control his emotions, his lips trembled. "You're a very mature man, I can see that. Probably because of our firm faith in things. That's good. What a man looks for is faith. To be frank, in the past I looked for it too. But religion couldn't satisfy me. . . ." He paused, waved a hand as if brushing away something in disgust and then suddenly changed his topic. "Last year I read an English version of the *Selected Stories of Maupassant* in Paris. There was a story about a deputy finally meeting the son he had left long ago and the son turned out to be an idiot. I couldn't fall asleep after I'd read it. And later on I often had visions of you, thinking you were in trouble. But now I feel at ease. Almost beyond my wildest expectations, you've become . . . a. . . ." He couldn't find the right word. The son however saw a satisfaction, a kind of consolation in his eyes. He knew that both he and his father were happy about this reunion since each had got what it was that he needed. His father's guilty conscience had been assuaged. And at a crucial moment, he had reviewed his own past and come, to some extent, to understand the meaning of his own life.

The sun had now sunk behind the hill and was shooting its last golden beams at the clouds above. In the reflection from the glowing clouds, the hillside pastures, the fields and village were covered in a gentle dusk light. He was approaching his school, the playground already in sight. From a distance it looked like a still lake surrounded by brown-patched grassland. Caressed by the evening breeze, he was swept by a wave of tenderness. In the end, he thought, his father had not really understood, although he had said that he himself had had a firm faith too. Intellectual knowledge without a basis in emotional experience was an empty thing. At some times and in some ways feelings were more important than ideas. What he had now acquired after more than twenty years of hardship, were the feelings and the understanding of a labourer. This was his treasure. Profoundly moved, he felt his eyes watering. In the end, he hadn't wasted all of those hard years trudging along that difficult road.

He saw the school at last. A few people in front of his house were turned in his direction. The white apron Xiuzhi wore sparkled like a star twinkling in the gathering dusk. The crowd grew rapidly and, recognizing him, ran towards the road. A little girl in a red jacket raced towards him like a leaping flame. She was nearer and nearer, her steps faster and faster. . . .

Translated by Hu Zhihui
and Wang Mingjie

绿 化 树

张 贤 亮

熊 猫 丛 书

＊

《中国文学》杂志社出版

（中国北京百万庄路24号）

中国国际图书贸易总公司发行

（中国国际书店）

外文印刷厂印刷

1985年第1版

编号：（英）2—916—31

00300

10—E—1767P